Queen of Emeralds

The Scottish Stone Series, Book One

Kelsey McKnight

Queen of Emeralds

Limitless Publishing, LLC
Kailua, HI 96734
www.limitlesspublishing.com

Formatting: Limitless Publishing

ISBN-13: 978-1-64034-035-0
ISBN-10: 1-64034-035-1

Dedication

This book is dedicated to my family. Told you my history degree would be useful for more than teaching...even if it's just to write some killer kilted romance novels.

"Taladh na mna Sithe"-*RC MacLeod*

Oh let me not hear of thy being wounded.
Grey do thou become duly.
May thy nose grow sharp ere the close of thy
day.

Oh! not of Clan Kenneth art thou!
Oh! not of Clan Conn.
Descendant of a race more esteemed; that of the
Clan Leod of swords and armour, whose fathers'
native land was Lochlann.

Chapter One

Charlotte Holloway picked the stray pieces of hay from her loose hair as her stepmother looked on, disapprovingly, from her place by the roaring fire. They stood at a distance in her father's lavish study, waiting for him to return from his business somewhere deep in the countryside. He had been gone for two long weeks and Charlotte had taken advantage of his absence by forgoing her tightly laced stays in order to watch the farmhands birth the late winter foals, and take lingering walks around the frozen lake of the estate until her cheeks were reddened and the hems of her dresses were damp with snow. Overall it had been a delightful time and Charlotte was more than saddened to hear of her father's impending return.

"Charlotte," her stepmother, Abigail, the Duchess of Glenwood, snapped, "do stop that fidgeting and try to look like a proper lady. I don't want your father to know that you've had the run of the estate like a common farm girl."

"Yes, ma'am." Charlotte rolled her eyes and

1

slumped into a plush red armchair surrounded by piles of books she had recently devoured, but had not put away. With Christmas only just over and the beginning of the London season a few days away, Charlotte attempted to display as much freedom as she could in what little time she had left. One of those freedoms was reading several of the newest novels her father had ordered for her from London. Her stepmother believed novels to be inappropriate for young ladies and would rather Charlotte spend her time practicing running the home or doing needlework by one of the many fireplaces for hours.

Charlotte, for the most part, detested all things having to do with being a proper lady and she was anything but. She liked her frocks to be as loose as her hair and didn't see the need to do any kind of needlework. She preferred to sneak into the kitchen to bake with the friendly cook, who was as quick to smile as she was to reprimand her small staff, and spend time outdoors doing all sorts of unladylike things.

In her youth, Charlotte was allowed these little freedoms, but it had been a long time since her father had willingly permitted her to gallop her horse at full speed or stay up late reading in the library. Now that Charlotte had approached the age for marrying, she was suddenly expected to be as still, and as boring, as her stepmother appeared to be.

The study's oak door swung open with a flourish as her father, George Holloway, the Duke of Glenwood, entered the room followed by a butler with a silver tray of tea. Her father's portly form was reddened from the trip up the stairs and down the long hall to greet his tiny family.

"Good evening, my two loves!" He gruffly pulled a reluctant Abigail into a hug before crossing the room to Charlotte.

"Hello, Father." Charlotte stood and planted a kiss on her father's cheek. "I hope your business went well."

"Quite." He sat down behind his desk with a sigh as the butler poured tea for the three of them. "But, judging by the hay in that auburn hair yours and the mud on the seam of your dress, I see that while the cat's away the mice will play."

Charlotte's cheeks heated at being caught so soon and she declined the steaming cup offered to her. "The stables had three new foals born since you've been gone. They're all a bit too early but lovely all the same. I can already tell they'll be in fine form to pull a carriage, but I do hope you'd consider one for the races. He has splendidly long legs and already canters so beautifully!"

"We'll see, we'll see." He dabbed the stray drops of tea from his walrus-like mustache.

Abigail came up to the desk and delicately took her cup and saucer. "Charlotte has been running around here like a fool. Fraternizing with the farmhands, locking herself away with books unfit for young ladies, and baking cakes in the kitchen with the staff...she hasn't even stood still long enough for me to have her fitted for this season's gowns."

"Has Charlotte anything new to wear to Christmas dinner at least?" her father asked over the rim of his cup.

"Not a stich." Abigail paused, taking a small sip of tea before passing her almost full cup back to the butler. "Charlotte has made herself quite scarce these past weeks. I do believe she has been hiding from me."

The duke turned to his daughter. "Is that true, Charlotte? Have you been avoiding Abigail?"

Charlotte shrugged, causing another piece of hay to be knocked loose from her curls. "Hiding from the seamstress, mostly. She pricks me with her pins on purpose and always tries to force these obnoxious gowns on me. They make me look like a pile of bed linens trimmed in lace."

"My dear, could you give my daughter and I a moment alone?" the duke asked his wife, wearily. Abigail complied and shut the door sharply behind her on her way out. "Charlotte, you're no longer a child and I've told you before that it is high time you stop acting like one. I can indulge your childish ways no longer."

She leaned a hip against the smooth desk and folded her arms. "It was just a harmless bit of fun. No one's about to see me riding or baking, so I don't see the harm."

"When you were five, it was a harmless bit of fun. You're almost nineteen and you are to be presented this season onto the marriage market. You need to learn to control yourself and begin acting like a young lady of your station."

"Marriage market. That term makes me feel like little more than a brood mare."

He sighed, bringing his hands to his brow and

massaging the tension. "We all have jobs to do, Charlotte. Men work and provide for their wives, bringing titles to the table. You, as a woman, will bring forth a large dowry and produce healthy heirs for a duke, baron, or lord. Your life of skipping about with your hem tied up to your knees is no longer acceptable. I expect you to conduct yourself like the daughter of a duke. Otherwise, no proper man would give you a second look."

"Oh, so I should be a perfectly boring porcelain doll with nothing better to do than attract a titled man and talk to other boring porcelain dolls about ribbons and feathered hats?"

"Yes, Charlotte, that is exactly what you should do." He deposited his empty cup on the desk and studied her for a moment, his expression almost unreadable. "You know that I've given you all that I could after the death of your sainted mother. I felt responsible for your happiness and hoped that, with my allowing you to grow up without the rules I should have, you would never feel the sting of being a motherless child. I know I coddled you in a most abhorrent way and now I am being punished for my soft heartedness. I've given you a youth of careless abandon and now you must put it aside in order to be a fine young lady who showcases your breeding and graceful charms."

"But, Father, I'm just not like that. Sewing bores me to tears and the other ladies Abigail brings about are only interested in talking about whom married whom, which lady has the most expensive fan, or what will be served for dinner at the next ball. It's perfectly horrid." Charlotte threw up her arms dramatically and sat back down in her chair.

"Now, see here!" The duke bristled suddenly, thumping his meaty fist on the desktop. "I will no longer have my daughter rolling about in the hay and playing in the dirt. Your launch into society is planned for a week's time and I expect you to behave in a manner that will not embarrass myself, nor your mother."

"Stepmother," Charlotte murmured just loud enough for her father to hear.

"My dear, Abigail has done her best these past ten years to be a mother to you. She has done her best to teach you how to behave and how to act like a lady of our social standing. She may have been a harsh teacher at times, but it was all done out of love for you. Abigail does not want to see you grow old without a husband and have nothing when I am gone. You would only receive the smallest of allowances given to spinsters of noble birth. You know well that the bulk of my fortune, and my title, will go to your cousin Franklin when I die. If you do not take a husband, you will be entirely dependent on Franklin's goodwill to feed and house you. And we both know that Franklin isn't the kindest of men."

"I'm aware that by being a female I have been declared utterly incapable of holding land or titles by myself. You do not have to constantly remind me of my apparent inferiority."

"Obviously, I do. Your dowry is enough to attract a good suitor, but it won't even exist if you don't marry. Dowries do not go to unmarried women. They go to dutiful wives."

"What about Abigail? When you met her, she lived on her own estate and by the number of servants she had about her, she wasn't in need of any financial help."

"She lived on the generosity of her benevolent brother, Michael. He allowed Abigail to live on one of his smaller estates and gave her a sizable allowance to spend on dresses, maids, and other such fripperies out of love. Do you think your cousin Franklin would be so generous to you?"

Charlotte remembered her cousin's pinched face and the way he sneered at her when he pushed her down in the mud or kicked her shins under the table at dinner. "No, Franklin is absolutely horrid and I wouldn't trust him to take care of a fish, let alone me."

"Then you see why it is imperative that you marry. When you do find a husband, you will be able to keep this estate and most of my other properties when I pass, although the title will still go to Franklin along with some of my fortune. If you decide to remain alone, then you get nothing."

"But I don't get to keep anything, really. It all goes to my husband."

"Which is exactly why you need to find a good man, one who will keep your inheritance intact and not gamble it away at the club or sell it off piece by piece like the husband of Lady Gertrude did to her. You should find someone we can trust, without question, who will not betray the family."

"So I am your property to do with as you wish until I marry. Then my husband will control me until his death. And finally, if I give birth to a son, he will hold my fate in his hands? Am I just the property of men until I, myself, am in the grave?"

The duke nodded. "Then you find yourself at the mercy of another man—God."

***

"It really won't be that bad," Charlotte's oldest friend Penelope said as she adjusted her parasol to keep the sun off her ivory skin. "There are dozens of eligible men looking for wives this season."

"Doesn't it feel strange? Being paraded about, hoping one of them will select us? It's very much like being a show pony."

"Well, I'm quite delighted being a show pony. This season I'll meet a wonderful man with a lovely country home and a townhouse in London so that I may go to the shops whenever I wish and hold picnics in the spring by my private lake. We'll honeymoon in Paris and he'll adore me."

"Everyone adores you, Penelope, and anyone who doesn't is a fool."

"You'll meet a nice man, too. Just try to keep an open mind."

"I wish I didn't need to worry about meeting any man. I wish I could just live my own life."

"And do what? Run about outside every day until you're as brown as a berry and live out your days a spinster?"

"What would be so bad about that? Not having to wear a corset and being able to lounge around in bed with a book one day, then jump in the lake for a swim on another sounds very nice to me."

"But what about a husband and a gaggle of children? I know you're fond of children. You spend every summer at that orphanage with all the little waifs."

"I would love my own children, but I do have a tender heart for orphans. I would very much like to improve conditions at those institutions." Charlotte tapped her pointed chin with the tip of a finger. "I could open a school, perhaps, or merely invite children to come ride the horses and see the foals. Country air would probably do them all a world of good."

"Your father would never agree to you collecting unwanted children. He could hardly stomach you giving the homes your allowance every month," Penelope pointed out. "Although it would be positively darling of you to open your home to them, if you could."

"It would never happen. You're right in saying that my father would certainly not allow it."

"But a husband might." Penelope grinned mischievously, pulling Charlotte to a stop. For such a polite young lady, she could be as cunning and as sly as a fox. "A husband might adore you so much that he would help you in your quest to open your estate to orphans or students."

Charlotte looked up at her friend in earnest, her eyes wide. "Do you really think a husband would be so understanding?"

"I do." She glanced about at the empty field before leaning in closer. "Remember Eleanor Gainsby?"

"Yes, we had the same French tutor, I believe. I

haven't seen her in years."

"Well, I saw her not too long ago in Mr. Penny's hat shop. She's gotten married to a wealthy Parisian man who indulges everything she does. Eleanor has always loved exotic animals, so her husband transformed one of his country estates into a menagerie of lions and elephants…all sorts of queer creatures."

"Elephants and little children are quite different. How would I know that any man I married would be interested in having strange children about, or even taking in a few foundlings?"

"That's the point of marrying a good man. A man who loves you would do anything to make you happy and a rich one would have the means to do so. Besides, even if he didn't want to indulge your ideas, you would have access to your funds as a properly married woman. While you wouldn't be able to take any into your home, you could be allowed to spend your time and money bettering the orphanages. Philanthropy is all the rage in some circles."

"Penelope, you're right!" Charlotte grinned. "I foolishly thought that by getting married I would be signing over ownership of myself to a man, but in reality I would be freer than ever!"

"Now, all we need to do is find you the perfect man and make him fall madly in love with you." She had a slightly dreamy glint in her fair eyes as she spoke.

"I don't know how to even talk to a man, let alone make one fall in love with me." Charlotte sighed, gazing out at the frozen waters of the lake.

"I just can't be a debutante like you."

"Oh, of course you can. Just wear pretty things and go to fun parties. It's not as if it's difficult."

"I can't imagine any man would be attracted to my wild ways. Everyone in society is just so boring and close-minded."

"Not me." Penelope tucked a stray blonde curl back into her bun. "Everyone adores me, remember?"

"Well, everyone *doesn't* adore me."

"That's not true. You're smart, funny, and you have the nicest hair of anyone else entering society this season."

"I need more than nice hair to attract a husband."

"You could try actually staying out of the sun and using your parasol for once. White complexions are all the rage."

Charlotte twirled the close lace umbrella by her side and shrugged. "What's the point of going outside if you have to stay out of the sun?"

"The sun is appropriate in small doses," Penelope stated in a matter-of-fact way. "As is this cold air. Although, I do believe we will both catch our deaths being out here like this."

"Nonsense. I spend hours outside in the snow and feel as right as rain. Besides, my stepmother will watch us like a hawk if we're inside."

"I don't know why you don't like her. She's always pleasant to me."

"That's because she admires your ladylike ways and hopes that your delicate manner will rub off on me. After a dozen years of having you as my dearest friend, you would think she would realize that I can't be influenced by anyone."

"You could give it a try, you know. Put on a bit of a show until the end of the season, or when you find a husband," Penelope suggested, adjusting her wrap. "Just put on a good display of being a timid little mouse and see how many proposals you receive.

"I don't think I could pull it off. I'm not dainty or charming like you. You already have suitors banging on your father's door for a chance to take you riding or to the theater when you come out. You already have a full social calendar."

"I could help you, you know. Teach you how to attract men."

Charlotte smiled and playfully tapped Penelope with her parasol. "You're going to teach me how to flirt? You're positively wicked."

"Come now, Char, it'll be great fun. You'll be my own little project and by the end of the season we'll find you a great lord to marry and he'll help you make your dream of opening an orphanage a reality."

"As long as he is kind and well-read."

"Does it really matter what books he reads?"

"I could never bring myself to marry a man who can't hold an intelligent conversation."

"Men don't talk to ladies about anything outside of the home, weather, and idle gossip. You probably won't find out if a man is well-read until after you're married." Penelope linked arms with Charlotte and steered her toward the house. "We can only try to do our best to find you a smart, titled, kind, handsome man…but for now we must work on you."

Chapter Two

"Do you remember what I told you?" Penelope whispered as she adjusted the diamond band that was twisted delicately in Charlotte's curls. "Never dance with a man more than three times tonight unless you really care for him and never ask him his views on politics."

"Why can't I do that, again?"

"Because it makes you look forward and men love women who are adorable little fools."

"I don't want to be an adorable little fool," Charlotte said crossly. "I want to be respected and talked to like an equal."

"Then good luck finding a husband," Penelope hissed. "At least your dress makes you look like a proper lady. The violet silk and gold trim does wonders to bring out your eyes. Although, I do wish you weren't as brown as a berry."

"It's too late to bleach my skin, so you'll just have to make do with your creation, as is."

Penelope rolled her cornflower eyes. "I'll be downstairs to watch you enter. Are you going to be all right by yourself?"

Charlotte nodded and Penelope slipped out of Charlotte's bedroom to join all of society in the Duke of Glenwood's London estate's ballroom. They had been at the London home for several days in preparation for Charlotte's coming out. Now it was the night of Charlotte's launch into society and she was more than nervous. After four grueling days of mimicking the way Penelope talked, walked, ate, and laughed, she felt as unprepared as ever.

"Charlotte?" Her father tapped lightly on her bedroom door before opening it. He stood in the doorway for a moment with a weepy smile on his lips. "You look just like your mother did when I met her."

"Do you really think so? Do I really look like Mother?" Charlotte studied herself in the mirror again, trying to see her mother in her own features. She supposed they both had the same wide hazel eyes and pouty lips. Charlotte might also have had her strong cheekbones, but she could hardly remember what her mother looked like. There was only one portrait of her mother hanging in her father's study, but he had it covered up with a sheet of black silk after her passing and refused to have it moved.

"The spitting image. She was always a great beauty and I'm very pleased that you took after her looks instead of mine." He laughed gruffly, trying to hide the emotion in his voice. "We could never get you married off if you had a mustache like I do!"

15

Charlotte smiled. She felt more at ease now, with her father joking as he used to. "It's strange doing this without her here. When I was younger I used to watch her get dressed in brilliantly beautiful gowns before the two of you went out to the theater or to dinner. She would let me wear her jewels and help her select which silk slippers she wore. I wish she was here to help me now."

The duke came up behind her and patted her gently on the shoulder. "You're doing well enough. You'll be the belle of the ball tonight. Now, let's get you presented as a proper lady at last."

***

"Presenting Lady Charlotte Lucille Holloway escorted by her father, the Duke of Glenwood," the butler called out as Charlotte and her father reached the top of the grand staircase. Dozens of the top socialites and eligible bachelors stood below them wearing their finest silks and jewels for Charlotte's coming out ball.

The Duke of Glenwood's ballroom was one of the oldest and best cared-for event rooms most had ever seen. Deep red brocade hangings and Holloway family portraits in ornate frames complemented the dark wood paneling of the walls and floor. Glittering chandeliers lit up the room and reflected off the many punch glasses being passed around by footmen in perfectly pressed livery. Even the floral arrangements were a sight to behold with exotic hothouse flowers pouring out of golden vases that were as tall as any man.

The duke and his daughter slowly made their descent toward the ballroom. Abigail stood at the base of the stairs in a modest, yet obviously expensive, gown. Her graying hair was twisted up in her customary sharp bun but she looked softer than usual in a dove gray dress edged in pearls. She nodded in approval as Charlotte gracefully released her father's arm from her grip. As the band began to play a lively song, George bowed to his wife for a dance. As they waltzed away to signal the official beginning of the ball, Penelope slipped through the crush to reach her friend.

"Oh, Charlotte, you made a divine entrance," she gushed as she gripped Charlotte's hand in her own. "And everyone who's anyone is here right now. Your stepmother must have invited all of London."

"Anyone we know?"

"A few girls from finishing school, but it's really mostly men. They're all dukes, marquises, or lords, I believe. I've heard there are even some from France, Ireland, and Scotland."

Charlotte looked around at the groups of men. For the most part, they all looked to be a bit older than her and several leered openly. "I feel like a cake on display."

"Oh, posh." Penelope waved her complaint away with her hand before linking arms with Charlotte. "They're all here for you. I've made a few introductions already so I'll introduce you." She pulled her toward an older gentleman with a bristly set of muttonchops and a dark purple morning coat. "Charlotte, may I introduce Percival Grant, the Baron of Eastly?"

He took Charlotte's proffered hand and bowed deeply. "My lady, it is lovely to meet you. I do hope you will honor me with a dance after you've made all the proper introductions?" His voice was much higher than she had anticipated.

"Of course," she replied seriously, holding in a giggle. "Please find me in a while and I'll be sure to accommodate you on my dance card."

"What do you think?" Penelope asked as she began to lead Charlotte toward the next single man.

Charlotte scrunched up her nose as she paused to take a little tart from one of the trays being carried about the floor. "He was much too old and rather silly sounding. I don't believe I could see him as my husband."

"They're all going to be older than you, for the most part."

"They don't need to be *twenty* years older than me. That's just ridiculous. Keep your matchmaking to someone our age, if you will."

"Fine. There's Charlie, the Duke of Fenton," she whispered as they approached a red-haired young man who was downing what must have been his third glass of punch. "He went to school with my brothers and I've always thought he was quite nice. His father died a few months ago, so he's come into his inheritance."

"Penelope!" Charlie grinned in a way that showed off all his teeth at once. "Do introduce me to the lady of the hour."

"Charlie, this is my dearest friend, Lady Charlotte Holloway. Charlotte, this is Charles Brandley, Duke of Fenton."

"Good to meet you, Charles." Charlotte held out her gloved hand to be kissed. "I've heard so much about you."

"Good things, I hope!" His freckled face was jolly as he brushed his lips against her hand.

"Always," she answered with a conspiratorial smile. She wasn't sure if he was marriage material, but she could imagine he might grow on her.

"Charlotte, Charlotte, do come here!" The Duke of Glenwood called from behind a group of tittering ladies.

"Please excuse me," Charlotte said, slipping her hand from Charlie's grasp. She made her way through the throng to her father who was chatting with a tall, older gentleman with a dour look on his long face. The man was imposing, to say the least— pale skin, black eyes, and black hair streaked with gray. He looked unhappy to be present at the lively ball, surrounded by men and women all in the throws of youth. In fact, he looked almost disgusted by it all.

"My dear Charlotte!" George's face was already reddened with drink. "Say hello to one of my dearest friends, Richard Howard."

"Good evening. Thank you for coming to my launch into society." Charlotte dipped a small curtsey with a perfunctory smile.

"Charmed." Richard looked down his long nose at her, studying her like she was a purebred greyhound or a tray of sweetmeats he'd like to sample.

George clapped his friend on the back. "Old Richard and I used to do business together. We owned some land in America and when I got out of the land business, I sold it all to him. He's quite the tycoon over there. As rich and famous as any old duke!"

"How lovely. I'm pleased that your business is doing well." Charlotte looked toward a waiting Penelope, hoping for an exit.

"Perhaps your dance card isn't too full this evening?" Richard asked.

Charlotte bit her lip. "No…"

"Jolly news," George declared as he begun dragging Richard over toward a footman with a tray of fresh drinks. "Save a dance for this old chap then, Charlotte!"

"Who was he?" Penelope whispered as she came up to Charlotte's side. She had been studying Richard from behind her ivory fan, her lips clenched tight.

"A friend of my father's. I'm supposed to dance with him."

"Oh, I hope he'll forget and you can go spend your time with some real prospects."

Charlotte shuddered. "He makes me uncomfortable. I really don't like the look of him."

"I don't blame you." Penelope looked around, then grinned. "There's Peter! He's Baron VonTren's oldest boy."

Charlotte spent the next few hours being dragged about the ball by Penelope and being introduced to all of her brother's school friends. Penelope barely let her get in a dance, or two, in between the numerous introductions. Charlotte's head was swimming with faces and names she could barely remember now. The endless small talk about how warm this winter had been and where the next dance would be held bored her to tears. To cope with the endless chatter she stole glasses of spiked punch, which made it considerably easier to endure the hours of dancing and presentations.

When Penelope was whirled away for a dance by some lord's youngest son, Charlotte took the opportunity to slip away from the crush and make a hasty exit out to a balcony door. Her head had begun to spin and she feared she might be sick from the drink if she couldn't get out of the stifling crowd. The balcony was large and its stone railing wrapped around most of the lavish building her father owned. The new electric streetlights illuminated the foggy London streets with a dim yellow glow. The large glass doors that led inside did surprisingly much to mute the loud music and Charlotte was grateful for the cold winter breeze and bit of privacy the balcony offered.

She pulled off the long white gloves she wore and leaned against the railing, inhaling large gulps of fresh air. "How I wish this was all over," she whispered to the empty streets.

"How can ye wish your own party to be done?" A deep voice asked from the most shadowed of corners.

Charlotte turned around, her light purple skirts flying with the quick motion. "Who's there?"

A tall man stepped from the darkened place where he had sat on a stone bench. His loose blond hair brushed his shoulders and his blue eyes seemed to flash brightly in the dark. He wore a black military jacket and a sharp yellow and black kilt that looped about his shoulder and was fastened with a silver and emerald pin. Traditional high socks covered his strong legs. A short sword was fastened to his hip by a rugged leather belt and his hand lay casually on its silver hilt. "Conner MacLeod. Chief o' the MacLeod clan."

"Charlotte Holloway, daughter of the Duke of Glenwood," Charlotte answered, stunned by the strange dress and deep Scottish lilt. She wasn't sure where he had come from, as he certainly would have stood out in the crowd of morning coats and ball gowns. She tried to advert her eyes from the bare swatch of leg that showed between his socks and kilt but could hardly bring herself to look away.

"I know who ye are, of course. This entire party is in your honor. But, I must ask…why do ye wish it over so soon?"

"I'm not much for balls."

"A pretty lass like you? How can ye no' be much for balls?" His lips curled in a mischievous smirk. "Do you not like the pomp and circumstance?"

Charlotte felt her cheeks grow warm and she wasn't sure if it was from the drink or the way the Scotsman looked at her from under his dark lashes. All the same, she sensed in him a kindred spirits of sorts. "I'm not much for society at all. I'd rather be out riding or reading a good book than be stuffed in this dress meeting every eligible bachelor in the city."

He laughed deeply. "I admire your honesty. Not many lasses are willin' to admit when a party does no' suit them."

22

"I assume the party doesn't suit you much either?"

"Not much. Us Scots have been tryin' to be more respected in our own right. One o' the ways to do that is to spend a bit o' time with the English. Make them see we're not all barbarians."

"Ah, fraternizing with the enemy?" Charlotte could almost hear Penelope chastising her for speaking so familiarly to a man, and about politics at that!

"Ye could say that." He brushed his hands through his hair and leaned against the railing beside her, looking over the side. "Ye aren't cold out here in the night air?"

"No, I rather like being outside no matter what the weather is." She took another deep breath. "Besides, I do think I drank a bit too much punch."

"And danced with a few too many borin' men, most like."

She giggled, despite being told a hundred times by Abigail that it was very unladylike to do so without shielding your face with a fan. "I suppose that might have something to do with it. But, that's the job of a duke's daughter."

Conner stepped toward her and extended his hand. "Well, since we are both trapped at this comin' out party, we may as well have a bit o' fun. Fancy a dance, Lady Glenwood?"

Charlotte took his rough, warm hand in her own. His palms were worn, much unlike those of English gentlemen with their silky smooth hands kept clean in powdered gloves. This man was obviously used to physical activity and hard work. She kept their

23

hands together before remembering she had removed her gloves and left them on the railing. "Oh, I'm sorry!" She pulled away from his grasp before slipping her fingers inside her gloves once more.

"You ladies and your gloves. Scared o' touchin' anythin' without a barrier o' silk?" he teased.

"I hate them, personally. However, one must play the part at times."

"And what part are ye playin'?"

"The part of a dutiful daughter."

"Then it looks to me that you are doin' a right fine job." He offered his arm, which she gladly took. "Now, my lady, let's go have us a dance."

***

The room hushed slightly as Charlotte entered on Chief Conner MacLeod's arm. Penelope watched, wide-eyed, as the couple began a lively waltz with the other colorful pairs of dancing guests. Conner was an animated dancer and whirled Charlotte around the floor with surprising ease for someone as rugged as he. She was enjoying herself so greatly that she hardly notice the strange looks some of the guests gave them, nor the look of disapproval on Abigail's tightly pinched face.

His hands clutched her closely, perhaps closer than was really appropriate. He grinned with the self-confidence that only good-looking men rightly had and gazed at Charlotte with true merriment in his sapphire eyes. Conner didn't attempt the usual small talk that most men would try during a dance, but just let their mutual joy at having a fine partner fill in the silence between them.

"What a crowd," Conner whispered into her ear as the music winded down and the dancing couples slowed to a halt. "Ye would think they'd never seen a pair o' dancers before."

Charlotte felt a chill go up her spine that she tried to ignore. "I suppose your appearance has caused quite the titter. I must say, we do not see very many Scottish Lords and it always is the surprise."

"I suppose the man approachin' us would agree with ye."

"I am here to collect my dance." Richard Howard's monotone voice greeted Charlotte's back.

Conner dipped a short bow and lightly kissed Charlotte's hand. Even through the silk of her glove, she felt the heat of his mouth on her skin. "A pleasure, my lady."

Charlotte blushed again and felt bold enough to ask, "If you stay longer, perhaps we might dance again?"

"Perhaps," he answered smoothly as he backed away into the crowd. "Perhaps."

"Quite the heartthrob," Richard said dryly.

Charlotte cleared her throat. "That was Conner MacLeod, the Ch—"

"I know who he is." Richard held out his hands. "Now let us have that dance."

She allowed Richard to take her by the waist and hand. She found that, while he was a passable dancer, he didn't move with the spirit that Conner MacLeod did. His moves were mechanical and his face held the same uninterested expression as always. The hand that grasped hers was also clammy and damp, the sweat seeping into her glove.

"Your coming out party has been a success," Richard stated as they moved slowly around the floor. "You must be quite pleased."

"Yes, the turnout has been very satisfactory and I believe the guests are enjoying themselves," she said evenly.

"And you're not?"

"I am not used to this sort of attention," she said carefully.

"If you hope to find a husband, I assume you will at least have to pretend that all this pleases you. Put on a good show."

His statement took Charlotte by surprise. "I…I…"

"No need to explain yourself. Your father has told me of your need to find a trustworthy husband. Besides, I do believe that finding a husband is what all girls hope to do before they're married and altogether too old and ugly to find a match."

"And you, Mr. Howard? Are you married?" she asked, hoping to draw attention away from herself. Blast him for claiming his dance at one of the longer songs.

"The late Mrs. Howard died several years ago."

"Oh, I'm so sorry."

"Don't be. She was a silly little thing and couldn't give me any sons. Just a handful of daughters," he spat with distain. "I was rather glad to see her go. She held on quite a while after the last girl was born."

Charlotte fought to hide the look of surprised disgust on her face. "Daughters can be quite lovely. As you know, I'm a daughter, myself."

He studied her face with a mixture of surprise and boredom. "As you are. I am going, in two days time, to see some new opera or other. Would you accompany me?"

"If I do not have any other engagements." Charlotte prayed silently that she could find a way to escape spending any more time with Richard Howard.

"I'll speak to your father about it before I leave. I see the music is ending so I will release you to your duties," he said with a curt nod as he abruptly stopped dancing. "I'll see you on Monday evening."

Charlotte quickly made her way toward Penelope, who looked more than irritated. "Thank goodness he didn't ask me for another dance. I don't think I could suffer it."

"He looks like he is constantly smelling something foul," Penelope said, taking Charlotte's arm and pulling her behind a large pillar. "But that Scottish man, however, is quite the sight."

"His name is Conner MacLeod. He's the chief of the MacLeod Clan." Charlotte noticed she no longer saw Conner in the crowd and wondered if he was back on the balcony.

"I've heard of him before." Penelope's voice was low and she looked around to be sure no one was close enough to hear them. "He's a ferocious fighter who owns much of Scotland, and is said to be quite the womanizer."

"I can almost believe it," she murmured, more to

herself than Penelope.

Penelope yawned and glanced around the pillar, eyes scanning the fatiguing crowd. "I do believe your Scotsman has left. Do you think it's almost time for us to retire as well? It must be near morning."

Charlotte paused and glanced toward the glass balcony door. As much as she wanted to find Conner, she refused to tie herself to a man who was unlikely to be faithful to her. "Yes. Let's slip away to bed before my father forces me to dance with another of his ghastly friends."

Chapter Three

The next morning, both girls awoke in Charlotte's bed with thick heads and sore feet. It was almost noon when they slipped out of their nightgowns and had their maids dress them in comfortable day clothes. Penelope decided she would go home to her parents' London townhouse after lunch while Charlotte would recover from her late night in her bedroom with a good book. The early afternoon light was bright and the floor-length windows in the casual dining room did nothing to help their headaches.

"Charlotte, Penelope," her father said as they took their seats at the long dining room table for lunch. "I hope you are not too tired from last night's events?"

"I'm positively drained," Penelope said as a footman placed some chicken and freshly baked rolls on her plate. "The music was divine and the turnout was wonderful."

"Glad to hear you approve. And you, Charlotte?" George asked.

"I do believe I met all of London last night but I can hardly remember anyone's names." She took a bite of chicken before continuing. "Was there any post for me this morning?"

He stood with excitement and retrieved a small pile of letters from the sideboard. "You've received invitations from several *very* influential people and two nice floral arrangements."

Charlotte flipped through the letters. She noted some invitations for different New Year's Eve balls and a few others for dinner or trips out riding. The names of the men sounded familiar, but she could hardly match any of the faces to them. "Who are the flowers from?"

Her father shrugged and sat back down in his chair. "I didn't look. I'll have one of the footmen deliver them into your bedroom."

"Perhaps one will be from your Scotsman?" Penelope grinned mischievously at her in between bites of steamed carrots.

Her father stiffened. "Scotsman? What Scotsman?"

Charlotte shot a sharp look at Penelope, who was suddenly very interested in her plate. "Just this Scottish chieftain who was in attendance last night. He was a very agreeable dancer."

"And why is he now *your* Scotsman?" Her father's ruddy face reddened.

Charlotte tried to look nonchalant. "He isn't *my* anything. He's just some man who was at the ball last night. Penelope is just stirring up trouble, as usual."

Penelope tried her best to look innocent. "You

know me, always the tease."

He nodded curtly. "Good. I'm glad to hear he's 'just some man.' You read horrid stories in the papers about those blasted Scots pillaging and causing a ruckus. Anyway, on to brighter things. I heard you've received an invitation from Richard, as well?"

Charlotte fought the urge to grimace. "He wants to take me to see a new opera on Monday night."

Her father's face broke into a grin. "Wonderful news! I know you'll have a nice evening together. Richard's a good bloke."

"I thought I might skip the opera," Charlotte said steadily. "I don't want to overwhelm myself with invitations so soon after my coming out. Besides, I don't believe that Richard and I get along too well, so I would hate to waste his time."

"You're going," her father told her abruptly. "Richard has extended you a courtesy and you shall oblige him. I'll have none of that nonsense. You will not refuse to go out with my oldest friend."

"Yes, Father." Charlotte pushed her mostly full plate away from her, suddenly devoid of her appetite. Her stomach seemed full of stones. "I find I'm still tired from last night. I think I'll go to my rooms now."

"I should be leaving as well." Penelope hastily followed Charlotte as she stood and left the room.

When they were safely away from the dining room and a carriage for Penelope had been summoned, Charlotte turned to her friend. "I can't believe my father is making me go to the opera with that old man Richard."

"Maybe play sick?" Penelope offered. "Certainly he can't force you to go when you have something terribly contagious."

Charlotte shook her head, making her curls bounce about. "He would know in an instant I was faking it. As a child, I would always play sick when my German tutor would come over so that trick is old hat."

"What will you do then?" Penelope asked as her maid put her fur wrap around her shoulders.

"I suppose I'll have to go."

***

Two large vases full of flowers sat upon Charlotte's small writing desk when she entered her bedroom. One was a playful display full of baby's breath and purple blooms of lilacs, wisterias, crocuses, and hydrangeas. It reminded her slightly of the dress she wore the night before. A little gold card was tucked into the blossoms. She opened the envelope and read:

Charlotte,

I hope to hide from the crowd with you again. Save me a dance.

-C

Charlotte bit her lip and read the card again, knowing it must be from Conner MacLeod. No one else would have written a card like that to her. Her heart sped up for only a moment while she tried to suppress the fluttering feeling in her breast. Conner was apparently a very skilled flirt, but she wouldn't allow him to use her.

Shoving the card safely in one of her desk's many tiny drawers, she went to the next arrangement. A simple bunch of spring daffodils sat in a vase. The grouping was small and unimpressive next to the vibrantly purple display. The white attached card read:

Lady Charlotte,
I will be at your father's home at eight o'clock to take you to the opera.
-Richard Howard

Groaning openly, Charlotte tossed the note to the floor and fell into her freshly made bed. She knew she had to go with Richard, but she would be sure that it would be the only time she was forced to go out with that man. Sooner or later a real suitor would come along who was young, handsome, and embraced who Charlotte really was.

Richard could hardly be interested in Charlotte. He was old enough to be her father and was blander than a plain piece of dry toast. If he disliked his daughters as much as he seemed to, she could barely think that he would desire to spend any time with her. Perhaps Richard felt the need to take Charlotte to the opera as a way to do something nice for her father. She hoped it was just a courtesy between friends.

Briefly, she thought back to the night before when Conner danced and laughed so easily she felt as if she was in a dream. It may have been the drink, or the absence of anyone even remotely amusing outside of Penelope, but she felt herself drawn to him. He made her chest feel tight and her heart beat faster as if it were trying to escape. When their bare hands touched for that brief moment on the balcony, Charlotte felt sparks between them that were strange and deliciously frightening.

But, all the same, she thought back again to the conversation she had with Penelope about what a mysterious Scotsman had done to an innocent lady. She wished, deeply, that Penelope had never told her that story and, more so, that it wasn't even true. She knew that she didn't really know Conner—one never knows anyone after only an hour—but she didn't think him the type to get a child on a woman and not do the proper thing. But, then again, maybe that was the way with the Scottish.

Chapter Four

"Your blue dress or the gray, my lady?" Charlotte's maid asked as she sifted through the hanging silk and muslin frocks in her large dresser.

Charlotte sat in front of her dressing table, brushing her long hair with a heavy hand. It was Monday night and she didn't have that long to get ready before Richard would come to take her to the opera. As soon as she had dinner with her father and Abigail, she had retreated to her bedchambers to begrudgingly prepare.

"Whichever one you think is best," Charlotte answered tiredly.

"The gray, then," Mary said with a nod as she whipped the pale gray dress off its hanger and laid it on the bed. "Do you mind which jewels?"

"The purple, I think." Charlotte stood from her seat and began lacing her corset.

Mary took her place behind her, tightening it even more until Charlotte felt as if she couldn't breathe. "Is everything all right, my lady? You seem rather sad."

"I'm just not fond of the opera," she lied. Mary was more worldly than Charlotte, although a year younger. No matter the situation, the maid's keen intellect spotted the truths behind the falsehoods.

"Me neither. Too much singing for my taste. I prefer to see a good show with a few jokes and some colorful costumes." Mary smiled as she pulled Charlotte's dress over her head and began doing up the buttons after arranging the pillars of crinoline underneath. "Is this a suitor you're going out with tonight?"

"Just a friend of my father's," Charlotte answered, putting a pair of pale purple jewels in her ears.

Mary dared to pry further. "Surely you must have met someone at your coming out?"

"No one in particular." Charlotte noted Mary's look of mischief in the mirror. "Why? What have you heard?"

"Nothing, my lady. I just noticed you had two bunches of flowers."

"And you wanted to know who sent them?"

Mary smiled sheepishly, her fingers twirling Charlotte's curls into a bun. "I was a bit curious."

"The smaller one is from my father's friend, Richard. He's the one taking me to the opera."

"And the other?"

"Conner MacLeod."

The maid let out a small shriek. "No, not the flirtatious chieftain!"

"You've heard of him?" Charlotte asked as she slipped her feet into slippers and pulled on her fur wrap.

"He's quite the heartbreaker. I've heard in the market, from some maids from different houses, that he's a warrior king who may behave with honor and class while in London but is truly a wild man with an even wilder *appetite*. I've also heard that he's looking for a wife, but that he ruins many fine ladies on his way to the altar."

"Oh, Mary!" Charlotte felt heat rise up her neck and settle in her cheeks. "Don't talk so wickedly."

Marry dipped a short curtsey. "I beg your pardon, my lady. I was just repeating what I heard from the market and got a bit carried away."

"It's fine. It just surprised me." She began toward her door but turned at the last moment. "Mary, if I ask you to do something, could you do it with care and discretion?"

"Anything, my lady."

"Can you listen at the market for any news of Conner MacLeod? Do not ask on my behalf, but just tell me if you hear anything."

Mary opened her mouth but decided against it, opting to bob down into another curtsey. "Of course, my lady."

***

"We have the finest balcony box," Richard told her as she slipped the wrap from her shoulders and handed it to an usher at the door.

"Lovely," Charlotte said shortly, adjusting her gloves. Couples slipped past them to find their respective seats and some glanced at Charlotte and Richard with confusion as if the mismatched pair

37

didn't belong in the opera house.

"It's very secluded and allows us the best view." He led her up a narrow flight of stairs where a butler waited to allow them entrance to their private booth. Two gilded chairs looked down onto the darkened stage and Charlotte took her place in the one Richard offered.

"Champagne?" A butler offered them each a glass as soon as they were seated.

"Thank you." Charlotte took a sip and surveyed the masses. She didn't see anyone she instantly recognized.

"Do you care for the opera?" Richard asked, studying her in that strange way he had.

"I prefer the theater, but the opera is nice in its own way."

"I detest both. The dramatics are ridiculous."

"Then why bring me?"

Richard shrugged as the lights dimmed and the curtains opened. "I thought you would like it. But, now, I see that I should have picked a different diversion to amuse your simple mind."

Charlotte looked at Richard, stunned by his casual rudeness. If he had merely taken her out as a favor to his oldest friend, then why would he do something he disliked just to try to amuse her, but then insult her in the same breath? Hopefully he wasn't trying to court her, and these were merely the actions of a man toward the child of a dear friend.

Tired of looking at Richard's bland expression, Charlotte turned her attentions back toward the stage and lifted her gold opera binoculars to her eyes. She had missed the beginning moments of the opera but the singer's soulful voices chilled her to the bone and brought forth tears of unnamable emotion. The feelings they stirred baffled her. When the dropping of the curtain signaled an intermission, Charlotte surprisingly felt as if she could hardly wait the half hour for the second act.

"Surely you must go powder your nose or something." Richard looked down his long nose at her tear-streaked face. "I can't have my date looking as if she has just attended a funeral in my opera box. Silly women, always blubbering for no good reason."

"Pardon me?"

"You are pardoned. Now run along and do something about your appearance. You're looking rather blotchy with female emotion."

Charlotte started at his harsh words and stood abruptly, her hooped skirt knocking over her chair in the process. "If you mean to tease me due to my being moved by this wonderful opera, then I mean to leave you to your misery, alone."

His bushy eyebrows rose but his face gave away no emotion. "You want to find your way home alone in the night? Rather unsafe for a woman."

"I mean to get away from you!" She picked up her skirts and spun around only to bump into the butler who had come in to see the cause of the raised voices.

"Well, considering your vile shrieking has created a more rapt audience than the vile shrieking on the stage, I assume that it is for the best that you show yourself out." Richard turned away from her and lifted his empty champagne glass to be filled.

Charlotte gasped in surprise at his coldness. She pushed past the butler and fled down the narrow stairs to the main lobby, brushing tears of anger and frustration from her face. She was sure that Richard had been correct in his observation that the scene she caused had drawn more than a few eyes to their booth. And she was even surer that her reddened cheeks and flyaway hair would draw just as much notice when she reached the lobby.

"Lady Holloway?" A strong hand grasped her arm as soon as she reached the landing and pulled her into the darkened cloakroom.

"Unhand me!" Charlotte spat through her tears as she pulled her arm free of her glove, leaving her assailant holding the bit of silk.

The deep voice laughed heartily. "Ye can never keep your gloves on around me, eh lass?"

"Lord MacLeod?" Charlotte squinted in the dark as his familiar form came into view.

He bowed deeply, offering her the glove in his outstretched hand. "At your service, my lady."

"Why did you pull me into the cloakroom?" she asked, snatching her glove out of his hand and pulling it roughly on.

"I saw the confrontation a few moments ago."

"Oh, that. You must think me a right fool."

"Never that." He grinned, sporting a pair of good-natured dimples. "Ye showed stones to tell that old man what for."

"I just got so angry! And now my father will be even angrier that I left his friend at the opera." Charlotte felt her stomach sink at the thought of her father's disappointed look as Richard reported how ridiculously she had acted.

"If your father was angry at anyone, it should be that old man up there. He has no right lettin' a young lady go out into the night unprotected." He dropped a warm hand on her bare shoulder and searched out her face in the darkness. "You are all right, though? He did no' hurt ye?"

"No, just my pride," she answered, trying to ignore the heat radiating through her body.

"May I take ye home? We can wait here until intermission is over, then I'll have my carriage brought around. We can escape without an audience."

A breath escaped her. "Oh, Lord MacLeod, that would be lovely. I really didn't give much of a thought to what I would do when I got downstairs."

"I figured as much." He looked around at the collection of coats and wraps. "Do you think ye can find your things in this mess?"

"I believe so. My lady's maid sewed my name into all of my coats and wraps so they never get taken by mistake."

"Smart lass." He began flipping through the men's outer jackets when Charlotte noticed he wasn't wearing his kilt, but a finely cut jacket and breeches.

"You look like a gentleman!" Charlotte exclaimed before realizing how rude she sounded.

He glanced her way with a deep chuckle. "And what did I look like before? A chimpanzee?"

"Don't tease." Charlotte turned her back to him and dug through the thick furs until she found her own. "I just didn't expect to see you without a kilt."

"I have to blend in some o' the time." He helped her settle the wrap around her shoulders. "All sorted, my lady?"

"Yes, I believe so." She placed her hands on her hair and felt the loose tendrils that had slipped from their pins. "Do I look frightful? Be truthful."

He took a step toward her, studying her in the dim light that seeped in from under the door. "Delightfully mussed, I'd say."

"Is it really that bad? I can't go out there looking a mess after the scene I caused. They'd think me a madwoman."

"Allow me." He reached up and began tenderly stroking stray curls back into place. He was so close to her she could almost hear his heart beating. But, on second thought, the loud hammering must have been her own. "I'm no hair dresser, but ye look much more presentable now."

"Thank you."

"Anytime." He offered her his arm, cheerfully patting her hand. "Allow me to escort ye to my carriage?"

"Any time." She smiled, finding that his jolly mood was quite contagious.

"Make my carriage ready." Conner ordered the nearest footman who didn't seem the least bit shocked at their sudden exit from the coatroom. "The duke's daughter is quite ill and needs to be returned home."

"I feel quite terrible for making you leave before the opera is over," she whispered into his shoulder.

"The show ye put on was much more interestin'

than anythin' on the stage. Besides, I told ye I hoped to hide away with ye again and I meant it."

"Oh, yes, thank you so much for the flowers. They brightened up my bedchamber significantly."

"They must have been only one arrangement in a hundred after your comin' out party. It was the talk o' the town." He began leading her out the door and toward an impressive carriage with men in bright livery guarding it and an intricate crest featuring a fierce looking bull adorning the sides.

Charlotte allowed him to help her into the carriage before he settled himself opposite from her. "I had no idea you liked the opera and even less of an idea that you owned any English clothes. They suit you."

"As I've said before, I wish to be respected by the English so I did adopt some o' their ways. Purple suits ye just as the English clothes suit me."

She lightly touched the amethysts at her ears. "Thank you. They were my mother's."

"Ye'd look even better with emeralds by your eyes, if that were possible." The deep brogue rolled off his tongue and hit her like the softest silk.

Charlotte cleared her throat to give her time to catch her breath. "Well, I don't own any emeralds, so I'm sorry to say that you will be disappointed if we meet in the future. Thank you again for helping me. You really did rescue me tonight."

"Do no' mention it. I would hope that someone would do the same for one o' my sisters if she was in your position."

"You have sisters?"

"Six. All younger than I."

43

"You must have been quite outnumbered in your youth."

"Still am," he answered as the carriage began moving down the cobblestone streets. "Four o' my sisters are married already."

"Four of them? There are certainly a lot of women in your family."

"Aye, a great group of lasses, my sisters are, and each o' the married ones have a gaggle o' daughters."

"Does that displease you?" Charlotte dared to ask, remembering Richard Howard's displeasure with having several daughters of his own.

"Displease me? No' at all. I love them. Wonderful lasses with big hearts and bigger mouths." His lips curled into a smile as if remembering something fond.

"I'm glad to hear you don't mind having so many girls about you."

He looked at her curiously. "Why would I mind? A lass is worth no less than a lad, after all."

"I wish all men thought that way." Charlotte looked out the small carriage window at the passing townhomes.

Conner leaned over in his seat and took her hands in his. "Anyone who says you're worth less than any lad is a fool and does no' deserve your time."

She looked back at him in surprise at his boldness. He leaned so close that it would only take her moving forward a few inches to make their lips meet. But then she would risk becoming one of the chieftain's many conquests. Charlotte pulled her hands from his grasp. "It is merely the way of things here. Men control women from birth until the afterlife and beyond."

Conner sat back in his seat, his sculpted face not showing any disappointment at his advance being spurned. "Strange way o' things. In Scotland, there have been many warrior queens who ruled in their own rights and women can own land and livestock the same as any man. In that way, *barbaric* Scotland is more progressive than *civilized* England."

"Truly?" Charlotte dared not dream that there was somewhere she would be treated as an equal instead of a possession.

"Truly." He nodded. "Scotland loves women."

She stifled a wry laugh at his statement. "So I've heard."

"And what have ye heard?" Conner asked as the carriage slowed to a halt in front of her home.

She shrugged, watching Conner exit the carriage and hold his hand out to her. "Just how much the Scottish love women. Even when it isn't good for the woman to be loved."

"What do ye mean by that?"

She looked up at him, deep into those bright blue eyes. Wondering how many other women had swooned like she had over his strong legs in a kilt or the way his Scottish tongue spoke her name, Charlotte hardened her heart against him. "You know what I'm referring to."

His striking face was blank. "I really have no idea."

"As you say," she said with a practiced

nonchalance. "I really must get inside."

He bowed over her hand. "May I call on you?"

His request caught her off guard. "Perhaps. But considering how angry my father will be with me over leaving Richard at the opera, I doubt I will be leaving the house or entertaining callers anytime soon."

He grinned at her as she made her way up the stone steps. "I'll take that as an 'aye'!"

Chapter Five

The house was quiet when she entered the night before. Her father and stepmother must have been sleeping and Charlotte didn't even dare to wake Mary to help her undress. Instead, she slipped out of the stiff gown and corset, falling asleep in her underclothes and amethyst jewels.

"Someone must have had a late night," her father proclaimed in the morning when Charlotte came to the dining room after having soaked in a rose water bath.

"I suppose." She looked at the pile of unopened post beside her father and wondered if Richard Howard had written to him about her behavior.

"How was the show? How was Richard?"

Charlotte dipped her spoon into her porridge, quite devoid of any appetite. "The show was lovely. Just as the papers had promised."

"I'm glad you had a nice time. I hope you minded your manners?"

She lowered her head, hoping to melt into the oaken table before making her confession. She wasn't in the habit of lying to her father and would hate to start now. "Well, Father..."

"Sir, I have a package for Lady Charlotte," the butler interrupted as a footman handed him a box carefully wrapped in brown paper.

"A package?" Her father looked curiously at the box. "No return address. Must be from one of those fancy stores you and Abigail order your lady things from."

"I wasn't expecting anything." Charlotte took the package and noted that the handwriting looked vaguely familiar.

"Are you all right, Charlotte?" George asked over his teacup.

"Just tired. I think I'll spend the day going through those invitations for New Year's."

"Good." He nodded absently. "It's tomorrow, is it not? I never celebrate the New Year. It's a young person's holiday."

"Two days, actually. I've put the invitations off for far too long."

"Nonsense. You're fashionably late and no one ever responds to invitations anyway. When your mother and I first began courting, we would go to two or three parties and dinners a night." He looked off at the far wall where a portrait of her mother used to hang before Abigail moved in. "She loved to dance and would be the first, and last, person off the floor. And no matter how late we stayed out, she would greet me in the dining room for breakfast looking as fresh as a rose."

"I remember." Charlotte smiled. "Sometimes I would stay up past my bedtime and wait for you and mother to come home. If she heard me, she would come into my room and tuck me into bed."

"She was a good mother. You know, Abigail does try her best."

"I know," Charlotte conceded. "It was just hard, as a child, to replace my mother with Abigail. Just look at this dining room. As soon as you met Abigail, you moved mother's portrait to the attic."

"I was just doing what I thought would be the best for everyone."

She reached over and placed her hand on her father's. "I know. And you did a fine job."

"You've such a kind heart, Charlotte. I do hope that whoever you marry sees that."

"Me, too, Father. Me, too."

***

As soon as Charlotte closed her bedroom door behind her, she ripped the brown paper from her package to reveal a black velvet box. She clicked open the gold clasp to find a pair of stunning emerald and diamond drop earrings along with a necklace of tiny diamonds framing a large emerald. The set, which was nestled in a bed of dark blue silk, must have cost the buyer a small fortune and she knew exactly who must have sent them.

Charlotte pulled the rope in her room that rung a bell in the servant's quarters, summoning her chambermaid, Mary. The girl scurried in with an excited look on her mousy face. Mary had always been a plain country girl but whenever she had heard a tasty bit of gossip, her face glowed with excitement.

"You look like you have a secret." Charlotte loved the girl's enthusiasm.

"Oh, my lady, I've just come from the market." Her gaze fell on the box of emeralds. "Well, I see you've already gotten some of the news."

"What have you heard?"

"I met a maid who works in Lord MacLeod's kitchens today, so I heard a bit of juicy chatter."

"Go on with it," Charlotte said, sitting on the edge of her bed.

Mary sat at the desk and took a deep breath. "Harriet, that's the maid, said her master express ordered a bunch of jewels and sent them out early this morning. She didn't see what was in the box but I assume it is you who received the gift."

"Is that all?"

"No! He's written home to his sisters to say he's staying in London longer than expected to do some courting."

"Is that so?"

"Harriet saw the lord pacing in his library all evening and she believes she heard your name when he was addressing his butler. But she only saw him for a moment before a footman chased her away."

"Do you think it's why he sent me this?" She held out the box.

Mary's eyes widened. "So it *is* true. He must mean to court you!"

Charlotte sighed, looking at the box of emeralds and diamonds—a show of intention from a known womanizer. "Send them back."

Mary blinked. "Really?"

"Yes. Send them back. No note. Nothing."

"As you wish."

***

"Charlotte! Charlotte!" Her father hammered a fist against her bedroom door, waking her from a fitful nap.

Charlotte sat up and took a moment to rub the sleep from her eyes and rearrange her dress before opening the door. She could only assume her father had spoken to Richard Howard and was coming to chastise her for her behavior. It was an event she was not looking forward to.

She opened the door to reveal her beaming father and a tightlipped Abigail. "What's going on?"

"You've received a proposal today, that's what!" he cried, taking Charlotte to sit on the edge of the bed with him. Abigail stayed standing in the doorway, looking less than delighted to be there, and remained silent.

Charlotte sighed, guessing that Lord MacLeod wouldn't take the returning of the emeralds as a no. "Father, I must decline."

"You don't even know who it was! I'm sure you'll be quite happy."

"Father, I know it's MacL—"

"Richard will be coming by later to give you your ring."

Charlotte felt the room spin and grasped her bedcovers to anchor herself. "Richard? Richard Howard?"

"Yes! He came to me this afternoon and said he

was enamored with you. It's perfect, Charlotte. I trust him completely to keep the estates intact and he has enough money that he'll never squander your fortune away."

"I can't," Charlotte whispered as tears fell down her cheeks.

"Nonsense. No need to be frightened by marriage. All young girls are a bit shy but—"

"No, Father. I can't marry Richard."

"You're refusing him?" His face fell.

"Of course I am!" Charlotte leapt up. "He's more than twice my age and we'd never get along. He's so unpleasant and hates his daughters!"

"He cares for you a great deal, Charlotte. He said the two of you got along tremendously at the opera."

"Well, he's a liar. He was quite rude to me and I left the opera house early just to escape him."

Her father ignored her confession. "I'll have none of your dramatics. Richard is a good man and he will give you a good life. Now, get yourself together and look presentable. He'll be here after dinner to make a formal proposal. I won't have you be an embarrassment," he spat, rising from his seat.

"I won't marry him. I can't!" She stomped her foot like a child and looked toward her stepmother for support. "Abigail, please."

Abigail stepped toward her husband and placed a bony hand on his arm. "George, we really can't force her to marry Richard if she doesn't wish to."

George turned to Abigail in surprise. "Surely you see what an offer he is making her?"

"Of course I do," Abigail admitted. "But, at the

same time, she has only just come out into society as a marriageable lady. At least give her until the end of the season to see if another man makes an offer."

"And betray my oldest friend?" George shook his balding head. "Never. He's a good man who will keep her inheritance intact. I trust him implicitly."

"Then give her until the New Year. Just a few days to think her prospects over," Abigail pleaded, her voice perfectly even. "A proposal is always a lot to take in, no matter who the groom might be."

George took a deep breath. "After the New Year. Then I expect you to give your hand to Richard. I will not accept anything else."

"And if I still refuse him?" Charlotte asked, crossing her arms tightly over her heaving chest.

"If you refuse to be the bride of Richard, then you shall be a bride of Christ," he said shortly, making both his wife and daughter gasp.

"But why?" Charlotte sobbed, falling back onto the bed and burying her face in a pillow. "Why give me two vile options?"

"I'm doing what's best for you and for this family. With your wild ways, no other man will attempt to tame you and anyone foolish enough to try would certainly only enter into an engagement with the sole purpose of draining the Glenwood Estate's bank accounts." George turned from his daughter and shrugged his wife's hand from his arm. "Go to your parties and have your fun, because in three days you will be an engaged woman."

Chapter Six

"Charlotte?" Penelope called from the other side of Charlotte's locked bedroom door. "Charlotte, please let me in."

Charlotte crossed the room to open the door and immediately fell into Penelope's open arms. "Oh, Penelope, how did you know to come to me?"

"Abigail sent for me."

"Really?" Charlotte pulled her inside and locked the door again behind her. "Then you know the horrible news?"

"No. She only wrote that you needed me and that I should pack to spend a few days with you until after the New Year's celebration. My maid's bringing up my things now. Is something amiss?"

"It's terrible. My father is behaving in a most horrid manner. He says I am to either marry Richard or go to a nunnery!"

Penelope gasped in horror. "No! It can't be!"

"It's true. He only just told me last night. I've been locked away in my room trying to think of a way out ever since."

"And what have you decided?"

Charlotte dried her tearstained face with the back of her hand. "I can't see another way out. It seems like I either have to spend my life with Richard Howard as my husband or promise myself to God."

"That lecherous beast or a nunnery? Those can't be your only options, I won't allow it!" Penelope sounded so earnest that Charlotte wished dearly that she could believe her friend had that sort of power.

"My lady?" A timid voice whispered at the door. "It's me, Mary."

"I'll get it." Penelope opened the door wide enough for the maid to slip in with a heavy tray and a bag.

"I thought you might want to have your dinner in your room." Mary placed the tray on a small table in front of the fire between two armchairs. "It's your favorite. London broil with all sorts of vegetables and apple pie for dessert."

"Thank you, Mary." Charlotte lifted one of the trays and inhaled deep. "I suppose my father hoped to lure me downstairs with my favorite foods?"

"No, my lady. I told the cook that you might be in need of a little cheering up, then snuck the tray up before they served dinner in the dining room. I hope that wasn't too forward of me?" She dipped a small curtsey.

Charlotte's lower lip quivered and she felt as if she could hug the girl. "No, you did wonderfully, Mary. It was so good of you to think of me."

Marry smiled shyly, holding out the plain cloth bag. "I have something else for you, my lady."

"What is it?" Charlotte asked as she sat at the

table and took the bag.

The maid began taking the tops from the rest of the plates while Penelope took her seat. "I went to Lord MacLeod's home this morning, like you asked."

Penelope looked up from the piece of meat she was cutting. "Lord MacLeod?"

"I'll explain later, Penelope. What happened, Mary?"

"I gave the box to a footman at the back door, with my regrets, and headed for home. I barely made it down the block when none other than MacLeod himself ran up behind me!" Mary took a breath, relishing in her rapt audience. "He was holding the jewelry box in his hand and told me to take it back. He said to tell you that there are no strings attached to the gift, that he merely wished to be kind. He also told me to beg—yes, he used the word *beg*—you to attend his New Year's Eve ball. He said if you don't attend, then he'll be forced to cancel the whole thing entirely, go back to Scotland, and give up trying to befriend the English."

"What a strangely romantic proposal," Penelope whispered, breaking the silence.

"My lady," Mary continued, "he ran after me in little more than his breeches and shirt."

"Not even shoes?" Penelope was fully engrossed in the tale.

"Not even shoes."

"Shoes or no shoes, I'm not taking the gift." Charlotte placed the bag on the table and began eating.

"What is it?" Penelope eyed the bag excitedly.

"What did the wicked Scot give you?"

Charlotte shrugged. "See for yourself."

Penelope slid the velvet box from the bag and opened it to reveal the diamond and emerald jewelry. "Oh, Charlotte, they're gorgeous!"

"And entirely inappropriate." Charlotte attempted to sound unaffected by the chieftain's grand gesture, but found nonchalance almost impossible.

"But surely you mean to keep them," Penelope pressed on, "and go to his New Year's party?"

"I don't know." She put down her fork. "What's the point? Conner MacLeod is nothing but a rogue and I am to be married off to a sour old man."

"But he's such a jolly bloke, even if he does have a terrible reputation. Mary, you've heard the rumors, yes?" Penelope asked the servant.

"Yes, Miss Penelope. I've heard some very terrible things from the other maids." Mary cleared her throat. "Pardon me for speaking this way, but do you know a Miss Elizabeth Shadley?"

Charlotte thought a moment. "Yes, we had the same French tutor." She briefly remembered hearing a whisper of Elizabeth getting herself in the family way. She had left for several months, supposedly to stay with a distant aunt, and returned with a thicker middle and a timid demeanor.

Penelope noticed Charlotte's stunned expression. "What is it?"

"Mary, you aren't saying that Conner MacLeod is the father of Elizabeth's baby?" Charlotte's words felt thick in her throat.

Mary pursed her lips. "That is what has been

said." She glanced toward the clock on the mantelpiece. "I need to return to the kitchens. Will you be in need of anything else?"

"No, Mary, you may go." Charlotte watched the maid slip from the room before turning to Penelope. "Do you think it's true?"

"Perhaps. Everyone did say that Elizabeth must have been with child. Her father had sent her away so suddenly that no one could believe it was anything else. Do you really think it was Conner MacLeod's child?"

"In all honesty, I don't know what to think right now."

"Do you hate him?"

Charlotte sighed. "Truly, I don't think I could. What he did was deplorable, but he's just so very likable. I can hardly believe he would do something like that."

"Maybe it isn't true."

"Unfortunately, all rumors have a basis in fact. I could see how someone would fall victim to his charms."

Penelope's lips curled into a grin. "I think *you* would rather like to fall victim to his charms."

"Oh, you're terrible." Charlotte giggled, in spite of herself.

"No, I'm *right*. He may be an appalling womanizer, but that just makes him the perfect candidate for your final fling."

"My final fling?"

"Why, of course! You really must have one last scandalous night." Penelope grinned. "What does it matter if the Scot has less than pure intentions, if you fear you'll spend the rest of your life trapped with your father's friend?"

"I suppose you have a point, even if what you suggest is terrible. There wouldn't be any harm in keeping the jewels and going to MacLeod's ball if I don't give a fig about my reputation."

Penelope fingered the jewels and looked up at her friend. "Speaking of rumor and reputations…Char, people have heard what happened at the opera."

Charlotte groaned as she resumed her dinner. "What have they heard?"

"Bits and pieces, I assume. Many saw you and that Richard man quarreling in the box. Then they saw you fleeing the opera house with the Scotsman."

"Well, that is what happened."

Penelope's blue eyes widened in surprise. "It is? How could you not tell me?"

"I'm sorry, it just happened so fast and now my father's marrying me off.…I just had more pressing matters."

"Tell me everything!" Penelope ignored her dinner and went straight for the dessert. "Did something happen between you and the Scot?"

"Nothing improper. He merely saw my altercation with Richard and offered to deliver me safely home."

Penelope's face fell. "That's it?"

"You look rather disappointed that MacLeod didn't ravage me in his carriage." Charlotte let out a small laugh, despite herself.

"Honestly, I *am* a bit disappointed. You had a

chance for a grand affair."

"Penelope, you're so wicked."

"No, I'm a romantic and only want you to have a bit of fun before your wedding."

"They way you say it, it sounds more like a funeral."

"Isn't it?" Penelope asked, looking at her friend intently.

"I suppose so. It's the death of my youth, my dreams, my freedoms. Oh, Penelope, this is quite the mess." She dropped her head into her hands. "What am I to do?"

"You do your best to be charming and free tomorrow. You wear your Scottish emeralds, a scandalous dress, dance too much, and drink even more." Penelope put down her pie, stood, and went over to Charlotte's wardrobe. "You will be the talk of the town!"

"Isn't that a bad thing?"

"It is never a bad thing to be the talk of the town, even if it is for showing too much skin and being a perfect little fool. Who knows? Perhaps sodden old Richard will be so appalled by your behavior that he'll revoke his offer of marriage!"

"If only."

"It wouldn't hurt to try." Penelope pulled two dresses from the armoire. "Now, let us find the perfect dress for your night of scandal."

Chapter Seven

"Char, you do look lovely." Penelope admired her as they stood in the lady's cloakroom with the other women.

Charlotte turned before one of the floor-length mirrors to admire herself from all angles. "It is a lovely gown for my final night of freedom." It was a cream dress trimmed in silver and green ribbons. Her corset had been hooked within an inch of her life and it helped to thrust her full breasts against the dramatically low neckline of the gown. Her auburn hair was twisted up upon her head, being held in place by green ribbons and a diamond band. Curls brushed the bare shoulders that peeked out from small gauze sleeves. The gifted jewels hung heavy on her neck and ears—a secret display of rebellion.

Penelope twirled her own blue and white gown. "I do say, with that neckline you will be quite the piece for gossip."

"That is the point, is it not?" Charlotte pinched her cheeks to redden them. "To be a grand

61

scandal?"

"Yes, I suppose it is. And judging by the looks some of the other ladies are giving you, I think you've already become the talk of the evening."

Charlotte looked around at the other women who eyed her low neckline and French-style ball gown with interest. She hooked her arm with Penelope's and gave her a smile. "Then let us make our grand entrance."

"Lady Charlotte Holloway, daughter of the Duke of Glenwood and Lady Penelope Elmsly, daughter of the Baron Elmsly," a rail thin announcer shouted to the crowd as the two girls entered the room.

The eyes of the partygoers were on them and many an older lady fanned herself upon seeing Charlotte's daring dress, while many a man viewed it appreciatively. Charlotte smiled coyly at the crowd, egged on by Penelope's unvoiced giggles.

As her eyes surveyed her surroundings, she found that Conner MacLeod's ballroom was impressive. Cream marble made up the floors and many pillars while tall windows trimmed with dark blue drapes probably let in a lovely amount of sun during the day. The MacLeod bull crest was placed prominently between each window that pointed up toward vaulted ceilings. The ceiling itself boasted a fresco of cherubs in flight through a cloudy sky and framed three identical chandeliers. It was clear by this opulent ballroom that Lord MacLeod was a very well-to-do Scottish noble.

"Should we begin the evening by dancing with all the most flirtatious of the bachelors or by having our first glass of punch?" Penelope asked while surveying the crowd.

"Punch, I think," Charlotte answered. She led the way toward a refreshment table where they were promptly given crystal goblets filled with spiced wine. "I believe I will need some Dutch courage to get through tonight."

"Careful, ladies, the punch is quite powerful." A familiar voice broke in between them.

Charlotte turned to face Conner MacLeod who was dressed in full Scottish regalia. Seeing his strong-boned face and hearing his deep brogue made her weak in the knees so she took a moment, just a moment, to compose herself before turning to meet him. "Good evening, Lord MacLeod."

"Good evening, my lady." Conner brushed his lips against the back of her hand but his eyes were firmly glued to the creamy skin she had exposed that night. "I see ye have decided to accept my gift?"

"A gift given in friendship is never to be denied," Charlotte said simply as Conner greeted Penelope.

"Then I hope ye will do me the honor of a dance after I've greeted the rest of my guests?" he asked, hopefully.

Charlotte looked down, trying to avoid his piercing blue eyes. "If my dance card is not too full."

Conner smirked. "As a chieftain, I think I had a bit o' right to push others aside to claim my dances."

"Not in England, you don't," Penelope cut in. "See to her soon before she is snapped up by some fabulous Count."

"I shall," he said, taking in her sultry form once again. "Excuse me, ladies. I'll find ye again soon."

"That kilt is almost as scandalous as your dress," Penelope whispered, watching him walk away.

Charlotte took a sip, noting that it tasted just as robust as Conner had warned. "I rather like it. It's so different compared to the usual suits every British man wears. So very…*primal*."

"Did you see the way the Scot looked at you?" Penelope took care to speak just loud enough for Charlotte to hear over the music. "He looked as if he would simply eat you up."

"I do believe he would if he could."

"And I do believe you would let him."

Charlotte nearly choked on the last of her punch. "Oh, hush, Penelope."

Penelope handed her a new, full glass. "Even now, he's watching you."

She looked over the heads of the society guests until she saw Conner, who was deep in conversation with some men. Their eyes locked almost immediately. He nodded in acknowledgment before she tore her gaze away. "Yes, I suppose he is."

"And here's Charlie!" Penelope smiled as the recognizable redhead made his way through.

"Ladies." Charlie dipped a bow. "So glad I ran into you."

"Have you been here long?" Charlotte asked.

"No, I've only just arrived." He grinned at Penelope. "May I trouble you for a dance?"

Penelope looked at Charlotte as if for permission. "Would you be all right here by yourself?"

"Of course," Charlotte said, draining her glass. "Go on."

"I'll bring her back safe and sound after I've taken her for a whirl." Charlie winked, taking Penelope by the hand.

Charlotte watched as the couple entered the dance floor. Penelope danced with such natural grace and Charlie looked to be a willing and jolly partner. It was hard not to be a bit jealous of her dearest friend's freedom and the ease with which she smiled and laughed. Charlotte doubted that she would be that effortlessly happy when she was married to Richard. In fact, she foresaw that her life would be quite devoid of all fun and merriment.

The third cup of punch went down much smoother than the two that came before. Tucked away near a large floral arrangement of leafy ferns and pure white roses, Charlotte was able to view the party over the rim of her goblet. Couples were twirling on the dance floor in a vibrant array of petticoats and silks. Penelope was almost lost in the crowd, but Charlotte spied her friend, head tilted back in laughter, beginning another dance with Charlie.

"Ye do no' look much like ye are enjoyin' yourself." Conner seemed to appear from nowhere but he stood before her as if he had been there all along.

Charlotte was rightly startled. "Goodness, you scared me!"

"I'm sorry. I did no' mean to sneak up on you."

"It's quite all right. You throw a lovely ball."

"Thank ye. I really am pleased ye accepted my gift. I meant it when I said you were made for emeralds." His voice caressed her ears and made her heart beat faster.

"Do you give all of your friends such lavish gifts?" Charlotte dared to ask, looking up at him. He did have a lovely sculpted face. He possessed a strong jawline, a straight nose, and those piercing blue eyes that peered at her from under thick lashes and a steady brow.

"No." He moved a step closer and reached out his hand to gently touch the emerald dangling from her ear. "Only you."

Charlotte turned her face away from him and noticed some of the guests looking at them from behind fans, openly and without embarrassment. "You are too familiar with me. It will make people talk."

"Dash other people. Put down your glass and dance with me."

She obliged and allowed him to escort her to the dance floor just in time for the next song to begin. "You do like to cause a scandal."

"As do you, if that dress is any indication of your intentions. I think ye want to cause a bit o' talk in your own right."

Her lips curled into a smirk. "And if I did?"

"Then I'd say ye are doin' a right fine job." He breathed into her ear as he held her much closer than propriety normally allowed.

Charlotte let him lead her about the marble dance floor as easily as he did the night of her launch into society. But tonight was different. Tonight he held her tighter and looked at her longer, more intently, than she had ever been looked at before. Wordlessly he read into her soul and allowed her no access into his own. All he gave her was a perfect smile on supple lips and the feeling like she was the most beautiful girl in the room. It was understandable why he was able to seduce ladies with such ease. The man was ruggedly handsome and made of muscle that Charlotte could feel between his jacket and shirt. She imagined him riding horses, bareback, over grassy hills to fight an invading force or hunt a wayward stag.

"Are ye all right, my lady? Ye look a bit flushed." Conner's face was filled with concern as he brought her to a halt.

Charlotte, suddenly aware that she had been blushing due to less than pure thoughts, had to good sense to begin fanning herself with her hand. "I'm quite all right. The dancing must have been a bit much for me."

"As was the punch, most like," he teased. "Let's take a step out o' the ballroom so ye might catch your breath."

They made their way out toward the empty main hallway. It was made up of exquisite marble, just as the ballroom was. The high, curved, ceilings displayed crystal chandeliers and a pale blue sky with more perky cherubs on fluffy clouds. A double staircase of dark wood led to the second floor while the MacLeod coat of arms was prominently displayed above. In a small alcove there sat a small lounger and two wingback chairs surrounding a low table.

As soon as they sat in the slightly hidden alcove, a butler came to them to take any requests. "Bring us a selection of finger foods as well as hot chocolate," Conner ordered.

"Hot chocolate?" Charlotte asked. "How very French of you."

"I sampled it last time I was in Paris. It's become a favorite o' mine."

"I don't drink it nearly as much as I would like," Charlotte admitted, settling into her chair. The plush cushions enveloped her comfortably, making her more aware of her spinning head. "My stepmother believes it gives you bad skin."

"Ach." Conner waved a large hand. "Nonsense. I have a cup or more a day and I'm the picture o' health."

The butler reappeared with a tray loaded with cakes, finger sandwiches, slices of sweet fruit, two glasses of hot chocolate, and an assortment of candies. "Do ye require anythin' else, Laird MacLeod?"

"No, Peters, ye may go." Conner dismissed his butler and handed Charlotte a cup.

"Laird?" Charlotte's brow scrunched in confusion.

"Laird is my status in Scotland and is akin to a sort-o' king in some parts o' Scotland," he explained simply.

"I'm having teacakes and chocolate with a king?" She giggled, inhibitions firmly lowered.

"It would appear so."

She stifled a burst of laughter. "Do remind me to tell Penelope I've had dessert with a king!"

"Are ye feelin' all right, my lady?"

"I do apologize." Charlotte took several deep breaths. "In all honestly, I never drink so much and find myself so very…very…"

"Drunk?" Conner offered with a grin.

"Very much so. But I will try to compose myself."

"As ye do," he said before taking a bite of a sandwich.

"You have a lovely home, Lord MacLeod." Charlotte reached for a strawberry and popped it into her mouth. "Do you always keep house in London, or are you just visiting for the season?"

"My father bought this building shortly after my youngest sister was born. My parents rarely used it, but I keep a staff when I wish to visit, or stay, for a time."

"Well, I very much like your style of decoration—classically English with a touch of Scotland."

"Is that what ye call it?" Conner seemed amused. "Well, ye should see my real home in Scotland. A medieval castle on a cliff, atop a steep hill no army could capture."

"How perfectly grand! Are the castles there much different than those you've seen in England?"

"The older in England match those in Scotland, for the most part. But large, modern, cities have grown around the castles in England while, in my home, they're still verra much the same."

"Fascinating. I would like so much to travel as you do. I've never been out of England."

"Shame. I think you'd take a fancy to some o'

the other cities I've been to."

"Where have you been?"

"All over. France, Spain, Ireland…well, my mother is from there, actually. So I've spent a fair bit o' time there with my cousins."

"Ah, is that why your first name is Conner?" Charlotte inquired. "In all the books I've read, I've never seen a Scottish Conner."

"Aye, that's where it comes from, but now ye *have* seen a Scottish Conner!"

She giggled. "I suppose I have. Tell me, have you been to the Americas yet?"

He shook his head. "No, it's one o' the only places I've yet to see."

"Nonetheless, you're ever so lucky," she gushed, placing a hand tightly on his arm for emphasis. "The art and architecture must be divine, not to mention the food! Of course many cooks study other places and bring in cuisine, but I bet it's much better in its country of origin."

He pushed the tray toward her from his perch on the edge of one of the chairs. "Try a crème puff."

She let go of his arm and selected one of the smaller desserts. Charlotte took a small bite of the confection, careful to not let the powdered sugar fall upon her dress. "So delightful. Your cook must be good."

"Verra. I never travel without her."

"Her? So you value her opinion very much."

"Aye, she's been with me for many years."

"You've said that women in Scotland are treated with respect like men, isn't that correct?"

"Verra much so." He leaned forward. "Tell me,

my lady, if ye could do whatever ye wished, what would it be?"

Charlotte was taken a bit aback. "I don't believe anyone has ever asked me that before."

"There's a first time for everythin'."

"Well, you might think me silly, but I'd very much like to open a home for orphans on my main estate. It has dozens of rooms and a rather large acreage."

"I do no' think that's silly at all. Fine idea."

"You really think so?" Charlotte asked, briefly wondering if he was agreeing with her because she was a woman, or his guest, or too drunk to argue with.

"Aye. There are far too many children without families and no' enough quality places to put them."

"That's what I've always said!"

"Why the interest? Surely a lady like yourself does no' come into contact with the unwanted?"

She shuddered. "Oh, I *hate* that term. Orphaned children are not 'unwanted.' They just merely haven't found a home yet. When I was young, my mother would take me to the workhouses to bring money and food as a charitable donation. I would go in a fine lace dress and play tag with children dressed in rags. It wasn't until I was much older that I realized how terrible it was for me, this little china doll, to play with these poor children who had nothing while I had everything and more. I mean, look at me." She gestured to her couture gown and heavy jewels. "What I'm wearing could feed a poor family for ages."

"So it's guilt that's drivin' ye to do good?"

"I hate to say that, but I suppose it's true, in a way. I feel that with my family's fortune, and the lands we own, I could house dozens of children and give them the proper food, education, clothing, and start that they deserve."

"So, what's stoppin' ye?"

"I'm a lady. Ladies can't own land or have money of their own outside of whatever allowance is given them by their male relations."

"Even when it's to undertake such a noble deed? Seems unfair."

"It is. The best a lady in my position can hope for is to marry a forgiving husband who indulges her philanthropic fancies."

"Is that what ye hope for?" His voice was quiet, as if he was taking great care to not be overheard. "A permissive husband?"

"It's the only thing I can hope for." Charlotte tried to not sound too bitter but she was afraid she failed. "After all, my father has the right to marry me off to whomever he pleases and I must oblige him."

"Terrible." He shook his head, causing strands of sandy blond to brush the tops of his broad shoulders.

"Never mind that. Sometimes one can never help their lot in life, but merely do their best to make something out of the one they're given." She stretched a bit. "I feel a bit better now that I've eaten. I'm so sorry I'm a bit of a mess."

"You are never a mess, my lady. Although I did warn ye about the punch." He looked around at the empty hall. "Would ye like to take a tour? Nothin' improper, o' course, just a turn about the main floor?"

Normally, Charlotte would have declined such an offer. Who knew what would be said the next day if she were caught with an unrelated man in secret? But, the entire point of going to MacLeod's New Year's ball was to drink herself silly and cause a bit of a stir, and she was certainly on the right path. "That would be most agreeable. Thank you."

He stood, smiling, and held out a hand to her. "You really must see my library first. I have the feelin' that ye would find it verra interestin'."

She took his arm as he walked her down the grand hall. At the end of the corridor was a set of white doors with golden handles that pushed open easily as soon as Conner gave them the lightest of taps. Charlotte audibly gasped at the size of the room.

Taking up two stories, the library was twice the size of her father's. Walls and walls of books lined the full shelves and a series of rolling ladders were added so that one might reach the upper shelves with ease. An impressive fireplace both warmed the room and set it with a cozy glow that beckoned her to take a seat in one of the dark blue armchairs that were piled with golden pillows. A portrait of a woman in a gilded frame looked down upon her from atop a horse.

Charlotte's slippers made no noise as she detached herself from Conner to take a better look at her surroundings. A large desk was tucked away in a corner and was heaped with papers and open books. The volumes on the shelf looked old, she noticed upon further inspection. Their leather bindings had suffered abuse and some had no binding at all, but were merely stacks of paper that were tied together with string.

Plotted between the books were numerous curious objects and Charlotte spied a Chinese vase, a golden globe, the model of a warship, and a jar containing some kind of animal among the collection. Overall, the space was even more impressive than she had thought it would be.

"What do ye think?" Conner asked, leaning against the back of one of armchairs.

"It's fantastic." Charlotte picked up a model of a suit of armor, smaller than the average songbird. "You have so many books. There's no way you could ever read all of them."

"I give it my best try." He smirked. "If ye think this is a lot, then you should see my library in Scotland. It's larger than this room with books from all corners o' the world in several languages. I usually buy and order my books here, then take my favorites back home with me."

"And the rest just sit here, unread?"

"I get a bit o' time to myself when I'm here so I read more than ye'd think."

"Honestly, I've never thought of you as much of a reader."

"Ye think I spend all my time raidin' and pillagin' like a Viking?"

Charlotte reddened. "Oh, no, nothing like that…just…hunting, maybe."

"O' course I hunt just like your father and his lofty friends. The difference is that in Scotland we eat what we kill. And, after I hunt my supper, I have plenty o' time to read."

"It must have taken years to accumulate such a library. These would be enough books to last me for years." She ran her fingers down the spine of a particularly faded book. "I bet these are all just so fascinating."

"Ye can borrow whatever ye like."

She turned to him, beaming. "Really? I can borrow your books?"

"Why not? Like ye said, they just sit around when I'm no' here. I'll have my butler made aware that you are to borrow whatever ye like. Ye seem like a voracious reader."

"Oh, Lord MacLeod, that is so gracious of you." She looked up at the rows of books and had to crane her neck to see the end. "I have positively no idea where to start."

"Conner," he stated, taking a few steps toward her. "Please, call me Conner."

"I don't think I should. It's ever so intimate."

His shoulder lifted in a shrug. "It's my name."

"So is Lord Macleod."

"Just try it, Charlotte." Her name rolled off his tongue like honey and sent a shiver down her spine.

She glanced toward the open door to ensure no one would hear their exchange. The effects of the punch were wearing off, making her almost painfully aware of the impropriety of the situation. "I don't know if I should."

He looked at her with mirth in his piercing eyes. "Ye come to a party dressed up to play the wicked lass, but do no' want to be wicked enough to say a simple name?"

"I didn't wear this to be wicked, nor will I shy away from your name," she snapped, suddenly aware of their proximity. While they had been talking, he had taken slow steps to be closer to her and now she was near enough to reach out and touch his face, if she wished. And, oh, how she wished.

"Then be a wicked lass and say it," he dared.

"Conner," she whispered, barely loud enough for him to hear.

"What was that? The wind?" he asked, looking about dramatically, as if her voice were softer than the beats of the ball's music, wafting through the halls.

Her heart raced and her breathing quickened at his request. She suddenly felt as if her corset was laced too tight as her bust strained against the silk. "Conner," Charlotte said again. She liked the way his name felt in her mouth and almost hoped he would ask her to say it again.

He came closer, still. "Charlotte."

"Conner," she breathed.

He lifted a hand to her face, gently cupping her cheek. "You are so beautiful, Charlotte."

She looked down, not accustomed to be spoken to in such a casual manner. "We should not be so familiar."

"And ye should never look down when you have the ability to show off those eyes." He slid his fingers down her cheek and under her chin to lift it up. "I've never seen such eyes. Green as the hills, gold as the wheat in the sun, and a bit' o' purple heather, all different in a turn o' the head."

She looked up at his face, fighting the twist of excitement in the bottom of her stomach. His hair, golden and deliciously tousled, swept his high cheekbones and the edges of his sculpted chin. His own eyes were full of lust and she could see herself in their depths. Her pulse leapt again as she felt his hand touch her lightly on the side, pulling her toward him. Her hands rested on his chest now and she could feel the beating of his heart, strong and as fast as her own.

"Conner, what are we doing here?" she asked, breathlessly.

His full lips twisted into a grin. "What's only natural when a man is with a woman like you...so young and pretty, so full of life."

"It isn't natural between a *lord* and a *lady*."

"Well, since I'm the *chief* o' a clan, I do no' think the rules apply to me," he said gruffly before pressing his mouth to her hers.

Charlotte found herself letting him kiss her, something she could barely imagine before. She had never allowed a man to kiss her, yet, here she was, alone with a Scot while they shared a passionate embrace. His lips were soft and warm, malleable to her own and perfectly suited. Her back was pressed against a bookshelf and she found herself pinned there by his hard body.

The force of their bodies shook loose several books but neither even glanced at the volume on the floor. Conner's tongue pressed against her lips and her mouth opened easily to allow him entry. The hand that once touched her face dragged its way down to her neck and he brushed his thumb lightly against her throat.

She instinctively thrust her chest toward him, an invitation for him to continue. When his lips followed down to her bare shoulder, Charlotte grew weak at the knees and clutched tightly to his jacket. Her breathing grew ragged. His mouth savored her creamy skin and he dared to brush his fingers over a breast, making her moan. With one final, hard kiss to her lips he pulled away, leaving them both breathless.

"Are ye angry with me now?" he asked her softly.

Charlotte shook her head, trying to clear her foggy mind. "No, not angry…merely surprised."

"How did I surprise ye?" He backed away but still kept a hand at her waist. "Certainly ye knew it had to be comin' since the first night I saw ye."

"How ever would I know to expect that?"

"I thought…" He pursed his lips and looked toward the door. "I'm no' sorry I did it."

"I'm not sorry you did, either," she admitted, surprising herself with her own boldness. She wasn't sorry that they hadn't been caught, either. She understood well that someone could have wandered in at any moment and seen them kissing.

He grinned. "Then I might be tempted to do it again."

"I would rather you didn't," she said primly, stepping away. She took a moment to straighten her skirts and compose herself again, taking a shaky hand to her hair.

"Then ye don't care to kiss me again?"

She narrowed her eyes. "I believe it was *you* who did the kissing."

"And I believe that ye were a fine participant. Verra willin'," he teased, attending to his own disheveled shirt and jacket.

"We...we should go back to the party. Soon someone will notice the host is gone."

"I suppose ye are right, even though I do no' wish to take ye back to the ball when I've had ye to myself all this time."

Charlotte bit a lip, fighting the beating of her heart and her own wish to stay in the library. "You know," she started, changing the subject, "I never did thank you for your gift. Although I did fight you on it, I do rather like emeralds."

A look of satisfaction crossed his face, all discussion of the library over. "Glad to hear it. I knew they would suit ye well. Now, it's only fair we show off these fine gems to the rest o' my guests before the clock strikes midnight." He offered his arm to Charlotte. "Join me in the ballroom?"

Chapter Eight

Old ladies tittered and fluttered their feathered fans as Charlotte glided by on Lord MacLeod's arm. She smiled politely at their judgmental faces as if she were a queen greeting her subjects and allowed everyone to quietly judge the dress on her body as well as the rake on her arm. Out of the corner of her eye, she saw Penelope holding court with a group of handsome admirers.

For a moment, she wondered if she would ever feel this happy and free again. She felt safe and rather much like herself while in the care of Conner MacLeod. If he weren't a scoundrel who seemed to enjoy ruining London's fine ladies, Charlotte wouldn't think twice about allowing him to pursue her—not that her father would ever allow it, anyway.

"Look at how they all admire ye," Conner whispered, his head tilted down so she could hear his deep brogue.

"I doubt very much that they are *admiring* me."

"Then ye do no' give yourself enough credit.

You are the loveliest lady here and, I dare say, the loveliest in London."

"Just London? Not all of England? Or Scotland?" she teased, throwing him a pout.

"No, my lady, I can no' go against my own country by sayin' ye are prettier than all the Scottish lasses, in front o' everyone. I might lose my crown!" He spun her so they were face to face on the dance floor. "But, as long as you won't tell the Scottish lasses, I'll tell ye that you are the prettiest lady in England, Scotland, and all the other lands I'm too lazy to name."

"Tell me, are all Scottish men such shameless flirts?"

"Aye, I do believe we are," he answered as he spun her jauntily around another couple. "And I do believe you lovely English ladies love it."

Charlotte's stomach dropped as she suddenly remembered the poor Miss Elizabeth and her bastard child. While they were dancing in finery, there was a small child out there in the world who had been utterly abandoned. She abruptly let go of Conner's hands. "I'm sorry. I do believe I have to sit down."

"Are ye all right? Should I send for a doctor?" His features showed concern as he took in her face, which had probably grown pale.

"No, I'm just going to have a moment to myself." Charlotte turned from him and stalked over to a row of chairs normally reserved for chaperones and the mothers of girls attending the dance.

Conner followed her to her seat. "Might I fetch ye a glass o' water or something to eat? Do ye need to go home?"

"No," she replied curtly, looking past him to find Penelope among the dancers. "You have guests. Go attend to them. I'll be fine."

He looked at her strangely for a moment before giving her a small bow and retreating into the crowd. Charlotte tried to take her mind, and eyes, off the Scottish Chieftain by searching for her friend. She finally caught a glimpse of Penelope by the refreshments table and rushed over to meet her.

"Everything all right?" Penelope asked. She fanned her cheeks, flushed from dancing. "You look rather unhappy."

"It's just Lord MacLeod," she whispered.

"He did something to upset you?"

"No, not really. He's just so charming that it makes me forget what a scoundrel he is."

"I saw you two disappear for quite some time earlier, and I'm sure the other guests have as well."

She rolled her hazel eyes and took a glass of punch from the table. "We just had a chat in the main hall and he showed me his library."

"Oh, is that what we're calling it these days?" Penelope slapped Charlotte playfully with her fan. "You little harlot."

Charlotte considered telling Penelope about the kiss they shared, but thought better of it as she would tease her the rest of her living days about 'her Scot.' "Do stop it. We really did only talk. He's a wonderful listener and even entertained my ideas about a children's home."

"So he supports your dreams and listens to you blather away all evening instead of spending it flirting with the other ladies?" Penelope asked in a sarcastic tone. "That scoundrel!"

"He *is* a scoundrel. No amount of intelligent conversation or handsomeness will negate Elizabeth and her baby."

"You're not looking to make a husband out of him, so who cares if he's a cad? He's terribly good looking and anyone who sees the two of you would think you were involved. You know, many fine ladies take a lover besides her husband," Penelope suggested. "Just because you have to marry Richard doesn't mean you must be faithful to him. It's not like you're marrying him for love, or even of your own free will."

"I know lots of people take lovers, but I could never do that. I intend to take my marriage seriously no matter who my husband is. Maybe Richard and I will grow to tolerate each other."

"How romantic," Penelope mused dryly.

"It's the best I can do." She thought of the kiss she shared with Conner and wondered how nice it would be to feel that kind of passion every day of her marriage.

"Then do it tomorrow. For tonight you must dance and drink and flirt like a common brewery maid, remember? Tomorrow you become a proper lady but tonight is your last night to be nothing more than the young girl you are."

Charlotte smiled. "You're right, Penelope. I'm letting thoughts about dreadful Richard and MacLeod's past ruin my last evening as a free woman."

"Then why not have another dance with your

Scot?" Penelope peered over Charlotte's shoulder. "He's been staring at you since you two came back from your little tour and he seems terribly distressed."

"There are a dozen other people he could be looking at right now."

"You're blushing!" Penelope clapped her hands together. "Now, if only there was a way to get him over here in time for a New Year's kiss. We have very little time left."

"Penelope, don't," Charlotte begged as her friend looked about with dramatic thoughtfulness.

"Lord Macleod!" Penelope called over her, waving her hand in the air. "Do come here a moment."

"You're a terrible friend," Charlotte mumbled.

"And you do love me for it." Penelope smiled as Conner came up to them. "Hello, Lord MacLeod. Charlotte was just telling me what a lovely tour you gave her of your home."

Conner raised a brow at Charlotte. "Is tha' so?"

"Oh, yes," Penelope continued. "I've heard you're quite the conversationalist so I thought I would ask you over here to entertain Lady Charlotte a bit more while I excuse myself for a dance. I haven't quite finished the list on my dance card."

He bowed at the two women. "I'm always at your service."

"Especially Charlotte's." Penelope poked Charlotte with her fan. "I think I'll wander over toward the Count of Bentler. I dare say it has been a solid five minutes since he's had a dance."

Charlotte watched her blend into the crowd

before turning to Conner. "I'm sorry about her. She loves to tease me mercilessly."

"I like her." He nodded. "Seems like a good friend."

"She's the best, really. I don't know what I would do without her."

"Charlotte." His voice lowered. "I didn't offend you earlier, did I? Ye ran off so suddenly."

"No. I just felt very dizzy and needed to sit and refresh myself."

"And ye are feelin' better now?"

"Quite, thank you."

"Then might I persuade ye to give me the last dance o' the year?"

Charlotte was momentarily confused. "Last dance of the year?"

He nodded to a large clock next to the refreshments table. As the New Year's timepiece, it had a place of honor where it was visible from almost anywhere in the room. "Almost midnight. I'd be honored to dance my emerald queen into the New Year."

"Your emerald queen?"

"Aye. No lady has ever looked finer in jewels made for royalty."

She held out her hand. "Then stop your flattery and dance with me."

He grinned and led her to the center of the floor, oblivious to the looks they garnered. Certainly some people noticed them both missing from the ballroom for quite some time and, undoubtedly, even more noticed how attached they were while in the crowd. If anyone saw what had occurred in the library…Charlotte blushed at the thought as Conner weaved her in between the couples and grinned at her unabashedly while they danced.

"Countdown to midnight! It's almost time!" A voice called from somewhere near the front of the room. "Ten! Nine!"

Everyone stopped dancing, as did Conner and Charlotte. "Eight!" They all called in unison. "Seven."

"How exciting a new year is," Charlotte whispered.

"Six! Five!" The crowd shouted, getting louder.

"Anythin's possible," Conner replied at her side.

"Four! Three! Two! One! Happy New Year!" Everyone shrieked in happiness as the band struck up a lively tune and footmen tossed confetti into the crowd from the balcony above.

"Happy New Year." Conner pulled Charlotte in for a New Year's kiss, deaf to the gasps around them.

Charlotte let herself be taken away by the moment while it lasted and smiled when he pulled away. "Happy New Year."

Chapter Nine

"How was your New Year's, dear?" her father asked over his usual morning paper.

Charlotte thought back to the evening before, to her scandalous gown and the even more shameful kisses with the Scottish chieftain. "Fine."

"Just 'fine'?"

"Yes." She took a bite of toast and almost wished Penelope was still staying with them to break up the awkward silence. Lord knew how difficult it was to keep her quiet. Just last night, Penelope rehashed Charlotte's New Year's kiss as if it were the crime of the century.

"You know, you're going to have to cheer up eventually. No one likes a sour bride."

"I don't much care who loves or hates me at this point."

"And that's too bad for you." He flipped to the next page in his paper, not even looking at his daughter. Even Abigail avoided looking at Charlotte. "You could at least pretend to put on a happy face when Richard comes this afternoon."

"He is to come today? Why?"

"To make a proper proposal."

"What's the point? You've already given me to him."

"Charlotte." He sounded weary. "This is a new year and a chance for you to accept Richard with love."

"I could never accept him with love because I don't love him."

"Then accept him for duty without acting like a child. He is to be your husband and he will be here after lunch to propose. Go take a bath and put on one of your prettiest frocks to accept him."

"Shall I also serve him tea on bended knee and sing him songs of longing while he stares down his nose at me?"

He groaned and put down his paper. "Charlotte, do try to behave yourself today."

Charlotte pushed her chair away from the table. "Of course, Father dearest."

***

"How was last night?" Mary asked as she added rose oils to Charlotte's freshly run bath. "I heard a bit from the other maids at the market."

"And what have you heard?" Charlotte asked, shivering in her light silk robe.

"That Lord MacLeod throws a great ball and a certain lady slipped out of the ballroom with him for quite some time."

Charlotte bit her lip and sat on the edge of the tub, dipping her fingers in the hot water. "Anyone say who it was?"

"The maid didn't know her name. Said it was a woman with auburn hair, a white dress, and emeralds on her ears and neck. Told me, in confidence, that a footman saw Lord MacLeod kissing this mystery woman in his library."

She paled. Charlotte was almost certain that no one had seen them. "Is that all?"

"Well, my lady, since I know that it was obviously you who was seen with Lord MacLeod, perhaps you know better than I what happened." She busied herself by selecting a towel from the bathroom's tiny cupboard while Charlotte slipped off her rope and gingerly sat in the porcelain tub.

"No other gossip?"

"Only that Lord MacLeod was in a jolly mood this morning, whistling as he roamed about and giving all the servants the day off even though his ballroom still needed a cleaning."

Charlotte smiled as she imagined Conner humming in the library over a pile of books. That cheeky rogue. "Anything else?"

"No, my lady, nothing else of any consequence." She placed the towel on a chair next to the claw foot tub. "So did you have a fine night?"

"It was...better than I expected." Charlotte touched her lips, trying to remember the feeling of Conner's against them. In his arms, even for a few short dances and that private embrace, she felt safe and cherished. It made her pulse race madly and her legs tremble. She would never feel that way again, so full of life and passion.

"Oh, my lady," Mary breathed. "You poor dear."

Charlotte was jarred from her thoughts, conscious now of the tears running rivers down her cheeks. "Mary, I'm sorry. I shouldn't let my emotions get to me like this. I don't know what's wrong with me."

Mary paused, placing a hand on her arm. "I'll go lay out your dress for today. Please call out if you need me."

Charlotte watched her dip a short curtsey and close the door behind her. She leaned back in the water, letting it cover her up to her chin. She was careful not to let her hair, which was piled upon her head, touch the fragrant water. Her private bathroom was small and basic—sink, toilet, a claw foot tub, and a cupboard where she stored towels, lotions, and other toiletries.

She used to find her bathing room a calm oasis, but now Charlotte struggled to relax and enjoy her last moments as a single woman. In a mere hour, Richard would arrive and her life would be over. She couldn't even bring herself to eat lunch.

Charlotte thought back again to the night before when she allowed herself a night of freedom—and freedom she did take. She felt as if she had drunk a dozen glasses of punch and she felt ill later from all the sweets and cakes Conner kept bringing to her, and Penelope, after midnight.

As soon as their New Year's kiss was over, all the guests had converged to the dining room where a fantastic spread of food was laid out for them to take and pick at. While she and Conner were not allowed another moment alone, she felt that he still took care to lavish attention on her by making up her plate, giving her a prime seat near the desserts, and bringing Charlotte her cloak himself when it was time for them to leave the ball.

Conner. It seemed so strange to think of him in such an intimate way, although they did share a rather warm moment in his library. But, still, it was just a moment of passion and now she would no longer be free to kiss foreign men in their libraries—or anywhere at all, for that matter. She would spend her days holed up in some bare study with Richard as he stared at her, coldly, from the other side of the room. She shuddered to think about having children with the man. Certainly she couldn't bear to have him touch her as Conner had. And as her husband, Richard would be allowed many more liberties.

Charlotte ran her hands over her body, the body she would soon be forced to share with him. She was always a slender girl, toned from her youth of climbing trees and secretly swimming in the lake behind her father's estate. Her stomach was flat and curved up to pert breasts. The night before, Charlotte had felt her body yearn for attention in a way she never had. Conner's light touch made her skin hot and tender. She pondered if she would never feel that carnal hunger again.

"My lady?" Mary opened the bathroom door. "It's time for you to get ready."

Begrudgingly, Charlotte exited the warm water and wrapped herself tightly with the towel. "It can't be time already."

"I'm afraid it is," she answered, ushering her into the bedroom. "I've laid out your pink muslin day dress. It gives you such rosy cheeks."

"Good," Charlotte muttered, fingering the large white sash on the dress. This would be her burial garb, the dress she would wear to the end of her short life when she accepted Richard. Then, Charlotte had a revelation. "No, not the pink."

"Then your blue and white silks, or maybe the gray?"

"No," Charlotte whispered, still stroking the cloth. "Bring me my black gown. If they want to kill my dreams and my happiness, then I will dress for the funeral."

Chapter Ten

"Dear, God, Charlotte!" George bellowed as she entered the formal sitting room. "What on earth do you have on?"

"A dress." Charlotte sat on the empty couch by the fire and straightened her skirts around her, her face a composed mask.

Her father reddened. "You look like you're going to a bloody funeral!"

"Aren't I, though?"

"Go change this instant!"

"There isn't time." Abigail entered. "I saw Richard's carriage as I came down. He'll be in any moment."

Charlotte smiled at her tiny victory. Here in the sitting room, among the pale yellow furniture, blue walls, and golden décor, she looked positively sinister in comparison. She watched her father huff and stomp around the room for a bit until the butler announced Richard's arrival.

"Richard, old man!" George cheered considerably. "How are you?"

"Quite fine." Richard shook his friend's hand, unsmiling. "I was hoping to have an audience with Lady Charlotte, if that would be agreeable to you?"

"An audience, you say?" He chuckled. "Well, an audience you shall have! Come, Abigail, let us go make ready the tea and leave them alone to chat."

Abigail glanced once at Charlotte, as if concerned, before following George out of the sitting room. Charlotte stared at Richard. His inky hair was slicked back and his beady eyes peered down at her over his humped nose. She recoiled when he took a step near her to take a seat on a chair next to the couch.

"Lady Charlotte, I hope the New Year finds you well," he said blandly.

"Quite well, thank you." She clutched the black muslin of her skirt in an attempt to stop the trembling of her hands.

"You look quite nice today. I approve of dark colors on ladies. Makes them more respectable and less flighty, I believe."

Charlotte momentarily cursed herself for her choice in wardrobe. Perhaps she should have gone with the pink. "Thank you."

"I assume you know why I am here?"

"Yes, my father informed me he was giving me to you a few days ago."

"Is that how he put it?"

"May I speak frankly?"

"I would prefer it."

"My father decided that I would either marry you, or go to a nunnery. He hoped it would end up a love match."

Richard raised a brow. "And you? What are you hoping for?"

"You really want to know?" She wondered if Richard had a heart after all.

"Yes, I believe I do."

"Well, I really don't want to marry you and I don't love you. I hardly even know you."

"I don't expect love, but I do expect respect and obedience in a marriage."

Charlotte's heart dropped. "Am I still to marry you then?"

"Obviously. You come with a good dowry. You're young and healthy enough to bear me a few sons. Besides that, your father is a close friend. I see no reason why we shouldn't be wed."

"You certainly don't love me."

"Love isn't essential for a marriage." He reached a hand into his pocket and pulled out a gold band with a sapphire displayed prominently on top. Charlotte looked at the dark blue stone, not bothering to hide her distaste. "I take it you do not like sapphires?"

"I really much think it doesn't matter what I like."

He shrugged and held the ring out to her. "If you want something else, it is easily remedied. I'll have my jeweler bring you a selection this week. Pick whatever you want."

"Is this it, then?" Charlotte asked, plucking the ring from his upturned palm. "We are betrothed?"

"I suppose so."

She pushed the band onto her ring finger and looked down at it dismally. "If you don't want to marry me, then you can always take this back and we can forget this ever happened."

"I'm sorry, Lady Charlotte, but I intend to have a son and I've decided that you are just the vessel to provide me with one." He sounded so matter-of-fact that tears began welling up in Charlotte's eyes.

"Why me? Can't you just marry someone else? Anyone else?" She hated the desperation in her own voice but saw no other option.

He stood and stepped over to her until his legs were touching her knees. "You find me so repulsive, you'd rather have some Scotsman pawing at you in a darkened room?"

Charlotte gasped. "How did you—"

"I have those who are loyal to me where I need them." Richard reached down and grabbed her by the wrists, pulling her up to him. "And I now know that my little wife will need some looking after when we are in London. Thankfully, in Virginia, Scotsmen are in short supply."

"Virginia?" Charlotte was horrified. "You mean in *America*?"

Richard's grip tightened. "Of course, you dolt. What other Virginia is there? That is where we are to live."

"Please let go, you're hurting me."

"Only after my little wife shows her betrothed the same kindness she showed the Scotsman." He leered down at her, surprising Charlotte with this open brazenness, where he was once a bland man without any sort of passion.

"Stop, sir, I beg of you!" She tried pulling her hands away. He released her only to grab her waist instead.

"What? Only kiss wild men in skirts, do you?" His hand roamed up toward her chest. "Only lift your petticoats for the Scottish?"

"I never!"

"Oh, but you would, in a moment, if I let you." He brought his pointed face toward hers. "Now, I wonder, would you lift those pretty skirts for me?"

"No!" Charlotte tried slapping his face away as he leaned in for a kiss, groping her chest and sweating with the effort.

"Stop being a little bitch and submit to me!" Richard roared, reaching back a hand and striking her in the cheek.

Charlotte fell to the ground, clutching her stinging face. "You…you hit me!" she cried in disbelief.

Richard straightened his cravat and smoothed out his disheveled hair. "You need to learn when to submit to my will. I am to be your husband and you are to be my wife. If I need to raise a fist to you to teach you how to be a proper lady, then that's what I shall do. Perhaps if your father weren't so soft with you, I wouldn't have to have such a hard hand. Now, compose yourself before your parents come back so they can congratulate us on our wedding."

"You're a monster," Charlotte whispered, rising from the floor. "Nothing but a brute!" She lifted her skirts and fled from the room, through the great hall, and outside to the empty streets.

Tears streaming down her face, she ran, the moisture obscuring her vision, her feet pounding on the hard ground. She slowed to a stop only when she saw that she had reached Regents Park. Her fine silk slippers, not meant for sprinting through damp streets, dug into her heels and she could feel the chill soaking through the fabric. A sharp pain in her side quickly worsened due to the tight pressing of her corsets. She focused on the uncomfortable sensation, willing it to overtake the sting on her cheek, which was only overshadowed by the deep heat of humiliation that settled in her chest.

Regents Park wasn't too far from home, but she knew no one would think to look for her there. In spring and summer, the popular park was a hotspot for society to take carriage rides, court, or sample the rowboats. It was the place to be for most of the crush and normally it was packed with ladies and gentlemen.

Now, in the dead of winter, Charlotte found herself very much alone. She walked, in solidarity with her thoughts, until she found herself at a bench facing a pond. The icy waters churned in the January winds but she barely felt the cold.

She looked down at her left hand where the gold and sapphire band pinched her finger. A beautiful weight that she wanted nothing more than to throw into the lake. She tried pulling the ring off but was met with resistance. The gold band wouldn't budge past her knuckle, although she tugged with all her might until her poor finger was red with trying.

"Charlotte?" a voice behind her asked.

She whipped around to see a man on a stately white horse. The man stood before the sun so she couldn't see his face. "Who's there?"

"It's me, Conner." He leapt from his horse, tying

the reins to the bench. "What on earth are ye doin' out here alone?"

"I needed time to myself." She wiped the tears of frustration from her cheeks. "There wasn't time for me to fetch a maid as a chaperone."

"Nor a coat?" Conner pulled his overcoat from his shoulders and placed it around her before joining her on the bench. "What's happened? Ye look like ye come from a funeral."

Charlotte had no idea how cold she really was until Conner gave her his warmed jacket. She clutched it to her, gratefully. "Haven't you heard the good news? I'm to be married."

Conner blinked, his face a mask of confusion as if he thought he heard her wrong. "Ye are to be what?"

She shoved her left hand at him. "Just now. No doubt my father will announce it very soon and there will be a grand wedding in the spring."

Shocked, he nodded his head slowly, examining her ring. "Well, I suppose congratulations are in order."

"Hardly. My father has as good as sold me to his brutish friend."

"Ye don't care for the man?"

"Care for him?" She turned her face toward him and lifted a covering of curls to show him her freshly bruised cheek. "He did this to me after I refused to let him paw me like an animal."

His mask of concern transformed into one of rage. "He *hit* you?"

"Yes. Apparently, Richard has people watching me so he knows about us kissing in the library. He was angry that I would kiss you and not him."

"That does no' give him the right to hit ye."

"When he's my husband he'll have the right to do whatever he wishes."

"I'll kill him." Conner swore, balling his hands into fists. "I swear I'll kill him."

"And then what? Be put to death for murder? I couldn't let that happen." Fresh tears pricked the backs of her eyes. "I won't let that happen."

"So what'll ye do? Marry a man who beats ye just because your father wishes it? How can a man give his only daughter away to a husband who beats her?"

"He doesn't know Richard hit me, but I don't think he would believe me even if I told him. I'll just have to learn how to live with Richard."

He shook his head and took her frozen hand in his. "That's not goin' to happen. You are not marryin' this Richard man." He lifted her gloveless fingers to his mouth and blew upon them, trying to warm them.

"And what will you do, *Lord* MacLeod?" Charlotte asked sarcastically. "Marry me yourself?"

He appeared to consider it for a moment, then brightened. "Yes, Charlotte, if that's what it takes, then that's what I'll do."

She blanched and pulled her hand from his grasp. "No, you will not!"

"Why not? I'd never raise a hand to you, ye know I would no'."

"I know you wouldn't hit me. But I won't have someone marry me out of pity." She sighed and rested her head in her hands, elbows on her knees.

"If only I could be smuggled out of the country on a pirate ship or something. Sail around Africa and East Indies."

"Is that what ye'd do?" He sounded amused. "Be a pirate?"

She shoved him, a smile spreading across her lips. "Stop teasing. I know I'll never be a pirate, or do anything of the sort. It would just be nice to escape."

"I can help ye escape."

"I'm not marrying you, Conner."

"Ye do no' have to marry me. I'm offerin' ye a way out o' this engagement and out o' England if ye'd take it."

Charlotte perked up and looked toward him, her mouth agape. "Are you suggesting what I think you're suggesting?"

"That depends. Do ye believe I'm suggestin' I take ye to Scotland with me?"

"But...but how would that work?" She imagined riding a horse freely over grassy hills, and being married off to a Scotsman in a loveless marriage in another. "I don't get any part of my dowry until I'm married, not that my father would agree for me to run off and marry some Scottish man. How am I to make a living? Where would I live? I'm just a woman in a man's world." Charlotte fought back new tears as she verbalized her shortcomings.

"Do no' be upset." Conner took her hands softly in his own. "Ye'll live at the castle with me as a guest o' the court."

"I can't take advantage of your hospitality forever."

"Aye, ye can. Live at the castle, learn the ways of the Scots, and if ye feel the need to earn your keep, then you can keep my sisters company on occasion. They'd benefit from bein' around a lass their own age. It's mostly my men and the castle staff at my home. Not many noble ladies come to visit."

"Don't tease me, Conner. I'm hardly the type of woman you'd want teaching your sisters anything."

"And why not? You are beautiful, opinionated, and have a right good sense o' humor."

"My opinions and humor are exactly why you wouldn't want me to influence your sisters. If you want them to be proper ladies, then get a proper lady to teach them."

"Scotland is different than England. Wit and honesty in a lass is somethin' to be prized, not shamed. Ye could live a good life in my homeland. Ye can live in the castle as a true lady and no' have to marry whatever man that father o' yours picks out."

Charlotte laughed wryly, looking down at their clasped hands. "It sounds too good to be true."

"But it's no'. Ye might even be able to go back to England when this all blows over. Your father will no' turn ye out. Just come with me for a year."

"I suppose a lot of proper ladies take a year or two to travel and learn a bit of foreign wares."

"When is he plannin' on a weddin'?"

"Not until the spring, I suppose."

"Then we have lots o' time to prepare. Do ye have someone you trust?"

"Penelope. She'd never betray my trust."

He shook his head. "I do no' know if ye'd want to involve her in this. It might become a scandal and ye do no' want to ruin her chances of having a good life here."

"You're right. I could never involve her in this kind of disgrace." Charlotte thought for a moment. "My maid, Mary."

"Your maid? She isn't loyal to your father?"

"No, she's been my maid for quite a while now and she's never once betrayed me. She's lied to my father for me and hidden quite a few secrets."

"Then use her to keep me updated on the progress o' this engagement. When the time comes, ye can use her to send massages or bring your luggage."

"You'll really do all this for me?" Charlotte asked, clutching tighter to his hands.

"O' course. I'd do anythin' for ye."

Chapter Eleven

"You're right frozen, my lady," Mary clucked as she began unlacing Charlotte's corset. "You'll be lucky if you don't catch your death."

"I'm fine, Mary, I just want to get this blasted funeral gown off and get into bed." Charlotte felt quite exhausted after her run to the park and plotting with Conner. While the thought of escaping Richard's clutches to the Scottish Highlands was an exciting and comforting notion, the reality was almost crushing. She knew her running off would anger and upset her father. He had tried her best at raising her, and Charlotte often trusted in his judgment. But marrying Richard was one thing she was unable to submit to. The reality of fleeing a forced marriage far overweighed any heartbreak her father might feel in her absence.

Conner also seemed to have a way of soothing her fragile soul. His deep voice lulled her as they planned her exit from London and he swore her father would one day forgive her. All the fears melted away in his presence, but when he left her by the back servants' entrance to sneak back into the townhome, Charlotte, once again, felt very alone.

"What happened, my lady? Why did you run off this afternoon?" Mary asked.

Charlotte stuck out her left hand. "And I have the bruise that goes with it."

"A bruise?" Mary gasped.

"Richard felt the need to show me who's in charge." She lifted up a strand of hair to reveal her cheek. "It looks like I'm not going anywhere anytime soon."

"Oh, that scoundrel!" Mary helped Charlotte out of the dress and laid it aside. "We should march straight downstairs and speak to your father."

"There's no need for all that. I have a plan but you mustn't tell Father."

"My lady, I've never once betrayed your confidences," she reminded her.

"I'm leaving England."

"Leaving England?" Mary shook out Charlotte's nightgown that she had warmed by the fire. "But how? When?"

"Lord MacLeod is taking me to Scotland with him. I'm to live at his home and teach his sisters until my father tires of this ridiculous notion that I'll marry Richard."

"So you'll marry Lord MacLeod instead?"

Charlotte scoffed. "Oh, no, he's just helping me."

"Pardon me if I'm speaking out of turn, but not many men offer to help a women sneak out in the night unless they fancy them."

"Things are different in Scotland," Charlotte stated, feigning knowledge. "Women are respected there and treated as equals."

"You're really going, then?"

"Yes, Mary. I don't have much choice."

"Charlotte?" Her father rapped on the closed door. "May we speak?"

"Open the door, Mary, then please go down to the kitchen and ask that they bring my dinner up to the bedroom.

"Well, let's see it, then," her father said, once they were alone.

"See what?" Charlotte asked, sliding into bed.

"The ring, girl, show me the ring!"

She stuck out her hand. "You'll be happy to know it's quite firm on my hand."

George glanced at her face before leaning in closer. "Charlotte, what on earth have you done to your face?"

"Ask Richard."

"Richard? What would he have to do with you bruising your face?"

Charlotte rolled her eyes and pulled her covers up to her chin. "It's quite the funny story. I'm sure his version of things will delight you."

Her father looked at her strangely. "Well, then, I'll be sure to ask him tomorrow at the club. You know he has requested a small wedding and a fast one, at that. It seems that he needs to return to business in America."

"And when will the blessed event be?" she asked sarcastically.

George ignored her. "You'll be married this

Sunday. Of course it's much faster than anyone would like, but Richard doesn't know when he'll be able to return to England."

"Fine."

"Fine? I tell you you're to be married in a few days and all you have to say is 'fine'?"

"Father." Charlotte sighed. "I wasn't given a choice in groom, a choice in wedding date or venue, or a choice in where I am to live. What exactly would you want me to say?"

Her father reddened, opening and closing his mouth several times in silence before speaking. "Richard is a good man and—"

"Your dearest friend," she finished for him. "I'm quite aware how you care for Richard. Just because you sold me to Richard doesn't mean I must care for him."

"Caring often comes in time. Abigail and I didn't begin to care for each other until well after we were married. Now we're quite fold of each other."

"Oh, what a dream, to be *fond* of my husband." Charlotte turned in bed to face the wall. "I'm unwell. I'm going to have dinner in my chambers and rest tomorrow, as well. Plan my wedding, plan my life, and plan whatever else you feel is necessary. Just let me be for tonight."

***

Charlotte was sitting at her small writing desk when Mary appeared an hour later with her dinner tray. She had penned a quick note to Conner stating that her wedding was to be that Sunday and, if his offer still stood, that she would be ready to leave whenever he was. She didn't sign the letter, for fear someone might find it, but still sealed it with wax to ensure it would be opened by no one but him.

"Hurry and eat, my lady, or your food will be cold," Mary cooed, placing a bowl of soup, a fresh slice of bread, and a plate of cookies along with a glass of water on the table.

"Mary, I have a letter for you to take to Lord MacLeod in the morning, as soon as you can."

"Of course, my lady. If it's very pressing, I'll take it to him straight away. Is there anything you'd like for your journey? This is all terribly exciting. Just like a dime novel, it is."

Charlotte smiled at her maid and tied her robe tighter around her before moving to her dinner. "I don't believe so. But I do hope I can get some of my things to Lord MacLeod's home before I have to leave. I would hate to leave everything behind."

"I can take it over in small amounts over the next few days," Mary suggested. "No one will think it odd to see a lady's maid carrying a bag of clothes. They would think I was taking it to be donated for the poor or to a seamstress to be repaired."

"Mary, that's a brilliant idea!"

She smiled and went to the large wardrobe, pulling a large travel bag from the top shelf and placing it on the bed. "We need to pack necessities first. Shifts, corsets, stockings, and a few sturdy day dresses."

Charlotte took a bite of the still-warm bread. "Very smart. I should take my jewels, as well. If I need to, I can sell them."

"I'll tuck them between the layers so they won't be tossed about." Mary placed some underthings in the bag and went to retrieve the jewels from a smaller dresser. "Did you discuss with Lord MacLeod how you were to get to Scotland?"

"No, I assume by carriage. I don't see him as the type to travel by steam engine."

"The Scottish are just as excited as we are to have the convenience of a train, my Lady. I wouldn't much be surprised if you were to take the train to his homeland."

"I suppose you're right." Charlotte pushed the remains of her dinner away. "Do you think I'm doing the right thing?"

"You can't marry a brute," Mary pointed out.

"You're right, but I'm afraid my leaving will cause great dishonor to my family."

"Dishonor and scandal may be the talk of one season but will be entirely forgotten the next. Plenty of fine ladies run off and elope with men their families dislike, and you're not even eloping. By next year no one will remember you running away and Richard will be far away in America."

Charlotte crossed the room and looked at her wardrobe, stuffed full of dresses. "It's rather scary to think of starting a new life in another country."

"Think of it more like an adventure. You'll be living in a foreign castle with royalty! Won't that be a lark?"

"What if you come with me, Mary? I'll be in need of a lady's maid and you'll keep me in good spirits."

Mary frowned. "I wish I could, but I dare not

leave my mother. You know she often finds herself ill. I need to be here in case I need to care for my little brothers and sisters."

"I suppose you're right." Charlotte's heart fell at the realization she would have no one with her in Scotland. "I will be so terribly alone."

"No more than if you married Richard and had to go to America. Then you'd be alone with a man who mistreats you instead of living in a castle with a jolly man who risks his reputation by helping you."

Charlotte pulled out three of her best silks from the wardrobe. "Well, I suppose if I am to live among royalty, I must look the part."

Chapter Twelve

"Charlotte, are you awake?" Abigail tapped on the door, her voice a whisper in the night.

Charlotte gasped. She was fully dressed in an outfit made for travel with her stepmother at the door. She shoved her small bag with the rest of her belongings under the bed and threw on her dressing robe, hoping it hid her traveling gown. It was the night before the accursed wedding was to take place and it was also the night Charlotte was to flee to Scotland. Mary looked at her in panic before opening the door.

"Good evening, Abigail, is everything all right?" Charlotte rubbed at her eyes, feigning sleepiness.

Abigail shut the bedroom door quietly. She was dressed for bed in a nightgown and shawl with her graying hair in a braid. "I know what you're doing. I know you're leaving here tonight."

Charlotte raised herself to her full height and mustered her courage. "And you're here to stop me?"

"No. I'm here to help."

"Help?" Charlotte mimicked dumbly. "You're here to help?"

"Yes. Mary, please leave Charlotte and I to talk," Abigail ordered. Mary looked to Charlotte for confirmation before leaving the room. Her stepmother pulled a small purse from a pocket in her nightgown. "This should help."

Charlotte took the purse and opened it to reveal a rolled up stack of bank notes and a pile of coins. "Abigail...it's too much."

"It's about two hundred pounds. Enough to get by on for quite some time."

"That's quite a bit of money. Won't Father notice it's gone?"

"No, because it is from my private funds. Your father never looks into my finances."

Charlotte was confused. Her stepmother was always so prim and proper. She never thought Abigail would help her cause a scandal. "I don't understand. Why are you doing this?"

Abigail sat on the edge of her bed. "Quite a bit of time ago, I was a young beauty just like yourself. Men threw themselves at me but I was a silly little thing who was holding out for prince charming. My father, tired of indulging me, married me off to a baron who was cruel behind closed doors. My father died before he could see what a terrible mistake he made."

"You were married before? I had no idea."

"There's a lot you don't know about me, Charlotte, but it seems that tonight is a night for telling secrets." Abigail took a breath and continued. "I heard one of the maids talking about a

112

bruise on your cheek. I've seen you with a dozen skinned knees from falling off a fence and a few sprained wrists from taking a tumble off a horse. I've never known you to bruise your face. It doesn't take a lot to deduce that Richard has a cruel hand just as my former husband did."

"What happened to your husband?"

"He died a few years ago, but we were divorced long before that."

"You got a *divorce*?" Charlotte couldn't help but gasp. Divorces were entirely unheard of in proper society.

"I did. It was done quietly without any dramatics. I ended up going to France and staying with an aunt for almost three years to avoid the gossip. Afterward, I retired to the country until I met your father."

"I still can't believe you got a divorce! I thought you wouldn't dare have the scandal."

"I found that I would rather have a scandal hanging over my head than be killed at the hands of my husband. My brother, who had inherited all of our father's lands and money, stole me away from my husband one day after seeing the bruises on my wrists and a bloody lip I had gotten. My brother was a good man then and is still a good man today. He gave me a dowry when it came time to marry and I haven't needed to touch a penny yet. It seems only right that I help one young woman escape marrying an abusive man than have you go through the torture I did. I want you to have the money, Charlotte."

Charlotte's lip quivered as tears fell down her

cheeks. "Oh, Abigail, thank you!" She threw her arms around her stepmother's boney shoulders. "I'm so sorry I was such a horrid child. I'm even sorrier I'm leaving before I really got to know you better."

Abigail awkwardly patted her shoulder. "It'll be fine, Charlotte. I don't know where you're going, but I'm sure we'll see each other soon."

Charlotte pulled away from her hug. "You don't know where I'm going? I thought you knew I was leaving."

"I did. I saw your maid slipping out of the house every night with a bag and returning without it. You also seemed in a very positive mood which is quite uncharacteristic for someone who is about to be married to that terror of a man."

"Was I that obvious?"

"Not to your father. He's too busy with the wedding to notice much else. Do you have everything you need for your trip?"

"Yes. Everything's packed and ready to go. Do you want to know where I'm going?"

Abigail smiled. "I do, but don't tell me. I don't want it to slip out when you've gone. Do you need the carriage, or a horse?"

"No, where I'm meeting my friend is within walking distance. By tomorrow I'll be far away from London and Richard."

Chapter Thirteen

It was well past midnight when Charlotte came to Conner's carriage in the darkened park where they first made their plan. The moon was full and illuminated the gilded carriage and jet-black horses. She knocked on the door before it swung open to reveal a grinning Conner.

"Fine night for a getaway!" he jested, helping her into the carriage. "Have everythin' ye need?"

"I believe so." She pushed back the hood of her heavy cloak and placed her bag on the floor. "Where are the rest of our things?"

"Already being loaded onto the train," he said as the carriage began moving.

"We're going by train? I had no idea trains ran this late in the night."

"Train is the fastest way to get to Scotland and there's always one available. I chose this one because we can be at my home by tomorrow afternoon."

"I've never been on a train before."

"Then you're in for a treat. We'll be in sleeper

115

cars so ye will get a good night's rest. There's also a fine dining car that's always open to order. Best way to travel, I'd say."

"Conner, thank you again for helping me. You could easily have ignored my plight and instead you've come to my rescue and cut your season in London short because of it."

He waved a hand. "Do no' even think of it. What kind o' friend would I be if I did no' help ye? Besides, this is a lot more excitin' than sittin' around at a fancy dinner while every woman in London tries to marry me to her daughters. I'll take a midnight getaway with you any day."

Charlotte smiled a bit at that. "I suppose you did meet all the eligible girls in England."

"Aye, that I did. A bunch o' prissy lasses obsessed with frills and lace."

"I'll have you know that *I* am a prissy lass, as is my dearest friend Penelope."

"You are no' prissy lasses. Ye have more stones than any man and Penelope is a right good time. Always full o' laughter."

"I'll miss her." Charlotte sighed. "She has always been a good friend to me and now I've run off on her without even a note."

"I've already sent her one."

Charlotte's hazel eyes widened. "You what?"

"I gave one of my maids a letter as I left, to pass along sayin' ye'd be safe and ye'd write shortly. Gave her all your love."

"Did you tell her where I was going?"

"O' course not. I didn't even write my name, but she'll know it's from me and she'll know we're

116

goin' back to Scotland. She's a smart lass, that one."

"You really do think of everything, don't you?"

"I have to or I would no' be able to hold my seat as chieftain."

"What do you mean?"

"Scotland's different than England. We get our seats passed to us just like ye do here, but we have to fight to keep them. Uncles, brothers, cousins all fight for the rights to be a chieftain. It might sound barbaric to the English, but that's just how we live."

"It sounds more dangerous than anything." Charlotte peeked out the velvet curtains to see the train station's clock tower looming ahead. "And your family? They won't mind you bringing me to live at the castle?"

"No' a bit. My mother lives out in another, smaller, estate and my wee sisters are always pleased to have another lass around."

The carriage fell to a stop. Conner leapt from it and held out his hand to assist her. They made their way through the station and were taken to their adjacent sleeping rooms by a station employee. Charlotte was pleased to see her bags had already been placed in the tiny cell. The room only held a bed to one side and a bench to the other. A dresser sat beneath the window and a door led into a petite private bathroom. Although it was small, the carpet was lush and the bedding was as fine as any hotel in London.

"Charlotte, I was goin' to go to the dining car soon to get somethin' to eat. Care to join me?"

"I think I'm just going to get some sleep. I'm

suddenly very tired," Charlotte said. She felt emotionally exhausted.

"All right. My room is right next door if ye need anythin'. There's also a bell beside the bed if ye need anythin' from the train staff." He smiled a bit before turning to leave. "Good night, Charlotte."

"Conner, wait." She took a step closer to him. "Thank you again for helping me. I would be getting ready to get married tomorrow if you didn't come save me."

"Save ye? Charlotte Holloway, you are no' a woman who needs savin'. Ye are too strong and too clever for that. Ye would have found your own way out if ye needed to. I was just there at the right time."

"And I'm really glad you were."

Conner reached out and gently stroked her bruised cheek. "As am I, Charlotte, as am I."

Chapter Fourteen

The rolling green hills passed by the carriage window as they trundled along the dirt road through the Scottish highlands. Wind whipped through the tall grass and wispy clouds floated through the clear blue sky. It was nothing like the sky in London, which was often gray and brown with the smoke and smog of the many factories that lined the waterfront. Charlotte could already tell that life for the Scottish was natural and pure, just as she imagined it would be. It was so peaceful. She thought it might be easy to forget that she'd come here to escape a brutish man, instead of simply visiting for the beautiful scenery.

"It's so green here." Charlotte stared out the carriage's open window. "Just hills as far as the eyes can see."

"Aye, it's as green as can be here if ye can ignore the bit o' snow. It rains more often than no' so we'll need to be sure ye have the right things to get ye by this winter."

"I brought my traveling cloak and furs. I should

119

be fine."

"All the same, I'd like for one o' my sisters to take inventory. I canno' have my honored guest takin' a chill."

Charlotte blushed at him calling her his 'honored guest' and resumed her watch out the window. Every so often, she would see a cozy stone cottage surrounded by a herd of fluffy sheep, thick with their winter wool. Clouds of smoke lifted from squat chimneys. She imagined a family sitting before the fire, snug and safe from the winter winds. The Scottish highlands were lush with life and charming in a way she had never imagined.

When she finally saw the MacLeod castle come into view, she was more than spellbound. Atop a rocky hill sat an enormous fortress unlike anything she had ever seen. Charlotte had imagined a fairytale castle with turrets and a moat, but instead she found an estate that appeared more terrifying and remarkable than any she had read about.

A thick stone wall, cornered by guard towers with dozens of arrow slits, surrounded the tall keep which must have been four stories or more. Bright yellow flags flapped in the wind atop the three tallest towers. Fearsome men patrolled the entrance on horseback and a black gate opened to them as they neared.

"Welcome to your new home." Conner smiled as they passed through the gate. The guards in kilts nodded as they passed into the front courtyard, broadswords clutched tightly in their meaty fists.

Charlotte grinned in response as they came to a halt once safe inside the massive walls. The keep looked kinder and more fairy-like than the fearsome walls that surrounded it. An intricately carved door, edged and crossed in steel, lead inside and up a set of wide stone stairs. A dozen maids and footmen in plain black clothing stood outside the castle's keep to greet their lord.

Once he assisted her out of the carriage, a somber man in livery came up to Conner and whispered something in his ear. He nodded and gave the man an order in Gaelic. He turned to Charlotte and offered his arm. "I've just been informed your rooms are ready and my sisters will come down to meet ye." He began leading her up the stairs past his staff and halted at the top, beside the door, to address them. "Good afternoon. This is Lady Charlotte Holloway, daughter o' the Duke o' Glenwood. As ye have been informed, she is to stay with us for a while as visitin' British nobility. Fulfill her requests and treat her as a true friend o' the MacLeod clan. Any command by her is as good as one from my own lips."

"Do you think it wise for you to tell the staff who I really am?" Charlotte whispered as they entered the main hall.

"I do no' think it makes a difference now. Even if your father knew where ye were, he has no authority in my lands. Do no' worry, Charlotte, you're quite safe with me."

She nodded as a maid removed her traveling cloak. She took in the main hall, with its great wooden arches supporting a tall ceiling and two large fireplaces raised on a platform, both warming the room with a cozy glow. Between the mantles sat the MacLeod crest and below that a hearty throne atop a pile of wolf skins raised on a platform.

Along the walls stood a dozen suits of armor all holding axes and Scottish short swords. It was all brilliantly medieval and made Charlotte shiver with excitement. She felt as if she was in the world of the famous Macbeth and couldn't wait to explore the castle further.

"This is the main hall o' the livin' quarters," Conner told her as they made their way through the room to an arched doorway beyond. "This also serves as a receivin' hall where I meet dignitaries and local noblemen who care for my lands when I'm gone. I'm to take ye to your quarters now to freshen up before my wee sisters attack ye."

The next room they entered was a spacious sitting room that contained a giant fireplace and a plush oriental rug that went well with the forest green walls and deep yellow furniture. It reminded her vaguely of many British homes, but there were dozens of weapons on the walls and the paintings were darker in color and more natural in theme, many containing more horses and men in kilts.

"This room is one o' the more comfortable. The door next to the fireplace leads to my primary study. I'll show ye the library later on if you're feelin' up to it. I promised ye it would be somethin' ye'd like."

"I'd like that very much, thank you."

"Watch the stairs. Some o' the stone is beginnin' to crack in places," he warned, pointing to a hairline fracture on the smooth step. Charlotte let go of his arm and allowed him to lead the way up the narrow staircase. She held tight to her hem of her traveling gown.

When they reached the landing, Conner gestured to the long hallway, which was lined with windows on one side and doors to the other. "My sisters have the first two sets of rooms and the door at the end o' the hall is to be yours. Your set o' rooms are one o' the finest in the castle. The old King James o' Scotland slept there several times during his reign."

"I'm to sleep in the same room as royalty?" Charlotte asked as he opened the door for her.

"Aye, it's the quarters we house all the high ranking dignitaries and royalty that happen to pass through the highlands. I hope it is to your likin'."

"It's perfect," Charlotte whispered, and she meant it. The room was gorgeous, done up in a deep yellow, the apparent color of the MacLeod Clan. The warm walls offset the golden-framed artwork and the deep brown of the floors and furniture. The tall windows were rimmed in red and yellow stained glass, sending bright speckles of color dancing along the floor.

The windows themselves looked down upon a rocky cove. Lush cliffs framed the twisting waters with small guard towers on either end. Charlotte had evidently been correct in guessing that the castle backed up to the North Sea. A small fireplace warmed the room that held a set of wingback chairs, a pillow-lined couch, and a bookshelf lined with the newest novels.

"This is the receivin' room. Ring this line next to the fireplace and a maid will be at your service to bring ye whatever ye need."

"And the bedroom is through those doors?" Charlotte guessed, looking at a set of closed double doors next to the shelves.

"Aye. I'll let ye get settled. Should I send a lady's maid to ye to prepare ye for supper?"

"That would be so lovely. Thank you for the rooms. They're quite beautiful."

"I only want you to feel at home. I hope ye will be comfortable and won't hesitate to tell me if ye need anythin'."

"Thank you, Conner."

He bowed to her, a smile on his lips. "I'll see ye for supper."

Charlotte closed the door when he left and eagerly went to the bedroom. It did not disappoint her in the least. A huge four-poster bed of dark wood bathed in blue and gold brocade bedding that was soft to the touch. Beautiful tapestries were displayed between the same stain glass windows that were hung with velvet dressings.

Her bags were lined up near an open wardrobe where she could see her gowns were mostly hung up to work out their wrinkles. She opened a smaller door to reveal a spacious bathroom with all the modern appliances like a toilet, sink, and a large bathtub that she was anxious to use.

Not wishing to wait for a maid or bother them with drawing her a bath, she turned the water on to fill the tub. In a tiny closet she found a pile of freshly laundered towels and vials of soap and fragrant oils. She stripped off her travel gown and gratefully plunged in the steaming bath. She scrubbed her body until her skin was quite pink and washed her hair until it was smooth and smelled of lavender.

For a moment, the engagement ring stuck on her finger caught the dim light of the setting sun. Frowning, she took some bath oil and dumped it on her hand. She tugged at the band, willing it to slide off. She pulled until her knuckle was red but still the ring was stuck. She sighed and hoped there might be a blacksmith or an ironworker who could carefully cut the ring from her finger.

When she exited the bathroom to dress, she found a maid sifting through her bags to place the rest of her clothing in the dresser. Her perfume and jewelry were already arranged neatly on a dressing table and a clean set of underthings waited on the bed. The plump maid hummed as she neatly folded Charlotte's clothing and piled the empty bags near the door to be taken away.

"Hello, I'm Charlotte," Charlotte said, clutching her towel to her. The wooden floors were cold beneath her bare feet and she hurried to the oriental carpet in front of the fire.

The maid turned and bobbed a small curtsey. "Good evenin,' my lady, I'm Maisie. The MacLeod sent me to prepare ye for supper."

"Thank you. I'm pleased to meet you, Maisie. And, please, call me Charlotte."

"Well, Charlotte, most o' the gowns are crumpled from the trip but the green velvet is still in good shape. I'll have the rest pressed and set right for ye by tomorrow."

"That would be wonderful." Charlotte eyed her shift, wanting to change, but not wishing to bare her form in front of a stranger.

Maisie appeared to sense her unease. "Do ye need me to help ye dress or will ye just need help with your hair when you're ready?"

"I can dress myself but I would appreciate help with my hair. I can never do anything nice with it by myself."

"Of course. I'll just take the gowns down to the laundry to be dealt with and be right back."

Charlotte waited until the maid had left before dropping her towel and slipping into her shift. She pulled her stockings up her long legs and cinched her corset just a bit looser than she usually wore it at home in England. By the time she was ready for her gown to be buttoned, Maisie returned.

"Let me take care o' those fastens." The maid hooked the tiny buttons with a quick hand. "That dress is right nice with your hair and skin, if I do say so."

Charlotte admired herself in the mirror. The gown did suit her. The velvet dress had a low sweetheart neckline and sleeves that reached her elbows. The skirts flared at her waist and brushed the floor with perfectly hemmed edges. It was simple, soft to the touch, and clung to her body in a beautifully sculpted manner. "It's one of my favorites." She sat down at the mirrored dressing table to allow Maisie better access to her hair.

"No doubt the MacLeod will be fond if it as well." The maid raised her eyebrows knowingly.

"He and I aren't...we don't..." Charlotte flushed, trying to think of the proper way to deny her involvement with Conner.

"The MacLeod has told us so, but it's hard to believe with such a lovely lass like ye."

"Why do you call him that?" Charlotte asked, trying to change the subject.

"It's what we call the kings in Scotland. The MacArthur, the O'Brian, the MacFinley are the other three. The MacLeod is the most powerful and enforces most o' the laws in Scotland. He also controls all o' the highlands."

"Sounds very impressive."

"I have a bit o' somethin' to put on your cheek, if ye'd like?" Maisie's voice was tentative as she eyed the blues and greens that marred Charlotte's skin.

She brought a hand to her face. "If you wouldn't mind?"

"No' at all." The maid took a small tub from her apron pocket and began gently sweeping the cream on Charlotte's bruise. "The MacLeod told me ye might have need o' this. A woman in the village makes all sorts o' concoctions. This should help cover it a wee bit until it heals."

"Thank you, Maisie." Although Charlotte knew that she had nothing to be ashamed of, she found herself embarrassed by the injury on her cheek. She thought it made her look weak, like a victim. As if she was a damsel in need of saving. But, yes, that was exactly what she was and it pained her to the core that she had neither the strength nor the masculine parts needed to rescue herself from an unwelcome marriage. Maisie's makeup hid her shame well and she was grateful for the maid's understanding.

"This is lovely." Charlotte admired her unmarred cheek. "Please tell me what it cost so that I might reimburse you."

"Ach, do no' mention it. The MacLeod took care o' it." Maisie began brushing Charlotte's hair with her ivory comb. "Have ye been to Scotland before?"

"No, this is my very first time out of England."

"What a treat, then. Ye are goin' to be thrust right into Scottish culture tonight. The MacLeod has a welcome feast for ye."

"Oh, I hope he hasn't gone to too much trouble on my account."

"Be flattered. The finest Scottish foods and pipes are on the menu tonight and you will be the centerpiece of it all."

Chapter Fifteen

Not long after Maisie had finished helping Charlotte dress her thick auburn hair into a neat mass of curls and braids, there was a knock on her bedroom door. Charlotte hastily stuck a pair of pearl earrings in her ears and slipped into her white slippers before going to see who it was.

"Good evenin'." Conner stood in the doorway looking both savage and debonair. His kilt was wrapped around his taut midsection and looped over his shoulder, held together by a pin in the shape of the MacLeod crest. In place of the formal dinner jackets that Charlotte was used to seeing, he wore a plain white shirt with his sleeves rolled up and the top buttons undone. His blond hair was held back with a piece of leather and a pair of boots had been tied up his shins. A gilded dagger hung at his hip by a worn leather belt.

"H-hello," Charlotte stuttered, feeling her face warm.

Conner gave a slight bow and rose, grinning. "Ye look lively this evenin'."

129

"Thank you. I do hope I'm not too overdressed?"

"Not at all. My sisters dress for dinner, although the men are a bit more casual than in England." He held out his arm to escort her downstairs. "We'll be eatin' with some o' my men in the feastin' hall."

"Feasting hall? What's that?" she asked as they made their way through the window-lined hallway.

"Before the introduction o' the British way o' dining, everyone sat together in a large gallery and ate together every day. It was a way for the chieftain to show his people that they were his equals and he would care for them, if need be. It's a tradition carried over from old times."

"And that's how you have all your meals here?"

"No' all the time." He took her down a different hallway than before. It was wide and dozens of pictures of men on horseback hung on either side. "My sisters and I often eat alone in a dining room, much like ye would at home."

Charlotte looked at the different halls and doors as they passed them. "I do hope you can give me a tour soon. I would so much like to explore. Your castle is positively massive and I'm afraid I would get quite lost."

"Ye can explore whenever ye like. Just be careful in the dungeon. There are pits and winding mazes."

"Mazes? In your dungeon?"

"The dungeons beneath the keep are large and deep. Almost the size o' the castle. In the event o' a siege, there are even secret places where the women and children can be locked up safe with stashes of food."

Charlotte bit her lip, thinking back to the historical books about the violent blockades in Ancient Greece. "You really need to be prepared for a siege?"

"The walls o' my castle have never been breeched." He looked down at the hand holding his left arm and brought her to a sudden halt. "What happened to your finger? It looks right raw."

Charlotte blushed and pulled her hand away. "I was trying to get this blasted ring off but it's stuck. I need a blacksmith, or someone, to cut it off my finger. If I loose an appendage to the cause, so be it."

"I do no' think it'll come to that. Let me see." She showed him her hand and he studied it closely. "I think I can get it off."

"Really? How?"

"Like this." He took her ring finger and carefully slipped it into his mouth. Charlotte's knees grew week as she felt his tongue against her skin. When he finally pulled away she could see her finger was free from the ring. He spat the piece of jewelry into his hand. "See? And ye can keep all your wee fingers."

Charlotte realized her breathing had grown shallow and her breasts heaved below her low neckline. For a fleeting moment she wished she could feel his tongue on other parts of her body. The mere thought of it both aroused and mortified her. "How did you do that?" she asked, rubbing the spot that once felt so constricted.

He shrugged, pocketing the ring in a small pouch at his hip. "I have my secrets. I'll give it to you after dinner so ye do no' lose it."

"I don't want it back," Charlotte said as they resumed their walk. "It's just a reminder of what my life would have been."

"But ye do no' have to worry about that now. You are safe in my lands and safe in this castle." His voice was soft and warm in her ears. "I promised I'd keep ye safe and I always keep my promises."

They walked in silence until they came to a stop in a small antechamber where two young women and a brawny man carrying a set of bagpipes waited next to a set of doors. The man bowed to Conner and went back to adjusting his instrument.

A girl with long, blonde hair down to her waist smiled as she saw them, her blue eyes wide with excitement. "Hello, I'm Flora. You must be Lady Holloway." Her soft voice held only a slight Scottish lilt. One might have thought she was purely British by the sound of her.

"Please, call me Charlotte." Charlotte found her to be a great beauty who reminded her of some of the finer paintings in London's museums. She was petite and willowy in a graceful way and a dress of the palest blue hung off her in waves.

"Flora is the older o' my two sisters livin' at home." Conner motioned for the younger to approach. "This here is my wee baby sister, Gwendolyn."

Gwendolyn stood slightly behind her sister, shyly peering at Charlotte under lowered lashes. "Good evening, my lady. You may call me Gwen, if it pleases you."

"Charlotte, please. And I would like very much if I could call you Gwen." Charlotte smiled at the shy girl and took in her looks with a kind eye. Gwen had bouncy gold curls framing a cherub face. Her round cheeks were freckled, and Charlotte thought she must have had perfectly delightful dimples when she smiled. Her silk gown was just as fine as her elder sister's, but she wore it without the confidence and grace that Flora did, much like a little girl playing dress-up.

Suddenly the bagpiper began playing, making Charlotte startle. Conner chuckled. "Ye'd better get used to the pipes, Charlotte. You will be hearin' a lot o' them. They mark my entrance into grand halls and such. And, seein' as ye are an honored guest, they play for ye, too."

They followed the piper into the feasting hall. Charlotte gripped Conner's arm and his two sisters followed them, whispering breathlessly to each other in muted Gaelic. The feasting hall looked like something right out of a medieval fairytale. The high ceilings were tipped in aged wood and iron chandeliers lit the room in strong candlelight. Tapestries of dragons, unicorns, and men in armor hung on the walls while giant swords decorated the space behind the main table. The main table itself was a giant oak one on a raised platform with four thrones seated behind it, facing the room. Six long tables occupied with dozens of men in kilts filled the room and they all roared as the little procession passed them.

Charlotte glanced at the men as they walked by, each appearing fierce but all wore jolly smiles as they held up goblets full of wine and banged their huge fists on the tables. She felt very much out of place, especially since she and Conner's sisters were the only women. In England, the men would be quiet and reserved, standing politely as she entered a room and nodding as she passed. These men were loud and almost terrifying. It thrilled her.

"All right there, Charlotte?" Conner asked as he deposited her in a seat to his right. His two sisters sat on his left and looked quite at home among the noisy crowd.

"Fine, thank you." She looked down at her table settings, surprised to see they were made of silver and all beautifully molded. In fact, everything was beautiful in a rugged sort of way. Even the tables were smoothed, carved, and shining.

Once they were seated, a dozen or more maids entered the room holding serving platters piled high with roasted meat, fresh vegetables, and newly baked bread. The maids came to their table first, offering their wares to the ladies. Charlotte selected a cut of gently seasoned beef and some sort of potato mash. Out of the corner of her eye she saw a particularly buxom maid trying to tempt Conner with a large slice of meat.

"MacLeod, won't ye taste my special meats? I've kept a slice just for you," the maid crooned, her voice girlishly high and wavering.

"Ach, Nettie, ye always take care o' me!" He laughed, stabbing the meat with his knife and slapping it on his plate.

Nettie, the maid, leaned down, showing off the tops of her creamy breasts. "I can come to your

134

rooms later and really take care o' ye," the woman whispered, but Charlotte could still clearly hear her. She wasn't sure why, but she felt her blood run hot.

"Away with, ye, Nettie." Conner waved his hand. "I'm no' takin' your lures, no matter how hard ye try. It never worked and never will! Now go back with ye before I tell your da what ye've been up to."

Nettie huffed and took her tray away to begin serving the rest of the men, occasionally pouting over her shoulder in their direction. Charlotte smiled to herself. It pleased her to see Conner denying the other woman's advances, even though she didn't exactly have a claim on him.

In fact, she would never have a claim on a well-known womanizing rogue like Conner MacLeod. He probably only sent Nettie away because he didn't want to offend his guest and little sisters. No doubt Nettie would be roaming the halls tonight to meet with him in secret.

After everyone had finished their meals and the men were talking amongst themselves, Conner stood, thumping his fist on the table. The men looked toward him in complete and sudden silence.

"Hello, my men and companions!" he began. "I hope ye all ate your fill and sated your thirst with the wine?"

The men thundered in the affirmative.

Conner continued. "I know ye all are probably wonderin' who our guest is tonight. Well, it's Lady Charlotte Holloway, daughter o' the Duke o' Glenwood. She'll be stayin' with us for the foreseeable future and I expect ye all to treat her with respect. Any request, demand, or order she gives will be akin to words from my own lips. If I hear any o' you lads givin' her a hard time, or treatin' her ill, then ye will have to answer to me. Hopefully, this fine lady will teach all ye scoundrels a bit o' manners!"

Charlotte blushed as the men clapped in her direction and excitedly raised their cups in the air. "Was that introduction necessary?"

"Verra necessary," Conner told her. "Now, if you are finished eating, I can escort ye to your rooms. I know ye must be tired from all the travelin'."

"I am," Charlotte said, allowing Conner to raise her up. She said her goodbyes to Flora and Gwen and left the feasting hall with Conner. She felt the gazes of the men upon her, their Gaelic whisperings almost musical.

"What did ye think o' your first meal among the fearsome Scots?" he asked once they were alone in the halls.

"Quite nice. The food was lovely and everyone seemed in a pleasant mood. Your sisters are quite charming as well. I look forward to getting to know them better."

"Good lasses, my sisters are. Gwen's a wee bit shy. I do no' know how she'll ever find a husband, as quiet as she is."

Charlotte bristled. "Gwen will do perfectly well without a husband. You, yourself, said that women in Scotland weren't traded and sold like live commodities."

"Ach, calm down." Conner chuckled. "The lass

wants to get married, but here in the highlands, a woman must be hard and strong to match up to a warrior. Even our common farmers need a woman o' iron to marry. Little Gwen is too soft for Scotland, perhaps."

"Then have you ever thought about bringing her to London to meet a match there? Surely, the English gentlemen would love a girl like Gwen. She seems perfectly angelic."

He nodded. "Aye, that she is. But I worry about her sometimes, and it would be hard on us to have her livin' so far away. Maybe next year I can take her into London and see how she fares."

"She'll be all right. If I end up back in London, then I shall be able to take care of her and make sure she meets everyone who is anyone. And you know that Penelope will care for her just as well."

"Do ye think you will go back to England so quickly?" he asked as they stopped in front of her door.

"I don't know. I can't stay here forever and take advantage of your hospitality," she whispered, looking down at the hardwood floors.

Conner sighed, reaching down and taking her hand in his. "Ye are a hardheaded lass, Charlotte. I've told ye time and time again that you can stay for however long ye want. A month, a year, a lifetime."

"A lifetime is a very long time to be someone's guest," she pointed out, smiling up at him.

"Then be more than a guest," he suggested mischievously. "Ye'd make a right fine queen o' the highlands."

Charlotte scoffed, pulling her fingers from his grasp. "Do stop, Conner. You're thoroughly embarrassing yourself."

"And ye have only been here a day. Mark my words, Charlotte, I'll have ye as my bride and ye'll come to my side willin'ly."

"Why the sudden jokes? Too much wine?"

"I'm as serious as serious can be." He tried to look solemn, but the corners of his lips twitched in amusement.

Charlotte rolled her eyes and reached for the door. If she was tired from her travels, then she was exhausted by his ridiculous attempts at proposals. "Really, Conner, you're too much. Now I'm going off to bed before you write me a sonnet or sing a song of deep longing outside my window."

"Would either work? Because, ye see, there's a fine balcony overlookin' the cliffs. Sure, it'd be a right sheer drop, but if it's a song or sonnet ye wish for, a song or sonnet ye shall receive."

"I'm going to sleep, Conner," she said with some finality.

"Ach, leavin' me wantin' for more." He sighed dramatically. "I suppose if a sonnet and song will no' be enough to win your heart, then I'll just have to try somethin' else." Conner bowed at the waist. "Until tomorrow, my lady."

"Until tomorrow," she agreed.

Chapter Sixteen

Bright sunlight snuck in through the gaps in the thick velvet drapes. Charlotte stretched beneath the plush comforter, knowing it was late in the morning but unwilling to rise from the comfortable bed. She looked about the room for a clock but noted that there wasn't one to be found. She just had to guess that it must have been close to noon. She never meant to sleep so late, but she found that as soon as her head hit the plump pillows, she immediately fell into a deep slumber, still dressed in her gown from dinner.

When she finally decided to rise from the bed, she was glad to see that the fire in her room was already lit. After washing her face, Charlotte went to the wall where the servant's bell was and pulled it. She needed to get dressed fast and didn't want Conner and his sisters to think all she did was lay about.

"Good mornin'," Maisie said as she entered the room carrying a tray. Another, younger, maid followed, carrying a pile of freshly washed and pressed dresses.

"Good morning." Charlotte looked at the tray, which contained a single cup and a silver teapot. "What's this?"

"The MacLeod sent it up for ye. Would ye like me to pour it?"

"I suppose," Charlotte answered, sitting down at the dressing table that contained her jewels and perfumes. She watched the young maid deposit the dresses neatly on the bed and open the heavy drapes before scurrying out of the room.

Maisie brought the tray to the table and poured a stream of hot chocolate into the mug. "This is a fine drink first thing in the mornin'."

"Oh, hot chocolate! I can't believe he remembered."

"Ye like it, then?"

Charlotte picked up the steaming cup and breathed in its rich aroma. "Yes, but I was hardly ever allowed to drink it at home. My stepmother believed it would ruin my complexion."

"The MacLeod is rather fond o' it too." Maisie began hanging the dresses in a large armoire. "Now, down to business. What will ye wear today?"

"I'm not sure. What do Flora and Gwen wear during the day?"

"Simple frocks, usually with a nice, thick, plaid wrap. They often go for walks if the weather allows."

Charlotte took a sip of her drink, finding it perfectly sweet. "Then I believe I have a pale pink dress somewhere. It should be casual enough."

"I know just the one."

"Is it very late in the day? I can't find a clock anywhere."

Maisie found the dress upon the unmade bed. "Only just ten in the mornin'. The MacLeod lasses aren't up yet, so do no' feel the need to rush. They're always late sleepers. I think the MacLeod will be in his study by now, if you felt so inclined to see him."

Charlotte reddened and busied herself by brushing her hair. "I'll see him in due time."

"I'm sure ye will." Maisie smiled coyly. "And I know he's eager to see you as well."

"Why ever would you think that?"

"He asked me about ye this mornin'," she told her, holding out a fresh shift and corset for Charlotte to put on. "Came right into the servant's kitchen to make sure I was takin' care of ye like a proper lady."

Charlotte stood and changed quickly into her clean clothes as Maisie averted her eyes. "He's just being kind to his guest."

"I think it's more than that. He's no' one to take such a special interest in his guests." Maisie buttoned up the back of Charlotte's dress and gently touched her loose curls. "Ye should leave your hair down. It's the most lovely color."

"Leave my hair down? I can't do that!" Charlotte gasped. She remembered Abigail telling her that only loose women and savages left their hair unbound.

"Most o' the Scottish lasses do it. I can no' remember the last time I put up either Gwen or Flora's hair as I did yours last night. They all wear it long here, more or less. But if ye'd like me to put it up, I will."

Charlotte looked at herself in the mirror, noticed the way the daylight hit the red in her hair and how the long tresses softened her face. "Do you really think it would be all right?"

"More than all right. Hair is a lady's crownin' glory." She sang as she took up Charlotte's brush and arranged her curls neatly. "Ye have lovely tresses and it'd be a right shame to hide them up in a bun."

"Then I guess I can give it a try. If it's the way of the Scottish, then I'm sure it's still right and proper." She looked at her long-sleeved dress in the mirror and admired the reddish sheen of her hair one final time before turning to leave the room. "Thank you for all your assistance, Maisie. It is really valuable having someone tell me how the Scottish do things."

"O' course, my lady. Ye have slept through breakfast, but if ye go down to the kitchen, I'm sure the cook would be more than pleased to give ye a bite to hold ye over to lunch."

Charlotte smiled and slipped out of the room, trying to remember how to get downstairs. Everything looked different in the bright morning light. The paintings were more vibrant and tapestries lively. She could hear movements in both Flora's and Gwen's rooms but opted not to greet them, hoping for a few moments to explore on her way to find the kitchen. She found the stairs easily enough and retraced the previous night's steps until she reached the feasting hall.

The feasting hall was quiet. Light streamed in through narrow arrow-slit windows. The tables were clean and bare and she wondered how many men over the years had sat at those worn tables. Each nick and scratch told a story. Without the sounds of the rowdy men and the banging of full goblets, the light tapping of her silk slippers echoed through the vaulted room.

She spied a small door she hadn't noticed the night before and opened it a sliver to peek inside. A set of narrow stairs led down. Charlotte remembered that in her father's country home the kitchens were below the dining room and ballroom to make it easier for the servants to bring up the food and drinks. Taking a chance, she walked down the stairs to find the kitchen.

As she came to the landing, she heard the familiar clanging of pots and pans. She had often spent her afternoons in the kitchen with her father's staff, learning how to bake pies with crust so flaky it melted in her mouth or how to make a succulent stew, perfect for the winter. With memories of her time in the kitchen fresh in her mind, she followed the noises until she reached her destination.

"Mary! Where are those rabbits for lunch!" A portly cook yelled over the clangs of the cooking wares. She was standing next to one of the three stoves, brandishing a wooden spoon at the several kitchen hands rushing about.

"Excuse me," Charlotte called out from the doorway.

The cook looked up, spoon still raised. "My lady!"

The other members of the staff froze, then dropped into deep bows and curtseys. Their unexpected stillness made Charlotte uncomfortable. "I apologize for disturbing you."

"No trouble, my lady. Whatever ye need, we can do for ye," the cook said eagerly, bobbing her red-haired head.

"Well, I was just hoping to get something small to snack on. Like an apple, perhaps? Maisie said you wouldn't mind."

The cook beamed. "A wee mite like you needs a decent meal!" She opened one of the ovens and peered inside before moving to another. "Do ye like sweet buns, my lady?"

"Very much so," Charlotte answered, moving deeper into the kitchen.

"I have some cinnamon ones that are just ready to come from the oven if it would please ye, my lady?"

"That would be lovely, thank you. And, please, call me Charlotte."

The cook motioned for the rest of the workers to stop gawking and continue with their duties. She pulled a tray of buns from the oven and began pouring icing over their tops. "I hope ye like my cookin', my lady—I mean, Charlotte."

"It's wonderful," Charlotte told her, looking hungrily at the pan. "I sampled some at Conner's New Year's Eve ball and he agreed that you were the finest cook he ever had."

The cook blushed and passed her a warm bun on a plate. "I'm glad ye both think so. If you ever want something special, or are in need of another snack, please come see me."

"Thank you." She took a bite and moaned, much to the cook's delight. She then handed the plate back to the cook. "I'm going to take this with me."

Charlotte turned back, out of the room. She went through the hallway and up the narrow stone stairs, then wandered through the feasting hall and over to a set of steps she hadn't noticed before, munching on her roll the whole way. The stairs were steep and windowless, but as she reached the top, she wasn't disappointed. There were two doors on either side of the landing. She opened the one to her right, which led out to a balcony. As Charlotte's eyes adjusted to the light, she took small steps outside, noting how much colder the air was compared to the day before.

The balcony itself was at the top corner of the keep, looking down on the open courtyard sandwiched between the keep and the outer wall. She could see maids hanging laundry in one portion of the yard, far from the front of the castle. She also saw men sparring with one another in a closer corner, the clanging of their swords echoing in the open space. A few had longbows and shot at targets with practiced aim. She walked to the portion of the balcony where she could get the better view of the men while she finished off her bun and licked the last bits of icing from her fingers.

"Again!" a voice called over the sounds of the clashing swords. Charlotte was surprised to see they used real swords instead of wooden practice ones like the few soldiers she had seen in England.

Charlotte leaned over the stone wall, trying to

ignore the chill biting at her fingers. Out of the dozen men in the courtyard, she picked Conner out easily. He stood in nothing more than boots and a plaid kilt, brandishing a long sword in his hand. His hair was tied back and his bare chest gleamed with sweat. Charlotte was glad she was two stories up and he hadn't noticed her observing.

She watched the men fight for several more minutes before Conner looked up, shading his eyes from the sun with one hand and waving his sword with the other. "Good mornin', Charlotte!" he bellowed.

Charlotte fought the desire to duck behind the balcony ledge. Instead, she straightened up and waved back. "Good morning, Conner!"

"Good morning, Conner!" a man jested in a mock falsetto voice. It was followed by hushed chuckles from the men.

"Fine day to be outside!" Conner yelled up at her.

"A bit cold. You should put on a shirt before you catch a chill!"

"Ye can only boss me about if ye marry me!" he answered brazenly. "What do ye say?"

Charlotte rolled her eyes. "Not for all the gold in England, you conceited fool!" The men roared in laughter, thoroughly enjoying her mocking their chief.

"What about all the gold in Scotland? I think I can offer ye that!"

"Is that so?"

"Aye, it is! Marry me and ye'll be the richest queen in the lands!"

"But with a silly oaf for a husband!"

Conner dropped his sword and clutched his hands over his heart. "Your words stuck me, fair lass!" He dropped to the ground dramatically, egged on by the ribbing of the rest of his kinsmen.

"Oh, get up! You're embarrassing yourself!"

He got up on one knee. "Should I sing ye a song, my lady? Melt your heart with my voice?"

"The poor lass will go deaf if ye do!" a bearded man said through peals of mirth.

"Then the poor lady must come down!" Conner retorted from his seat in the dirt. "Oh, fair maiden, grace me with your fine company."

"Only if you promise not to sing!" she answered, a smile on her lips. After he had assured her that he would keep his musical talents out of the equation, Charlotte quickly came down to the main floor of the castle and out to the courtyard.

"Ach, Charlotte." Conner came striding into view, wiping the sweat from his brow with a tanned forearm. "Why are ye out here in nothin' but a dress?"

"You're one to talk." Charlotte tried adverting her gaze from his bare torso, but found it difficult to ignore the hard muscled body before her.

"What's the matter, Charlotte? Never seen a man before?"

Her cheeks pinked and she trained her eyes on his face. "Don't tease me."

"Have a good look, Charlotte," he jested, thumping a fist to his chest. "I will no' be the last shirtless lad ye see in Scotland."

"Do you mean to say that all the men here forgo

shirts?"

"Aye. Trainin', farmin', and fightin' are all hard work. Verra seldom will ye see a fully clothed man outside o' the feasting hall."

"Oh, good Lord." Charlotte crossed her arms in both exasperation and chill.

"Ye English are all dramatic. But, ye will catch your death out here if ye do no' put on a cloak. Ye aren't used to the winters yet."

"The cold does not bother me. I'm quite content to be out in a brisk breeze."

He studied her a moment. "All the same, I'm callin' for a good cloak for ye. I'll have my sisters' seamstress get one together."

"But I already have a winter cloak. I just bought it last year."

"No' one that'll be any use to ye in Scotland."

Charlotte huffed. "Fine. Just send me the bill then, I suppose."

"A bill?" Conner seemed confused. "You are a guest in my castle and my guests never need, nor want, for a thing."

"You've already done so much and I have my own funds."

"Then keep your own funds. I promised I'd care for ye and care for ye I will."

"You're being ridiculous."

Conner studied her for a moment before reaching out a hand to touch one of her loose tresses. "And your hair is lovely this way."

"You always change the subject on me."

"I can no' help but get distracted when we speak."

"You're such a horrid flirt." Charlotte felt heat pool in her face. The lock of hair burned her skin when he dropped it back to her cheek, adding fuel to the fire within her.

"But I do mean it. Your hair is lovely down around your face like this. Ye look like a selkie."

"A selkie? What on earth is that?"

"It's a beautiful woman who wears the skin of a seal in the sea, shedding it upon land to steal hearts."

"So you're relating me to a seal?" Charlotte asked with a hint of merriment. "No one has ever told me I remind them of a ocean creature who eats fish."

"Think o' it like one o' your British mermaids then, if a selkie is no' to your likin'."

"A mermaid sounds much better, thank you." Charlotte cleared her throat, attempting to compose herself again. "Maisie said this is how the Scottish women wear it so I thought I'd give it a try."

"It suits ye greatly. Much better than the English way."

"I'll have you know I happen to like the English way. I just wanted to see how to do things the Scottish way. You know, 'when in Rome' and all that."

"Marry me and ye can do everythin' the Scottish way."

Charlotte sighed, growing tired of his game. "I've told you a few times now, Conner, no. So stop asking me. I'm rather done with you teasing me like that."

"But I rather like seein' ye get all flushed."

"And stop proposing in front of *everyone* just for a lark," Charlotte scolded, planting her fists on her hips. "You're making a mockery of marriage."

"I'd never mock marriage. Especially to you," he said with all seriousness.

"Oh, please. You're doing it for the laughs it gets from your men and I don't appreciate it." And she didn't. The charming Scot wooing her and trying to propose was strangely romantic, but she knew he wouldn't take it seriously and knew that it was nothing more than a jest for him. Whatever poor woman did end up marrying the Scotsman would be trapped in a marriage with lots of passion, but a marriage bed probably filled with other women.

"I don't do it for laughs, Charlotte. I mean every word."

She scoffed. "I'm sure you mean every proposal you make."

"Ye mean every proposal I make to *you*?"

"I mean every proposal you make to *everyone*."

He scratched his head. "Everyone?"

"Just forget it." Charlotte told him. "I think I'll go inside now and see if your sisters are downstairs."

Conner still looked at her strangely. "Charlotte, is somethin' goin' on that I should know about? Or is there somethin' bein' said about me that I should hear?"

She debated telling him that she knew about his womanizing, but thought it better to not bring gossip into her host's home. "No, nothing."

"Good, because we're friends, you and I. I care about ye a great deal and I do no' want there to be any secrets between us."

Charlotte's attempt at a hardened demeanor cracked. Her hands fell from her hips and hung loosely at her side. "I know, Conner."

"Good. Now, please, go inside and get warmed up. Do ye remember how to get back to the sittin' room?"

"Yes, I think I can manage." She turned from him to go back toward the stairs. She could hear his boots fading off behind her and felt her stomach drop in the most peculiar way. Charlotte ignored the feeling and went inside to find the girls.

Chapter Seventeen

"How long will you be staying here?" Flora asked over their casual lunch in the family's private dining room. Compared to the feasting hall, this small, wood-lined, room with the delicate chandelier and cloth-covered table was positively dainty.

Charlotte shrugged. "A year, perhaps. I'm not sure."

"Well, I like having another lady around," Flora told her. "It's only been Gwen and I for the past few months and we get terribly bored."

Charlotte took a bite of a steamed carrot. "Do you visit your mother often?"

"No," Gwen cut in. "Our eldest sister just had a baby so she's been quite distracted, as of late."

Flora looked around before leaning toward the table, and Charlotte. "Are you here because of Conner? Will you two marry?"

Charlotte nearly choked on her food. "Oh, goodness no. We're just friends."

"Pity." Flora sighed. "I thought he rather liked

you."

"And I heard he shouted proposals to you this morning," Gwen said, her voice a shy whisper.

"He was just joking about," Charlotte assured them. "He didn't really mean it."

"I think he did," Flora told her with a certain confidence. "He's not one to bring home English ladies for no reason."

"Yes," Gwen agreed, nodding her head enthusiastically. "He's never courted before and you're ever so pretty."

"And he talked about you a lot in his letters," Flora added.

Charlotte looked up from her food. "He did?"

Gwen grinned, showing off her deep dimples. "Oh, yes. He went on and on about what a fine lady you were and how he was going to bring you for a visit."

"I'm glad he thinks so highly of me," Charlotte said evenly. "But, the truth is, I'm not really here for a social visit. Your brother helped save me from a terrible marriage."

Flora gasped, positively scandalized. "You're *married*?"

Charlotte held up her hands. "Oh, goodness, no! I mean to say that Conner saved me *before* the wedding. My betrothed was a terrible brute and would have been a monstrous husband."

"That would explain why he came home so early," Gwen murmured to her sister.

Flora sighed and looked at Charlotte with a dreamy expression. "It sounds so romantic. An English lady saved from an evil man and swept away to a castle. It's just the kind of thing one might read in a French novel."

"That's not quite how it happened," Charlotte said, feeling the heat creep up her neck.

"Oh?" Flora perked up. "Then how did it happen?"

Charlotte opened and closed her mouth several times, looking for the right words to say. "Well…I suppose that it is how it happened, actually."

Flora clapped her slender hands. "That's lovely. All that's needed now is a splendid wedding and you would have your happily ever after."

"I'm sorry, but I'm not marrying Conner. He proposes merely for the enjoyment of the men." Charlotte looked down at her plate of cold food, her appetite almost entirely gone.

Flora pursed her lips and slid her gaze in Gwen's direction for a moment before continuing. "If you really did think he meant it, what would you do?"

"Flora, you can't ask her something like that. It's not polite," Gwen scolded.

Charlotte felt her face redden and looked at the two girls on the other side of the table. She hadn't thought all that seriously about Conner's proposals. She merely chalked them up to be the dramatics of a perfectly horrid flirt. If Conner really were interested in getting married and having a family, then he would have done right by one of the other women he ruined long ago.

"What are ye ladies goin' on about in here?" Conner asked from the doorway. His hair was damp as if recently washed and he wore a clean, white shirt with his kilt. He walked over to the small serving table in the corner and began piling up a plate with food. "I hope my wee sisters are no' givin' ye any trouble, Charlotte?"

Charlotte tried to compose herself and hoped that he wasn't privy to the girls' entire conversation from his spot by the door. "None at all. They've been the perfect hostesses."

He brought his plate to the table and took a seat next to Charlotte. Flora and Gwen each smiled mischievously at one another, causing Charlotte to see a certain MacLeod family resemblance in their impish smirks. She peered at Conner from the side of her eye and watched him as he ate and talked to his sisters. She wasn't listening to what he was saying, but actually just observing him.

This, his castle, was his natural habitat. Although he seemed very comfortable while in London, he smiled and spoke so easily in his own home. His mannerisms were casual and the way he addressed his sisters and his kinsmen was warm and friendly. Conner, although a flirt, was a very good friend and Charlotte was more than pleased to be there with his family. She resolved to try to forget the things he had done in his past, and focus on how he had certainly saved her from a terrible life. She owed him so much and it was almost shameful how she judged him.

"Do you ride, Charlotte?" Gwen's soft voice brought her back to the present.

"Yes, I love to ride. But I don't believe I've brought my riding habit."

Conner raised a brow. "Ridin' habit? Ye do no' need somethin' fancy just to ride in. Ride in what ye have on."

"In my day dress?" Charlotte motioned to her freshly pressed frock. "I couldn't do that."

"You just put on one of your normal day dresses and ride out," Flora said. "You don't get too messy riding horses. If you need to, you could borrow one of mine. We look to be almost the same size."

Charlotte shook her head. "I'll make do with something from my own wardrobe. Thank you for offering."

Gwen stood from her seat. "So we'll all go riding, then. Conner, care to join us?"

He pushed away his place. "Aye, sounds like a fittin' activity for this clear day. I'll meet ye ladies in the stables."

Chapter Eighteen

Charlotte had gone to her rooms and retrieved her thick winter cloak from her closet along with a pair of black leather riding gloves. Mary had the foresight to pack her riding boots, at least, for which Charlotte was very grateful. When she passed Gwen and Flora's rooms she found them to be quiet inside. She assumed they had already gone down to the stables, so Charlotte descended the stairs to the main hall. When she stepped out in the afternoon sunlight, she realized she had no idea where the stables were.

The courtyard was now empty, not teeming with men practicing their skills nor maids hanging clothes out to dry. She could see guards in the towers keeping watch but, other than that, there were no signs of life. Charlotte walked around the side of the castle, hoping to run into the stables eventually, and after about ten minutes she came upon a long wooden building with a slanted roof and two wide doors.

"Flora? Conner?" Charlotte called as she pushed

157

one of the doors open. "Are you out here?" She could smell newly thrown hay and felt the heat from healthy horses. She almost shivered with anticipation over being able to ride again. "Hello?"

"Hello," Conner's voice said from behind her.

Charlotte startled. "Do stop sneaking up on me all the time!" She was then confronted by two of the largest horses she had ever seen. One was a powerful bay whose shoulders would tower over a tall man. He stomped about impatiently as if he would burst without a good gallop. The other sported a white streak on her forehead and peered at Charlotte through intelligent, brown eyes.

"Ever ridden one o' these?" Conner gestured to the animals he led.

"No. They're huge."

"They're Clydesdales, the largest of all the horse breeds. Native to Scotland."

Charlotte examined the beasts. "I didn't know horses could be so…gigantic."

"If you are scared to ride them, I have a sturdy pony in the stables that would do fine for a lady."

Charlotte scoffed. "If you think I would be scared of a horse then you obviously don't know me very well.

"Is that so?" Conner grinned and patted the Clydesdale with the white streak. "Then I hope ye can handle Molly, here. She can be quite spirited."

She held out her hand for Molly to sniff and smiled as she felt the horse's hot breath against her palm. "What a lovely creature."

"Aye, I thought you and Molly would get on well. Ye can use her whenever you please while you're stayin' here."

"Really? Thank you, Conner, that's ever so kind. Are your sisters already out riding? I didn't hear them in their bedrooms when I came down."

"They're no' comin'."

Charlotte furrowed her brow. "They're not?"

"Aye," Conner said as he adjusted her horse's bridle. "Apparently, they both grew ill after lunch. Those meddlin' lasses."

"Maybe they really do feel ill." Charlotte couldn't help the sudden feeling of dangerous excitement that grew in the pit of her stomach. Of course this ride wouldn't be the first time she was alone with Conner, but being in Scotland with him created a new set of feelings she still couldn't quite identify.

"If ye no longer wish to go ridin' I understand. English ladies are rarely seen without a chaperone. Or I could see if the cook could spare a lass who can ride along with us?"

She waved her hand. "Oh, posh. I don't think I've ever been around you with a chaperone and I'm not about to start now."

"I do no' have a lady's side saddle, either. Ye have to ride like a man."

"I detest side saddles. One can never canter or have a good gallop without feeling like they'll slide right off."

"All right, then. I'll lift ye up. It's a high jump for a wee lass like you." He placed his hands on her waist and swept her over his head and onto the horse before Charlotte could protest. The ease with which he moved her made her feel like a 'wee lass'

159

indeed.

She looked down at him, noting that the top of his blond head just reached her thigh. "This isn't nearly as high as I thought it would be. I rather like feeling tall for once."

He laughed and went over to his own mount to make the final adjustments to his gear. "Glad ye feel stable. The Clydesdale is no' a horse many enjoy. But, Molly's a steady ride."

As Charlotte arranged her skirts to hide as much of her legs as possible, she couldn't imagine how anyone could dislike being on such a gentle giant. The horses she was allowed to ride at her father's country home were just timid little ponies. The only time she could have real fun while riding was when she took Penelope's brother's horse. Now Conner had been kind enough to allow her a formidable beast of her own.

He swung himself onto his warhorse as if he were simply sitting upon a chair. He looked like a proper Scottish warrior atop that formidable animal. In addition to his kilt, shirt, and well-worn boots, he had donned a wolf skin cape that only made him all the more fearsome. The addition of a long sword tied to the back of his saddle was a nice touch.

"Ready to ride out?" Conner asked. "I thought ye'd like to see the loch."

"I'd like that very much." Charlotte tapped Molly with her heals and together the pair began their walk to the front gates. "What is your horse called? I hadn't thought to ask."

He stroked his horse's neck. "Bear. He's my favorite horse."

"I can see why. He's beautiful." Her eyes strayed to his sword again. "Is it really necessary to bring that?"

"My sword? Aye. Wolves get brave in the winter when hunger strikes them," he answered casually. "They normally do no' bother humans, but I do no' like to take a chance like that."

Charlotte paled. She had never seen wolves outside of the London zoo. "Do you come across them often?"

"Where do ye think I got this cloak?" Conner chuckled, waving to the guards as they left the front gates.

Oddly enough, she found herself slightly less frightened by the idea of meeting a wolf in the hills. Conner was obviously an accomplished swordsman and, if his cloak was any indication, a very good hunter.

Once they were outside the heavily guarded walls, Charlotte was reminded of how breathtaking Scotland really was. The emerald hills went on as far as the eye could see and the January winds moved the grass in such a way that the rolling lands looked alive. In the distance she could see clusters of sheep and small patches of trees. To her left and right, the violently churning sea was visible, but Conner led her down the hill and toward the inland. However, they didn't follow the worn path the carriage had taken when she first arrived at the castle, instead trotting over untouched grass.

"Fancy a race, my lady?" Conner's blue eyes flashed with eagerness. "If ye follow me, we'll be at the loch in no time."

Charlotte returned his grin with a smirk all her own. "It wouldn't be much of a race if I followed you the entire way." She then kicked her heals to Molly's side, willing her forward into a brisk gallop. Charlotte felt so free on the back of that magnificent beast. The thundering of Molly's hooves reverberated in her chest and feeling her hair flying behind her in an auburn wave was almost too much for her to bear.

She knew they had been riding for more than half an hour, but the thrill of the gentle giant's galloping, and the lush scenery around her, made the race feel much shorter. Before she knew it, they had reached a large lake and Charlotte had won, although she guessed Conner had let her win out of chivalry. He and his horse were a well-matched team that could probably outrun any other. She looked back at Conner who had leapt from his horse with the graceful ease of a gymnast. His hair was tousled and she could see him taking in deep breaths of fresh air.

"What do ye think, Charlotte?" he asked as he came upon her horse.

"It's beautiful. The water is as gray as the sky."

"Aye, and colder still."

She turned her face down to him. "So, are you going to help me off, or do I need to jump and break my ankles?"

Laughing, he held out his arms to her and slipped her effortlessly from her high perch. "You are a verra bossy lass."

"Telling people what you want is what gets results," Charlotte stated primly, gently shaking the

162

wrinkles from her skirt, "not keeping quiet like a well-mannered lady."

"Ach, ye'd be a sight in London society today," he said, looking her over.

Charlotte patted her hair. While it had once been a smooth cascade, it was now a tangled mass. She wished she had thought to braid it before setting out to ride. "Is it really all that bad?"

"Not at all. Ye look right fine like this. Bein' a proper lady is overrated."

"Oh?" Charlotte raised a brow. "And what would you know of being a lady?"

"It's all tea parties and fancy frocks." He mimicked a curtsey. "Balls and ribbons and...well, I guess that's about it."

"And Scottish women have more interesting pursuits?" Charlotte took Molly's reins and began walking closer to the water.

"Aye." He followed her without Bear. "Take my sisters. They still like pretty little things and dancin', but they're also good with a bow and better with a dagger."

Charlotte noted Bear wandering over to a particularly lush smattering of grass. "Won't he run off if you let him walk about like that?"

"Bear? No, he's a fine beast. All my horses stay with me when we're out."

"So I can just let go of the reins and my horse will stay close?"

"Aye. And even if they do run off, they'll come back when called. Besides, Bear and Molly have takin' a likin' to each other. I doubt they'd wander too far."

"How impressive," Charlotte whispered, releasing her hold on Molly. The massive horse trotted over to Bear and began happily munching beside him.

"I'm glad you are a rider. There's no' much to do here for a lady." He started walking toward the lake with Charlotte at his side.

"I'm sure I'll keep busy. Riding, reading, and exploring are all very interesting pursuits."

"Then I have to show ye the library soon. It'll be sure to keep ye busy for years."

"I doubt I'll need to stay amused for years. Hopefully in a few months, I'll be able to return home."

"Did ye think about writin' your father? I'd do it myself, but I'm sure he'd like to know you're safe from your own hand. "

Charlotte sighed. "No, not yet. I left a note at home just apologizing and asking his forgiveness, but I can't imagine what else I could say right now. I keep trying to think of the right thing to pen, but I can never word it correctly."

He put a heavy arm around her shoulders and pulled her to his side. "It'll be all right, Charlotte. Families have a way o' workin' these things out."

She stiffened for a moment, startled by his constant familiarity, but found herself focusing on their physical closeness instead. Her shoulder was pressed against the side of his chest. His wolf skin cloak tickled her cheek. The warmth from his calloused hand heated her arm and she could feel each individual finger as if there weren't several layers between them. Charlotte inhaled his scent of firewood, hay, and rainwater. It was a rugged aroma that no English gentleman would ever possess.

"Are ye all right, Charlotte?" He looked down at her, a puzzled expression on his handsome face.

"Yes, I was just thinking." It was hard to ignore how contented she felt with his arm around her—an almost natural sensation she had never felt before, which gave her a sense of belonging that was hard to disregard. Just the mere memory of their indecent kiss in his London library was enough to make her heart race.

But the thought of Elizabeth and the child made her angry with him at the same time. If he was such a debonair outdoorsman who cared for his clan, how could he not care for his own flesh and blood? And that night, on New Year's Eve, he claimed to take an interest in orphans and foundlings just as she had and his words melted her core. Charlotte had the nagging suspicion that it had all been a lie and he merely fed her what he thought she wanted to hear. He feigned interest in her dreams while ignoring the child another woman bore him. She felt like such a fool.

"I want to go back to the castle," Charlotte told him, twisting smoothly out of his grasp.

"Why? What's wrong?" He followed her as she stalked toward the horses. "Charlotte, talk to me!"

She turned on her heel, filled with fury. "About what? About Elizabeth? About what happened to her? About your true intentions with me?"

Conner looked dumbstruck. "What are ye talkin' about?"

"Don't play stupid, Conner, it doesn't suit you."

"I really do no' understand what your goin' on about."

Charlotte heaved a heavy sigh and crossed her arms. "I'm saying that I know all about the child you abandoned."

"The child I abandoned." He repeated it, slowly.

"Yes, and I think it's abhorrent that you get a woman with child then leave them to fend for themselves in the cruel world of men. I've tried to ignore it to keep our friendship, but I don't believe I can stand it anymore."

"Charlotte, I do no' know what ye are talkin' about," he said, grasping her shoulders, forcing her to face him. "I've never even *lain* with a woman."

Charlotte balked. "What? But…Elizabeth…she was…" Her head spun with confusing thoughts. She had heard the rumors of Elizabeth being scorned by her lover and left with a seed in her womb. Charlotte had watched her return from abroad a quieter, sadder girl who had almost left society altogether.

"I barely know her. It's true she had a son by a lover, but I was no' he." Conner ran his hands through his loose hair. "Elizabeth used to be close to my eldest sister. When she fell pregnant and had to give up her child, she came to my sister as her dearest friend. I offered to help out o' kindness. I found a good home for her son with a distant cousin o' mine who lives in France. I made it so Elizabeth could visit her child whenever she wanted. I helped her because no mother should be parted from her child, no' because her child was mine."

Charlotte stared at him for a few moments,

although it felt like an hour. The only sound she heard was the lapping of the cold waters of the lake and the wind as it flew past them. She couldn't believe what she was hearing. All this time Charlotte had been pushing Conner away because of a lie—stupid gossip she had thought to be true. All the while he had never done anything worthy of her scorn.

"Charlotte, say somethin'," he pleaded. "Say ye believe me."

"I-I'm so sorry," she gushed, tears pricking the back of her eyelids. "So many people told me you had gotten her with child then abandoned them. You flirted so openly with me that I thought you were just trying to seduce me like you were Elizabeth. I'm so sorry, Conner. I'm so ashamed."

"It's all right, Charlotte, no harm done," he murmured softly, running his hands around her back, bringing her to his chest. "I can see how people might see my compassion towards her as an admission o' guilt."

She wiped at her eyes with her leather gloves, embarrassed at the burst of emotion. "I feel so horrid. You've been such a good friend with me and all this time I supposed you were such a terrible person."

"Come, now," he crooned. "Let's get ye back to the castle."

"I'm sorry." She wanted to stay by the lake, trapped in their own private bubble, but she also felt so emotionally drained. How could she have been unable to see that the charming, kind Scottish chieftain wasn't one to throw away his own blood?

She had believed the rotten chatter and now she wept into his wolf-skin cloak as he rubbed her back and shushed her.

Charlotte felt abashed and contrite as he beckoned the horses that came at once.

They rode back in silence, not sparing a glance in the other's direction. The once painfully short jaunt to the lake now felt as if it lasted all afternoon. Gone were the freeing, galloping steps of before and the exhilaration of the open land. The sensations were replaced with the sinking pang of dread, which weighed in her stomach like a rock. Each thump of the horse's hooves echoed the beating of her breaking heart.

Charlotte couldn't imagine how she managed to make such a mess of things or how she could have ever thought so poorly about the man who saved her from a violent marriage. She wasn't sure if Conner could ever excuse her behavior. He had only shown her compassion, concern, and a thrilling new feeling she hadn't felt before meeting him. And how had she repaid him? By holding him at arm's length and acting both hot and cold toward him, in the most abominable way.

"I'll take the horses in," Conner offered as they reached the stable. "Ye should go inside and warm up." He helped her off her mount and immediately brought the horses inside, leaving Charlotte standing alone in the courtyard.

Swallowing a sob, Charlotte ran around the keep to the front door and hurried up the stairs to her chambers. As she passed Gwen and Flora's doors, they both popped their heads out to see her dashing by in a flurry of tears. As soon as the door was closed behind her, she threw herself on the bed without bothering to remove her cape, nor her muddy boots.

There was no way Charlotte could continue staying in the castle after coming clean with Conner about what she had thought of him. She rolled over onto her back and looked up at the ancient ceiling. She needed to leave the MacLeod keep as soon as possible. There was nothing more to be done.

Chapter Nineteen

"What are you doing?" Flora asked from the doorway.

Charlotte looked up from the bag she was hastily shoving her clothing into. "Packing."

Flora gasped. "Leaving? Why would you go and do a thing like that?"

"I've made a mistake by coming here." Her voice cracked as she spoke and she pushed her tangled hair away from her damp face with the back of her hand. "I've made an utter fool of myself in the most disgraceful way."

Flora took the bag Charlotte had been packing and placed it on the floor. "Did something happen at the loch?"

"Yes. I'm such a stupid fool."

"Just tell me what happened so I can help. Is it Conner? Did he do something to offend you? I know he can be quite boisterous and often forgets that not everyone likes being joked with."

"No, it's not him. I heard a rumor in London that I thought was true and because of it I haven't been nearly as kind to him as he deserved."

"Is that all?"

"Yes," Charlotte said miserably.

Flora clamped her mouth shut as if trying to control a flood of giggles. "Is that really it, then?"

"Well...yes, I suppose," Charlotte admitted, becoming confused.

"All this crying and packing over a rumor?"

Charlotte flushed, feeling more like an idiot than ever. "I told Conner what I heard and it wasn't even true, but he looked ever so upset with me."

"I can't imagine Conner staying mad at anyone for any reason." Flora patted her hand. "This was all just a misunderstanding."

"I insulted him greatly. It feels like a slap in the face to continue to take advantage of his generosity now."

"Charlotte, what rumor did you hear that upset you so?"

She swallowed a fresh wave of tears. "I heard that Conner had gotten a woman with child and I believed the gossip."

"That *is* an awful rumor." Flora frowned. "Can't you just say you're sorry?"

"I already have but it's not enough. I've made Conner think that I dislike him when that's not the truth at all."

"Oh?" Flora smiled a bit, once again showing the MacLeod family resemblance. "And how do you feel?"

"Don't push, Flora," Charlotte scolded, trying to control her own lips from turning up.

"Now, Charlotte, you do look a fright. Your hair

is a bird's nest, your dress is spattered with mud, and your face is as red as a ruby. Dinner is to begin shortly and if you want Conner to accept your apology fully, you need to look a bit more enchanting than this."

***

An hour later, Flora had Charlotte primed and polished to look like the proper lady that she was. Charlotte wore a cream colored silk gown which hung off her shoulders and dipped low on her chest. The skirts had tiny pickups that accentuated her slim waist. Her hair hung long with her natural curls oiled and brushed to surround her face like a red-gold frame. Lastly, she donned the emeralds Conner had given her as a gift. They hung heavily upon her neck and ears, almost as heavily as her heart felt in her chest.

Charlotte knew she had a quarter of an hour before they were to assemble for dinner in the feasting hall and she had to find Conner before then to make things right. Taking one last glance in the mirror, she took a deep breath before sneaking out of her rooms and down the hall to the stairs.

She wasn't sure where Conner would be. She wasn't even sure where things *were* in the castle. Working on a hunch, she ran through the halls and up to the top of the stairs she had been in that morning. Instead of taking the door on the right, which led to the balcony, she slowly pushed open the other.

As her eyes adjusted to the light, she saw she

was at the top of a beautiful staircase and standing at eye level with a crystal chandelier. And all around her were hundreds upon hundreds of books. As she looked down at the lower levels, she saw more volumes lined up neatly on shelves. She shut the door behind her and glided down the steps, her gaze overwhelmed by the thousands of books before her. The library was just as striking and ostentatious as Conner had promised.

She walked past a colossal fireplace that had a mouth so large she could easily stand inside. She even saw that the mantle was held up by two marble statues of exquisite women who were both just her size. There were dozens of paintings on the walls and even more weapons scattered about. A huge mahogany desk sat in one corner, its surface covered in piles of books. In another corner a table held maps on easels and even more piled up in orderly rolls.

The library was stunning, but also without any other occupants. Wherever Conner was, it appeared he wasn't here. If he had already left to the feasting hall for supper, it might be too late for Charlotte to find him. She debated going to his chambers, but remembered that she had no notion of where his rooms were either. Deciding to continue her search outside, Charlotte stepped back to the stairs, hoping to get a bird's eye view from the balcony.

"Charlotte?" Conner stepped from a darkened corner she had not yet explored.

She spun around, her skirts lapping at her ankles like a silken wave. "Conner! I was searching for you. I didn't know why, but I had a feeling that I'd

173

find you here."

"Is somethin' amiss? I was about to go fetch ye, and the lasses, for dinner." His deep voice was relaxed and the sound reverberated in her chest.

Charlotte took a deep breath. "I needed to talk to you about what transpired today."

"What about it?"

"I listened to gossip and believed terrible things about you that I know aren't true. Because I was such a silly little fool, I treated you most monstrously. I needed to tell you how very wretched I am for thinking ill of you and I do hope you could forgive me." Once she had finished, she waited for Conner to say something, anything. He merely stood there in silence, staring at her, taking her in. "Oh, Conner, do say something, please?"

"Ye silly lass," he whispered, pushing back his hair with his hand. "Ye ran all the way up here to give me an *apology*?"

"I-I...yes. I couldn't see you again without telling you how sorry I was and I certainly couldn't do such a thing at dinner."

"Did ye really think me so fickle as to be angry with ye over somethin' like that?"

Charlotte furrowed her brow. "Well, I just thought...you seemed so distant after my stupid outburst and I thought you were angry with me."

"I was never angry with ye, Charlotte. I just finally understood."

"Understood why I was so callous and treated you so strictly?"

"No, I finally understood why ye try no' to love me."

174

Charlotte let out a breath she wasn't aware she was holding as she fought back fresh tears. "Oh, Conner, I'm sorry I was such a fool."

"Stop the tears, Charlotte." He grinned as he enveloped her in his arms. "And stop sayin' you're sorry."

"But you seemed so cross with me." She cried.

"I thought ye believed me to be a heartless rogue," he countered, stroking her hair with a heavy hand. "I dinna want ye to think that o' me. I thought I should give ye time alone."

Charlotte clutched his white shirt and planted her cheek against his chest. "Oh, no, never that!"

"Then we do no' have a problem." He brought her to arm's length and wiped away her tears with the pad of his thumb. "Charlotte, are ye happy here with me?"

"What?"

"Are ye happy here, living in the castle with me?"

"Well, yes, I mean I have only been here a short while…"

"Then stop makin' a fuss when there is no fuss to be had."

"I'm sorry. I just feel so foolish to have thought that way about you."

He shook his head and held out his arm to her. "If ye stop talkin' nonsense and London gossip, we can stop all this and go down to dinner."

As they reached the door, the thick wood swung open to reveal Nettie standing in the doorway. Her small eyes darted between Conner and Charlotte, her lips pursed with unhappiness. "Sir, I've come to fetch ye for supper."

"Thank you." Conner spoke to Nettie but his face was still turned toward Charlotte's own heart-shaped one. "Come, Charlotte, we canno' keep the hungry lads downstairs waitin'."

Charlotte frowned as she watched the maid walk before them, an alluring swing to her hips. She wondered. Just how long had the maid been standing there, and just how much had she heard?

Chapter Twenty

Charlotte awoke the next morning feeling refreshed and as if she had been given another chance. Conner had forgiven her fully and now they were friends again. But, were they friends? She threw off the comforter and stared at her small feet dangling beneath the lace hem of her nightgown. Conner had implied that Charlotte was trying not to love him, but she wasn't sure if any of his words were true. Her heart beat faster when he was close and the thought of seeing him filled her to the brim, but was it love?

The sound of several blaring horns jarred Charlotte out of her musings. Curious, she pulled a robe around her and slipped out of her room, padding down the hall barefoot until she reached a large window by the stairs that looked out over the main courtyard.

In the dim morning light, Charlotte could make out a group of a dozen riders and one large carriage. Squinting, she looked toward the group, wondering who they were. Judging by their livery and English ponies, they certainly weren't Scottish. Charlotte assumed they were merely looking to trade or to pay court to the lord of the highlands.

Charlotte turned to go back to her room as Conner came bounding up the stairs. "Charlotte, wait!"

She clutched her robe closer around her, wishing she had thought to comb her hair or get a proper dress on before wandering the halls. "Conner, I'm not dressed!"

"No time for all that," he growled, pulling her into her bedroom. "We need to talk."

Charlotte pulled her arm out of Conner's firm grip. "What's going on? Why are you acting so strange?"

"We have visitors."

"Well, unless you're going to be receiving them in my bedroom, I don't see why you feel the need to talk to me about it before I'm properly clothed."

"It's Richard Howard."

Charlotte blanched and felt her knees weaken. "No…it can't be."

"Well, it is. He's under the impression that ye have been kidnapped by a bunch o' ruthless Scots."

"I…I think I'm going to faint…"

Conner grasped her around the waist as her legs gave way. "Are ye all right? Do ye need a doctor?" He carried her over to one of the plush armchairs in her sitting room before pulling on her bell to summon a maid.

"Richard can't be here. Oh, Conner, what do I do?"

"Do no' worry, it'll be fine. I have one o' my

men talkin' to him now to see what he wants."

"He has to be here for *me*! There's no other reason for him to come all this way!"

Conner knelt next to her chair and held one of Charlotte's limp hands in his. "He will no' get to ye, I promise ye that."

"What will I do? What if he demands I go with him?" Tears began streaming down her pale cheeks. "I can't marry him, Conner."

"Charlotte, he has no power in Scotland. He is in *my* country, on *my* land, and is in no position to be makin' demands." His voice was foreboding and held much more vigor than Charlotte could ever hope to have in that moment.

"I...I don't think I can face him."

"Then ye won't. I'll have him sent away. He will be dealt with."

The bedroom door crept open and Maisie entered the room as she had every morning, but today she paused as she saw Conner in Charlotte's bedchamber. "Oh, my lord, I apologize. I thought the Lady Charlotte rang for me."

"I rang for ye," Conner answered. "Charlotte needs somethin' hearty to eat. There's an unwanted visitor here and she needs her strength. See to it she'd fed and cared for. Send for me if she faints again."

Maisie bobbed a curtsey. "Aye, my lord."

Once they were alone, Conner turned to Charlotte once again. "Are ye sure ye feel all right?"

"Yes, I'm fine. It was just a bit of a shock."

"Will you be all right if I go downstairs to take

care o' this? I'll come back as soon as he's gone."

"I'll be fine. I'm just going to have a bath and get dressed. I'll come downstairs when I'm ready."

Conner nodded and stood. "Send Maisie for me if ye need me." He leaned down and pressed his lips to her forehead. "Everythin' will be all right."

Charlotte wished, deeply, that she could believe him.

***

After a hot bath and a few tentative bites of toast, Charlotte dressed herself in a pale blue dress. Her hair hung down in waves and she tried to pinch a bit of color into her white cheeks. Not wanting to wait all day for any news, Charlotte decided to sneak downstairs to try to find out what was going on. She didn't hear anything from either of the girls' chambers as she passed and pondered if they knew that outside was the very man she ran away from.

When she reached the lower landing, she saw Maisie peeking out from behind a tapestry, motioning for her to come forward. "My lady, thank goodness you are here."

"What is it?" Charlotte asked as she was pulled behind the tapestry into a small alcove. If anyone were to pass by, they would have no idea the women were there.

"There be a man here askin' for ye. He's talkin' to the MacLeod now."

"I know of the man. That's why Conner was in my chambers this morning."

"The man wants to take ye back to England. He

180

brought soldiers with him. Says ye belong to him."

Charlotte paled and let out a deep sigh. "I don't belong to him. He's the man my father wanted me to marry. He's the reason Conner whisked me away here."

"Shall I take ye down to the servants' quarters? Perhaps ye could hide there?"

"No, I don't believe that will be necessary." Charlotte gently pulled the heavy fabric aside and looked around at the empty room. "I think I'm going to try to see what's going on in the grand hall."

"I'll come too. There's a way to see in the hall without havin' to go in." Maisie grasped her hand and pulled her out of the alcove and into the hallway, opening a door. The room she led them into was the sitting room Charlotte saw the first day she came to the castle. Maisie locked the two doors on either side of the room with a set of iron keys taken from a pocket in her dress. "Now, no one will disturb us. Come here, to the clock, and help me move it aside."

"The clock?" Charlotte was puzzled but followed her to the large grandfather clock and pushed it away from the wall. What she saw behind it shocked her. A small grate had been hidden behind the timepiece and Charlotte could hear the sounds of angry men's voices emanating from the wall.

"Keep quiet," Maisie whispered as she took the grate away. "They can't see us, but they might hear us."

Charlotte stood up on her toes and peered into the hole to find that it led to the great hall. While the window was small, it allowed a fair view of the proceedings. Conner sat upon the great throne, wrapped in his clan's tartan, a large and menacing sword at his side. Several of his best and largest warriors stood beside him, their faces intimidating and their hands upon the hilts of their weapons. Richard was before them, a small fleet of English soldiers at his rear. The British company looked almost pitiful next to the warriors of the highlands.

"Her father and I had an agreement," Richard said, holding out a piece of paper. "He wrote his intentions to give me his daughter in this note. I brought it as proof."

Conner motioned toward one of his men, who snatched the letter out of Richard's hand and gave it to Conner. He promptly tore it up, dropping the pieces upon the wolf skins under his chair. "The note proves nothin' and means even less in the highlands."

Richard gaped. "It proves that she is *my* betrothed and I have come to collect her. Her poor family thinks the girl is dead or ruined. I intend to bring her back to the civility of England and make an honest woman out of her."

Conner said something in Gaelic, making his men roar with laughter. He turned to the angular man with a grin. "Do ye think she'd ever agree to go back to England with you? She left England to escape your clutches!"

"I sincerely doubt that. I've made an official claim to the courts that she's been seduced by a savage and needs to be taken back to England to be reeducated."

"Reeducated, ye say?"

"Yes. I assume she has been brainwashed, or tainted by you and your…people and I intend to save her."

"She is no' a prisoner here. If she wished to leave she could at any time. She does no' need any savin'."

Richard turned and spoke to one of the soldiers in a hushed tone before turning back to Conner. "I have permission from the magistrate of London to search your property and retrieve the girl in order to return her to her family."

Conner let out a chuckle and the other Scotsmen howled with laughter. "Your magistrates have no authority in my lands. I only let ye in to give my men a good laugh. Be gone with ye, silly old man!"

"How dare you!" Richard held out a fist. "I have half a mind to challenge you to a duel."

"Oh, a duel! I'm so frightened!" Conner mocked him in a mock falsetto, making Richard all the angrier. "You're wastin' your time here. The lass does no' want to leave."

"I sincerely doubt that she would rather stay here with you *savages* instead of going home to the comforts and civility of England."

"Is that so?"

"Yes, and I would hear it from her own mouth!"

Conner said something in Gaelic to the men at his right and then turned his attention to Richard. "I'll have Charlotte brought down to see ye. But I'll have ye know that she is under my protection as the Laird o' the Highlands and I'll no' have ye scarin' her."

Charlotte's knees weakened and she turned away from the hole. "I don't wish to even *see* Richard. I can't!"

"But ye must. Laird MacLeod is sendin' for ye." Maisie stepped toward the door, motioning for Charlotte. "No harm will come to ye as long as he is by."

Sighing, Charlotte followed the maid from the room and to the door of the great hall just as it opened. One of Conner's kinsmen, a man called Big Angus, looked startled to see her there.

"Lady Charlotte," Big Angus began, nearly bending completely at the waist to reach her level. "The MacLeod wishes to see ye."

"I know," Charlotte said, ignoring the strange look she received. She squared her shoulders and straightened her skirts. "Let's get this over with."

Big Angus nodded as Charlotte took his arm. He patted her hand as a show of comfort and led her into the great hall. Charlotte ignored the English soldiers as they passed, keeping her head high and trying to control her shaking body. As she passed Richard, she saw a look of pure surprise on his face and heard him gasp.

She kept her gaze on Conner's passive face until she came to the throne. Charlotte let go of Big Angus's arm and made her way up the steps until she was at Conner's side. She noticed a chair had been placed at his right. It was a smaller version of his own throne and he motioned for her to take a seat.

Once she was seated at his side, Conner turned to her and held out his hand for her to take. "No need to be frightened. The man only wants to see ye are no' a captive here. If he sees ye safe and healthy, he can tell your father that everythin' is well."

"Charlotte!" Richard bellowed, his face flushing in rage. "Get down from there at once and come to me!"

Charlotte fixed her eyes at a spot over Richard's head, trying not to let him see how frightened she was. She knew there was no way he could force her to go back to England, but seeing him before her still chilled her to the bone. She tried sitting straight and keeping her face level, regal, like a queen.

"Ye can see she's fine," Conner said to Richard. "Now ye all can go back to England and leave us be."

"I refuse this." Richard blustered about, trying to contain his anger. "I refuse this! Charlotte, get off that ridiculous pile of animal skins, put your hair up like a proper lady, and get out to my carriage, now!"

"No." Charlotte's voice sounded firmer than she felt.

Richard bristled. "I won't take no for an answer. I promised your father I'd bring you home and here you are looking like one of those savages. Your father raised you better than this!"

"I said I'm not going. You can go and tell my father that I'm perfectly safe and this is where I've chosen to be at this time."

"You want to stay *here*?" Richard asked. "You would rather be *his* whore than *my* proper wife? Preposterous!"

Conner stood, his eyes full of fury, his hand on the hilt of his sword. "You will no' speak to

Charlotte in that manner while on *my* land and in *my* home. Ye English have no rights in the highlands and I could have my men upon ye in an instant for speakin' to her in that despicable manner. Be gone from my sight at once and go back to England!"

"How dare you!" Richard was about to take a step toward Conner when one of the English solders grabbed his arm, whispering something in his ear. Richard tore his arm from the man's grasp and straightened his suit's coat. "This isn't over. I'll be back with more soldiers, Charlotte's father, and the bloody king of England if need be!"

"Go on then with ye, then!" Conner waved a hand at him and fell back into his seat with a satisfied smile on his lips. "Run back to England!"

"Run back!" the Scots taunted. "Run back to England!"

Richard turned on his heel and marched from the room, his soldiers hot on his heels. As Charlotte watched him go, she didn't feel any sort of lightening in her chest. While she should be glad he left, she had the nagging suspicion that she hadn't seen the last of him.

Chapter Twenty-One

"Who was that old man?" Flora asked over their small dining table the next afternoon. "All the maids are talking."

"They said he was your suitor," Gwen added, an excited gleam in her eyes. "Is he the one who made you leave England?"

"I suppose you could say that," Charlotte answered grimly.

Flora pushed her finished bowl of stew aside. "You weren't actually going to marry him, were you?"

Charlotte nearly choked on her bread. "Oh, heavens, no! He's more than twice my age and all together an insufferable beast."

"Yes, don't be daft, Flora," Gwen said. "She's going to stay here and marry Conner, anyway. Who cares about that old man?"

"Yes, when are you and Conner going to marry?" Flora asked.

Charlotte reddened. "Oh, we're not! I mean, we're just friends and my father would never—"

Flora snorted. "Your father? He's the one who almost had you married off against your will!"

"He's still my father."

"I suppose he knows you're here now." Gwen looked over at Charlotte. "Did he send that dreadful old man to fetch you?"

"I'm not sure," Charlotte said, picking the remains of her roll apart. "I would think he would come himself if he knew where I was. I don't imagine he would send Richard in his stead."

"I suppose he'll find out soon enough when his friend comes back to England with his tail between his legs." Flora frowned. "Do you think your father and Richard will come back together to try to get you?"

"I hope not." It was a dismal idea—her father and Richard linking arms in Conner's throne room, both demanding her return home to England and to a bitter marriage bed.

Flora scrunched her nose. "I could never imagine marrying someone like that spindly old man."

"Nor I," Gwen agreed. "He is so ugly!"

Charlotte giggled at their overly disgusted faces. "Yes, he is. Hopefully none of us will ever have to see him again."

"No, ye won't." Conner entered the room with Big Angus at his side. "The English were seen riding south. I do no' think we'll hear from them any time soon. But, until we are sure they're gone from our lands, none of ye are to leave the keep without tellin' Big Angus first. I can't have ye ridin' off without an escort, just in case."

Flora shrugged, rising from her seat. "It's too

cold to ride now, anyway," she said, leaving the dining room.

"No walks either," Conner called after her.

"Are you sure they've left?" Charlotte asked quietly.

Conner gently brushed her cheek with his knuckles, her bruise entirely gone. "They're gone. We believe they took the train into Scotland and hired horses once they were here. I've sent two scouts to ensure they leave for good."

"Thank you." Charlotte leaned into his hand.

"Do no' thank me." He raised her up toward him. "I made ye face him when I told ye that ye would no' have to."

"Yes, but I'm glad you did. I needed to tell him that I was here because I wanted to be and I hope he tells my father that I'm all right."

"Walk with me, Charlotte?"

"Of course." She placed her napkin beside her plate and gladly took his arm.

As he led her down several halls, she reflected on how grateful she was for him in his entirety. While he might not think standing up to Richard Howard was such an immense feat, she knew how the British government looked down on the Scottish and how they might really take on Richard's cause to "free" her. He offered her his protection and strengthened his claims with a show of power against he who wished to harm her. She clung tighter to his arm, making him glance down at her in surprised pleasure.

"Are ye all right, Charlotte?"

She nodded. "Very much so."

"I'm glad to hear it." He stopped at a door before opening it. "I thought I'd show ye a bit of the pathways in case ye ever need to take use of them."

"You don't think we'll ever need to seek refuge there, do you?"

"No, I do no' believe ye will. But if ye decide to stay in Scotland, I want ye to know every passageway and secret tunnel o' this castle in the event ye do."

There was naught but darkness before them, but Charlotte could see that it was clearly a set of stairs before them. "We're going down there?"

"Aye." He took an unlit torch from a hook on the wall and reached for some tinder in the sporran at his waist. "If anythin' ever happens I want ye to be just as prepared as my wee sisters."

"They've been down here, too?"

The torch grew a warm flame, lighting the steep stairs. "Aye, o' course. Some know o' the door but most do no' venture far. The old jail cells frighten them."

"Jail cells?" Charlotte took Conner's arm as they began their descent, her slippers unsteady on the damp stairs.

"Every castle of any great measure has them. Quite a few people have been kept down in these depths and terrible things have befallen them." He flashed a jack-o-lantern smile, lit by the fire. "Some even say it's haunted."

"Oh, posh." Charlotte laughed.

"Many men died here since the castle was built. Men died buildin' it, defendin' it, and tryin' to escape it if they were caught."

"Did you torture people here?" Charlotte asked tentatively.

"Did *I*? No, but it was used in the darker times when kings fought for power and information was sought."

"Interesting." Charlotte bit her lip as they reached the floor. Three tunnel mouths stood before them, each as dark and slimy as the next. "Now where?"

"Depends on where ye want to go. To the right are the jail cells, the middle will take ye to the inner keep where we store goods in case of a siege, and the left takes ye to the cliffs."

"The cliffs?"

"Aye. It's an emergency exit o' sorts."

"Is that what you're going to show me?"

"Aye." He steered her toward the left. "But watch closely, as it's no' a straight path. Take a wrong turn and ye'll find a dead end or end up at the jail cells."

The hall was narrow with sturdy with gray stone walls that were slick to the touch. She saw several patches that looked newer than the others where an old doorway may have been patched up. When they got to the third such part in the passageway, Conner stopped her.

"This is it." He held the torch closer.

"What?" Charlotte looked around. The entranceway looked to be firmly cemented shut, but she had a suspicion that Conner was about to prove her wrong.

"Hold this fast and watch me," he said, passing her the light. He counted up ten stones from the floor, in the center of the door, and pushed.

"Oh, goodness." Charlotte gasped as the stone slab shuddered open, letting out a small burst of dust.

"Impressed?"

"Very. You could never tell there was a door here. Incredible."

Conner took the torch back and ushered her into a new, smaller, passageway with ceilings so low he had to stoop as he walked. "If ye come down here alone, ye should close the door behind ye."

"I do hope I never have to use this."

"Me too."

The hall grew damper and Charlotte stumbled a bit as they reached the end of the neatly stacked stones to see the natural formation of the cliffs making up a new passageway. "I can hear the ocean."

"That's because we're at the ocean." Slowly, the corridor grew brighter and Conner set the torch on the ground, letting it extinguish upon the moist floor.

Charlotte shielded her eyes from the sunlight. They were at the mouth of a cave overlooking the sea. Below them was a field of jagged rocks that would mean instant death if one were to fall. "Where are we?"

"On the cliffs, beneath the castle. There are handholds ye can use to climb up to the top o' the cliffs. Head east and ye'd find a cottage hidden in a patch of woods. It could keep ye secreted if anythin' happened."

"You mean I would have to climb the cliff?"

Charlotte paled and edged toward the mouth of the cave.

"Look to the right. Ye'll see a ledge ye can use to bolster yourself up."

Charlotte gripped the wall and peered over the side, seeing the small shelf and dozens of tiny steps that looked like they had been carved. "These aren't naturally made, are they?"

"No, someone chiseled them in a hundred years or so ago when they made the passageway to the cliffs."

"How frightening it would be to have to climb those." The top of the bluff was a good forty yards above them and terribly sheer. The mere thought of it made her dizzy.

"Ye won't, but ye'll know where to go if anythin' happens. It's also a right fine place to see the sunset."

She looked over the water, noticing the beginnings of a pink and purple sky building over the sea. "It must be quite pretty."

"Would ye like to stay a moment and see for yourself? Or are ye cold?"

It was true that Charlotte could feel her chilled skin prickle through her gown, but the view was so lovely she didn't wish to go. "Let's stay for a while, at least to see a bit of it. It's been some time since I've really watched a sunset."

"Then come have a seat with me." He sat down at the threshold of the cave, his legs dangling over the edge.

"Oh, that looks ever so dangerous."

"Come." He held out a hand, amused at her pale

193

face and nervous demeanor. "I will no' let ye fall."

"I hardly think you can promise me that."

"I can. Trust me, Charlotte. I have never let a guest o' my home fall to their deaths off a cliff and I'm no' about to start with you."

Charlotte paused for a moment, deciding whether she should take the risk. "All right. I suppose you're sturdy enough to act as a nice rock."

"Nice compliment." He laughed and helped her creep to the edge.

"Oh, it's much colder when you're put in the wind like this," she said as she pulled her skirts down to cover her legs.

"Ach, I did no' think ahead." He unpinned his plaid and draped a loop about her shoulders. "Better?"

"Much, thank you." Charlotte turned her head to hide the reddening of her cheeks.

They sat in companionable silence, their shoulders brushing beneath the thick tartan that covered them. Charlotte looked over the water at the setting sun and inhaled a deep breath of salt air. She'd never seen the ocean like this, only crowded shipyards teaming with sailors and old women selling fish, dumping their fetid remains into the murky water. The Scottish sea was a churning blue and clear as far as the eye could see in the distance, without a single boat in sight. Instead of the scent of sweaty bodies, crabs, and the stale odor of stagnant ships, she only breathed in sweet salt and the faint fragrance that was Conner.

He smelled of hay and horses, the tang of a bonfire, and something earnest and calming

Charlotte couldn't quite figure out. The heat between them warmed her to the core, making her feel as if she sat outside on a calm spring day instead of during the frost of winter. She dared a glance toward his placid face. He gazed into the sun, watching the sky deepen to a hew of reds and purples, his boots thumping lightly against the rocks as he swung his legs.

"Are ye ready to go back?" he asked, turning to look at her. "Ye've been starin' at me a good moment."

"H-had I?" Charlotte twisted away from the precipice and out of the folds of the plaid. "It must be time for dinner soon. I suppose it would be rude to be late."

Conner stood and stretched. "Aye, we should go back for supper, but I fear we'll have to do it in the dark."

"In the dark?"

"I do no' think this will light," he said, holding up the soaked torch. "There used to be another kept here for the journey back but it seems as if someone has taken it without putting a replacement back."

"Can you find your way back in the dark?" Charlotte looked apprehensively toward the pitch-blackness of the tunnel from which they came. "Please don't tell me we're going to have to scale this cliff!"

"Dinna fash. I know this castle like the back o' my hand. Just hold tight to me so ye do no' trip."

Charlotte grasped his arm as they entered the darkness, leaving the dying sunset behind them.

***

When they finally reached the brightly lit castle corridor, they could hear echoes stemming from the feasting hall. It seemed as if dinner had already begun and, judging by the sound of the men's chanting, they were waiting for Conner to arrive in order to eat.

"We'd better hurry," Conner said, refastening his pin to the fold of his kilt. "I've quite a hunger."

"Me too. But do I look a fright?"

Conner glanced over her. "No, ye look right as rain."

She brought a hand to her tangled hair and looked down at her waterlogged slippers. "I look as if I was *caught* in rain."

"Ach, no, ye look bonny with your cheeks pink from the cold and bit o' wind in your hair. But I can no' have ye walkin' about in those wet shoes." He stopped and bent down, grasping her ankle.

Charlotte gasped and floundered, struggling to keep her balance. "What on earth do you think you are doing?"

"Getting these off before ye catch your death." He pulled off one slipper before moving on to the next foot. He lined up both shoes next to a large tapestry of dogs chasing a boar. "I'll tell a maid to clean them for ye. Ach, your stockin's are soaked through."

"I can—" Charlotte was about to inform him that she could handle her own stockings when his hand disappeared beneath her petticoat and steadily pulled off a strip of delicate silk. In silence he freed her of the next one and regarded her from his perch upon his knee.

"Are ye all right, Charlotte?" He grinned, a hand still cupping her bare calf. He seemed to be waiting for her to shriek, slap him, cry out about her honor—but Charlotte refused to give him the satisfaction.

"Quite," she said with practiced dignity. She shook him free from her skirts and began stalking down the hall. "Do hurry, Conner."

"Aye, my lady."

The stones were cold under her feet and she felt very underdressed without any shoes or stocking. She also knew she should feel ashamed that she had allowed Conner to touch her naked legs, but she found herself quite thankful that he had pushed for her to remove her waterlogged things. She had always felt more at home without the pinch of silk shoes, but had never gone about so publically bared. She hoped no one would notice her unclad feet beneath the hem of her gown.

"Abou' time!" a hearty voice yelled as Conner and Charlotte entered the feasting hall.

"Ach, sit down, Jasper!" Conner called back, steering Charlotte toward the head table. "Ye could use to miss a meal anyway!"

The men roared with laughter, ribbing Jasper with good-natured jests. Jasper tipped an empty goblet toward his lord. Charlotte found herself smiling at their easy nature but still felt sorry that the men had to wait on their dinner.

"And where have you two been?" Flora asked once they were firmly seated. She had taken advantage of their absence to change about their places so she was seated on the far right, next to Charlotte.

"I showed our guest the cliff door." Conner motioned for the maids to bring out the platters. Plates laden heavy with cuts of seasoned beef, bowls of soup, piles of crusty breads, and slices of vegetables cooked soft were passed about. "Ye need to eat more, Charlotte."

"I eat well enough." She picked up a slice of bread, breathing in the yeasty heat.

He stabbed his fork into a particularly juicy cut of meat and slapped it onto her plate. "Eat this. Ye need some meat on your bones. A gust o' wind could knock ye straight off a horse."

"I will *not* blow away." She lowered her bread and began cutting the newest addition to her plate.

"He's just trying to fatten you up a bit." Flora grinned, her voice a whisper. "Everyone knows you need some padding in order to bear healthy bairns."

"Bairn? What's a bairn?" Charlotte asked between bites.

"Children!"

The meat suddenly became trapped in her windpipe. Charlotte coughed, caught complete off guard. "*Children*?"

"Aye." The girl threw back her mane of blonde hair. "You and I are both slight. Conner just wants us healthy for when the time comes."

Charlotte reddened. "Who said anything about children? I'm not planning on having any time soon."

"I think your suitor has different ideas." Flora's

eyes narrowed in the merry way her elder brother's did.

"Do stop teasing me." Charlotte wagged her fork. "No one here is having children any time soon!"

"Who's havin' children?" Conner asked, hearing quips of their conversation.

"No one," Charlotte growled.

Flora daintily sipped her wine. "Just yet, anyway."

"Ach, women's talk." Conner chuckled.

"If you must know," Charlotte began, "Flora here is talking about getting nice and fat for when she has a baby."

His eyes darkened. "Flora, what are ye goin' on about? A bairn?"

Flora's face was just as composed as before. Her brother's cold glance did nothing to ruffle her feathers. "Not *my* child. Yours and Charlotte's."

A loud gasp from behind them made all three turn in their seats. The busty maid Nettie stood clutching a jug of wine, her cheeks red and her mouth open in surprise.

"A *bairn*?" Nettie looked between Charlotte and Conner. "This English lass is havin' a bairn?"

"Who's having a baby?" Gwen asked, just now noticing the commotion on her other side.

"No one," Conner barked. "Nettie, no one is havin' a child so go back to your duties." He dismissed her with a wave of his hand before turning back to Flora. "Lass, stop teasin' Charlotte."

Flora scoffed. "She knows I meant nothing by it, don't you, Charlotte?"

"Of course I know you're joking as I am the one who knows when, and if, I'm having a baby." Charlotte picked up her plate and dumped the beef onto Flora's own pile of food. "So, instead of worrying about my reproductive plans, set about plumping yourself up for childbirth instead."

Flora giggled at Charlotte's frosty face. "I wish it *were* time for me to have a baby!"

"No more talk o' bairns. Especially from you, lass." He pointed at Flora. "Ye do no' even have a man yet."

"I would if you would allow me to have a man." Flora dropped her fork. "Charlotte, you left England to escape marriage, don't you think it should be up to a woman to decide when she's ready to wed?"

Charlotte paused. She was unsure if she should insert herself into this family conversation. But she knew she had no business keeping silent about matrimony when that was the entire reason she was in Scotland. "Well, yes, I do think it's a woman's right to decide her own fate, not a man's. When she reaches her majority, I think she should be free to choose to take a husband or remain unmarried."

Flora shot Conner a smug look. "See? Even Charlotte agrees with me! She thinks I should marry!"

"Marry?" Charlotte held up her hands. "I just told you my views. I have no idea if you should marry yet. Do you have someone in mind?"

"She does, but she has no business doin' it," Conner said before his sister could answer.

"Who is it?" Charlotte asked excitedly.

Flora leaned forward. "Do you see the man

sitting to the left? The one with the red hair?"

Charlotte peered around at the sea of men, most of whom had fiery heads. "Please be more specific."

"Him! His name is Jasper." Flora moved closer to Charlotte and pointed at a particularly burly man who was currently taking chunks out of a turkey leg and yelling out in Gaelic to someone on the other side of the room. "Isn't he handsome?"

Charlotte watched him wipe his mouth with the back of his hand and laugh loudly at something said at his shoulder. She could tell he was a joyful man and not too terrible to look at. Upon his cheek was a deep scar that marred an otherwise pleasant face. "Yes, he seems nice."

"Do no' encourage the lass," Conner murmured.

"Well, it would be quite hypocritical for me to run away from an arranged marriage in order to be my own woman while, at the same time, not supporting another grown woman when she says she *wants* to be married." Charlotte looked at him thoughtfully. "I thought you said women had the choice of a husband in Scotland."

He nodded. "Aye, they do."

"Then why don't you support your sister in her romantic pursuits?"

"Because she's such a wee lass." He sighed, looking over toward Jasper. "And he's a grown man, a fine warrior and hearty archer."

"Well, that didn't answer my question. Besides, wouldn't that be a positive that he can handle a weapon?"

"He's near thirty years old, much too old for her," Conner said. "And he only has a wee farm, just enough to get him through the winter and trade a bit. Flora is a lady o' breedin' and grace. She can no' work the fields and tend the hearth."

"How would you know what I'm capable of?" Flora crossed her arms. "I might have been to finishing school, but I can ride a horse and use a sword like any man."

"Bein' able to ride a horse without a side saddle is a far cry from bein' a farmer's wife." He drained his cup, watching his sister over the rim. "Do ye even know if he'd have ye?"

Flora blushed. "Of course I do! He's said so himself."

"Has he, then?" Conner's stare whipped back to Jasper.

"He's said that if I wasn't the sister of the chief, then he'd ask for my hand."

"But you *are* the sister o' the chief," Conner said. "He might say pretty words and woo ye, but he's no' in any shape to take a noble wife. He'll marry a farm girl soon enough and you will move on to a new bonny young lad."

Flora stood, pushing her seat away from the table with a loud scrape. "You're just cruel and short-sighted. I thought that since you brought Charlotte here you'd be more open to speaking about my marriage, but you're clearly still nothing but a single-minded hypocrite." She stalked from the feasting hall, Jasper's gaze trained on her back as she left.

"She's right," Charlotte told him. "She says they care for each other and your argument is that he isn't rich enough for her."

"He can barely turn a profit on his land."

"So you'll have her married off to a rich husband? You'll wed her to a man like Richard?"

Conner balked. "Ye know I would never!"

"Does she have a dowry?"

"Aye, a good one I've prepared myself."

"Is it enough to maybe buy a better plot of land or a farm hand to help?"

"I do no' want my sister's dowry to go towards buildin' another man's fields if he could no' take care o' them himself."

"But it's what she wants. She wants to marry Jasper and wants to be a farmer's wife." Charlotte reached over and placed a hand on his arm. "Wouldn't you want a sister who is happy with a poor husband than one who is miserable with a rich one?"

He rubbed his temples with a hand. "Aye, I know you're right. I just have a hard time seein' her holdin' a shovel and plantin' crops."

"I haven't known your sister long, but something tells me she and I are a lot alike. If you keep pushing her away from Jasper, she might end up running from you, too."

"Do ye really think she'd run off with him?"

"If he loves her, then yes, I do."

"As much as I like ye bein' here, Charlotte, ye know ye certainly are causin' trouble."

She smiled. "Or making things better."

"Aye, or that."

Chapter Twenty-Two

Charlotte placed her cheek against Molly's soft coat. She barely reached the Clydesdale's shoulder but Molly certainly was a gentle giant. The horse stamped her hooves a bit until Charlotte reached into the pocket of her day dress to give Molly the carrot she had taken from the kitchen after breakfast. The soft whiskers tickled her palm.

"There's a sweet dear," Charlotte cooed. "Such a lovely lady you are."

The horse nuzzled her chest, searching for more snacks.

"I'm sorry, I've only one carrot for you. Any more and the cook would certainly be angry with me." She patted her leg. "Perhaps after lunch I can take you a nice apple."

"The cook's makin' pie for after supper, but I think she'll spare one for ye." Conner stepped in front of the stable's door, holding a bundle of fur in his arms.

"Good morning," Charlotte said. "Your sisters and I missed you at breakfast."

204

"I bet Flora did no'. Is she still cross with me?"

"Of course she is. Last night you told her she was too silly to marry and her choice of husband was all wrong."

"Ye make it sound so harsh."

"But that is the reality."

"Flora's a soft lass who has no business tillin' fields."

Charlotte sighed. "I'm not going to tell you you're be hardheaded, although you are, only because I'm quite sick of talking about Flora and Jasper. I *will* just say that you're also wrong, being judgmental, and aren't putting the desires of your sister first."

"Is that it?" he asked, a bemused smirk on his lips.

"For now."

"All right then, are ye busy the rest o' the mornin'?"

"No, I was just visiting with Molly and then I was going to see Gwen and Flora."

"Could ye spare me some time? I've an errand I need a woman's touch for."

"Oh? What kind of errand?"

He held up a finger and called out, "Duncan! Duncan, where are ye, lad?"

A thin boy with curly brown hair and a ruddy complexion popped his head out from the rafters above. "Aye, MacLeod, what can I do ye for?"

"I need the wagon horsed as soon as you are able."

"Aye, MacLeod." The boy scrambled down a ladder and began pulling two horses from their stables. Charlotte noted they were both of average size and not towering Clydesdales.

"So you do have normal horses in Scotland." She poked his arm. "And here you are, saddling a behemoth for my use."

"What fun is a small horse in the highlands? A Clydesdale is all the better. So will ye come with me?"

"Where to?"

"I had a tenant and his wife taken by the fever in the night," he explained. "They left behind a son in need o' a home. He's with a neighbor but I'll be takin' him in until I can find somewhere permanent for him."

"Oh, poor boy. I'll fetch my cloak and we'll be off at once."

"No, I have a cloak for ye." He held out a pile of fur she hadn't noticed he was carrying. "I told ye that ye needed somethin' heavier for the winter."

The fur was soft and slippery in Charlotte's hands. "What animal is this from?"

"A wolf." Conner pulled his own mantle round his shoulders. "Shot it myself before I came to England."

"Goodness, a wolf." Charlotte fastened it around her neck, surprised at the warmth. "Thank you, it's...fierce."

Conner grinned, pleased with himself for his choice of gift. "Makes ye look like a warrior queen. Suits ye. Now, come. We must be off."

Charlotte followed him out of the stable to see that young Duncan had the cart ready for their departure. As the wind whipped a loose strand of hair around her face, Charlotte was grateful for her new furs. Once Conner helped her into her seat, she tightened the coat about her, burrowing into its folds.

"Do no' worry," Conner said as they began out into the hills. "The homestead is no' far from here."

"I feel so terribly for this little boy. Who will care for him?"

"I think he has an aunt who married a man down south. I sent a rider this mornin' before breakfast to see if she's able to take him."

"What if she can't?"

He shrugged. "I suppose I can find a place for him here. He can be a kitchen boy or work in the stable like Duncan."

"Is Duncan an orphan as well?"

"Aye. His ma died in childbirth and his da fell durin' a raid. I took him and had him brought up and now he has a place in my household as long as he wants it. When he's older, I'll have him schooled a bit and give him a piece o' land."

"That's charitable of you."

"He's one o' my people. O' course I take care o' him. I told ye the Scots look after their own."

The hills and farms passed quickly, smoke rising from the chimneys of squat houses and laundry fluttering in the wind. The people here were so simple, happy with their families and crops. It was so different than England where even the countryside was a hurried bustle of elaborate estates and an ever-encroaching city. She wondered if the green highlands would ever be taken over by factories and crowded houses.

"This is it." Conner stopped at the wooden fence of a stone house. He hopped out of the wagon and swung Charlotte to the ground.

Together they walked up the yard passing stray chickens pecking at the ground and ending up at a worn wooden door, the old red paint wearing off around the edges. Conner knocked quietly and the door opened to a harried looking woman whose red hair was escaping her kerchief.

"Oh, MacLeod! Thank the Lord ye are here! Me poor neighbors taken in the night, leavin' this poor bairn all alone in the world." She hustled them both into the warmth of her cottage that was dimly lit by two small windows and the sparks of a tidy fire. "I'd keep him, Lord know I would, but with my husband, I have six o' me own to feed."

"I understand." Conner patted her on the shoulder. "Which one is he, now?"

Six heads popped out from under a blanket in the home's single bed—five redheads, and one a child with shiny black hair.

"There he is. Come here, Ian." The woman plucked the black-haired boy from the bed. He was a slight child with large brown eyes and a pale, mournful, face. Charlotte didn't think he was any older than four.

"Hello, lad. I'm Conner MacLeod." He stooped down to the child's eye level. "Are ye all right to come with me and Lady Charlotte?"

The boy looked at her, and her heart tightened. "Hello, dear. Just call me Charlotte," she said.

"Is my aunty comin' for me?" Ian asked in a small voice.

"Aye, I believe so." Conner picked up the boy under his arms. "Thank ye for lookin' after him, ma'am."

"O' course." The woman clutched her apron. "Will he be all right, MacLeod?"

"Aye, I'll care for him. Have no fear." He passed her a small purse, clinking with coins. "For the bairns." He then turned from her and started toward the door. "Come, Charlotte, we'll hurry back and see that the lad gets settled for lunch."

Once they were in the cart and heading toward the castle, Charlotte nestled Ian into the folds of her new cloak, tucking his tiny body between hers and Conner's. He was quiet and still, much more so than other children she knew, but he had just gone through a horror no child should face. She held his hand and smiled when he reciprocated, his small fingers clutching hers.

"Do you like books, Ian? Or dogs?" she asked, coaxing him to speak.

"Dogs, misses," he answered.

"How lovely! There are many dogs at the castle."

He looked up at her. "A castle?"

"Yes, the MacLeod lives in a big castle and you will stay there with us. He has lots of dogs and a cook who's making apple pie tonight."

"Ye know, Ian," Conner looked away from the road for a moment. "I think one o' the huntin' dogs had puppies a few weeks ago. I'm sure they'd like a lad to play with."

"I do like puppies." He grinned.

Charlotte looked over at Conner and smiled. "Well, it looks like your new young guest has a lot

209

to look forward to tonight."

***

When they came back to the stables, Duncan and Conner took the horses to be watered, leaving Charlotte alone with the boy. He stood tucked within her cloak, his small hands clutching her leg. He looked up at her with mournful eyes, waiting for something.

"Well, Ian, are you hungry? I'm sure the cook will have something and I'm certain she won't care if you have a bite before lunch."

"Aye, misses."

She swooped down and picked him up, careful to envelope him in the warm furs. "Well, then, let's go and see what we can find to nibble."

Ian allowed her to carry him into the castle, casting wary looks at the armed guards brandishing broadswords and bows. He relaxed visibly once they were inside the keep, and seemed to be taking in the mix of vibrant tapestries, giant fireplaces, and lavish furniture.

"Oh, what have we here then?" The cook stood with her hands on her hips, her fingers wrapped around her wooden spoon.

"This is Ian," Charlotte said as a kitchen maid took her cloak. "He'll be staying with us for a while and I hoped you had something for him. He's had a tough time of it."

"Me mum and da are in heaven." Ian wriggled from Charlotte's arms and plopped to the floor. "They gone to be with me wee sister."

The cook's eyes widened at Ian's candid explanation. "Oh, ye poor bairn. What would ye like to eat? I'll make ye somethin' tasty. Porridge? A meat pie? Some stew?"

"A meat pie!" Ian exclaimed, climbing up on a stool to reach Cook's counter, making himself very much at home.

Cook smiled softly and began poking about in the oven at the half-baked pies she had been preparing for lunch, tittering as she went about poor orphans.

"Cook makes the best food I've ever eaten," Charlotte told the boy, sitting beside him at the worn wooden top. "Perhaps tonight she'll make you some hot chocolate."

Ian scrunched his pug nose. "Hot chocolate?"

"Oh, it's delicious. I promise you'll like it. It's a warm drink made from sweets."

"Mum says sweets are only for Christmas," Ian said solemnly. "And sometimes my birthday."

"Poor dear," Charlotte whispered. "I'm sure your mother wouldn't mind a treat, just now. Cook, would you mind having someone brew me a hot cup of tea?"

"O' course. Nettie, make Lady Charlotte a hot cuppa," the cook ordered the maid as she filled a cup with fresh goat's milk. She slid it toward Ian. "Drink up, wee one. Your pie will be just a minute!"

"Thank ye." Ian kicked his feet and drained his glass, grinning as Cook pulled the pies from the oven and plated two for Charlotte and Ian.

"Careful, they're hot," she told them before

turning to tend to her duties.

Charlotte sliced his pie in half, handing him part of the steaming pasty. "Be careful you don't burn your mouth." She took her own lunch and began eating, watching Ian as he devoured his food. It was clear he had been well taken care of by his parents; his clothes, though worn, had been mended with care, and despite his small form, he was lean from the youthfulness of a boy and not from hunger.

"You could do with a bath," Charlotte noted, peering at the smudges on his cheeks and the dirt beneath his fingernails.

"Oh, no, misses!" Ian said with a full mouth. "No baths!"

"But you'll be ever so nice and clean."

He shook his head. "No baths."

"Yes, baths." She took their empty plates to the sink and helped Ian from his perch, her new cup of tea in her hand. "After you've had a bath and some clean clothes, I'll see what we can do about finding those puppies."

***

"Will these do?" Maisie asked, holding up a pair of breeches and a thick woolen shirt. "I have a pair o' stockin's in my pocket as well. They'll be a bit big, but it's the best I could find in the village."

"They're perfect." Charlotte continued scrubbing at Ian's head, ignoring the boy's protests.

"I'll go tell the MacLeod the boy's all sorted then." Maisie winked at the boy before leaving.

"Now then, Ian, we're almost done. This isn't so

bad, is it?"

"It is!" The boy pouted as she poured a pitcher of fresh water over his head.

"You don't think it's fun to take a bath in a tub with lots of bubbles?"

"No, misses."

She held out a clean towel and pulled him from the water, wrapping him up tightly. "You can call me Charlotte, you know." She pulled the shirt over his head. It was on the larger side and hung to his knees. "Are you cold?"

"No, mi—Charlotte." As soon as he was sufficiently dressed, he toddled over to the two puppies curled up by the fire. He grabbed each about the middle, struggling as they squirmed in his arms. "The wee puppies want to nap with me."

"Is that so?" Charlotte asked, pulling back the blankets on her own bed and helping him deposit each dog on top.

Ian climbed onto the pillows and dragged each dog beside him. "The MacLeod says I'm to take care o' the puppies and they're my 'sponsibility."

"I'm sure you'll take very good care of them."

The boy smiled as he sleepily burrowed into the pillows, a puppy nestled on either side. "I'm tired. Will ye stay with me?" He yawned.

"Of course." She lay atop the blankets and smoothed his hair from his forehead. The boy closed his eyes and his breathing became shallow. Before he slipped into sleep, his hand curled around her fingers.

Moments later, the bedroom door opened and Conner slipped in. Charlotte waved her hand as he opened his mouth to speak. "He's just fallen asleep!" she whispered.

"Sorry." He crept up to the edge of the bed and sat beside Charlotte's feet. "I've heard he's been fed and bathed."

"Yes. The poor lamb was so fatigued he went right to sleep."

"Ye did well. Thank you for caring for him so. I'm havin' a room set for him now."

Charlotte looked down at the sleeping boy. "I don't know if he should go into another room. What if he gets frightened in the night?"

"I do no' want to inconvenience ye."

"It's no inconvenience, really."

He thought for an instant. "I could give him a room beside yours."

"Are there any free? I thought your sisters had the two rooms beside mine."

"There's one between. I wanted to give ye space from their shrieking and nonsense."

"In that case, perhaps it would be best to put him in that room if he wishes, but if he'd rather stay with me, that's all right."

"Do ye know what a small boy like him would need?"

Charlotte bit her lip and looked about the room. She assumed it was furnished similarly to her own and noted how formal it all looked. "I suppose some toys and books would be a good start. To be honest, I don't have much experience with small boys outside of the orphanages and they didn't have anything at all."

"I'll see what I can find for him. Will ye be

stayin' up here then?"

She glanced down at Ian's hand in hers. "Yes, I will. I wouldn't have him wake up to an empty room."

***

Ian quickly melted into the seam of the castle as if he'd been there all along. Every morning he followed Big Angus to archery practice and brandished his own little wooden sword. He could often be found running the halls, a puppy under each arm, or hiding away in the kitchen, begging Cook for something sweet.

But every evening he would, without fail, find Charlotte at dinner and sit upon her lap to be fed from her plate. And after dinner they would sit together in the library and poke about Conner's collected oddities and books. Truth be told, she was almost pleased that Ian's aunt hadn't come to collect him yet, even though she wanted him to have a stable, loving, home.

"Ye look deep in thought." Conner jolted her from her contemplations.

She sat on the floor before the fire in the library, the book of ancient Chinese maps before her still bared to the same page. She looked over her shoulder at Conner who leaned forward on his armchair, a bemused look upon his face.

"Sorry, I was just thinking of Ian."

"What about wee Ian?"

"I'll just miss him when he's gone," she admitted. "He's such a charming little boy and eager to learn."

"Ye know he'll always have a place here if he needs it."

"I know. It's just that he has such potential. I know you've given other orphans, like Duncan, a job here, but I just feel that Ian could be so much more than a stable hand."

"What do ye propose then?"

She brought her knees to her chest. "I don't know. Don't you have squires or something? A position where he could be well-educated and continue living here?"

"A squire?" He chuckled. "Ye mean a wee lad who would carry a sword for a knight? Sorry, lass, but we do no' have squires here."

"I'm sorry I asked. I know I should be grateful for him to have a place in the stable."

"You are so kindhearted."

"So are you. For the king of ruthless Scottish warriors, you certainly do have a soft spot for children."

"Ian would be the first lad I've taken into my home. Do ye really want Ian to stay here? In the keep, I mean if his aunt does no' come?"

"Would it be terrible of me to say that I would? I know it's intruding on your good will and I have no say in the matter, but he's just so happy here."

"Then he can stay."

"Really?" Charlotte perked up. "You mean he can retain his new chambers and live among your family?"

"If it's what ye will then aye, he can stay on as my ward. If ye will oversee his upbrinin', o' course."

Charlotte leapt up and threw her arms around Conner's neck. "Oh, Conner! That's so generous!"

"Calm yourself, lass!" He laughed and held her at arm's length, looking down at her body perched upon his knee. "I told ye that I care for my people, and my guests. If ye want the boy to be raised in my home, I'll take him gladly."

"Thank you ever so much. I'm so glad he'll stay here with us!"

"And you? Will ye stay?" His hands rested on her hips and he looked deep into her eyes.

Charlotte was caught completely off guard. While she had thought about what the future might hold, she never thought about staying in Scotland forever. She untangled herself from his lap and stood, taking several steps toward the fire. His questioning brought her back to the reality of their inappropriate embrace. "I…I don't know. I have a family and a life in England. I had hoped that once this business with Richard and my father was over, I might go home."

"I know ye miss your home." He rose up and went to stand behind her as she looked into the flames. "But ye have a home here now, if ye want it. England is only a short train away. It's no' as if ye'd never see England again."

"Yes, but it's so new. I'm a guest in a strange land taking advantage of your hospitality. I can't live here forever."

"I will no' push ye to make a choice." He grasped her arm and turned her to face him. "I asked ye when ye first came here, so I'll ask ye again. Are ye happy here?"

"Of course. These last few weeks have been wonderful. I feel so welcome and safe in your home."

"Then I'd like to take the time you are stayin' in Scotland to know ye better. I'd like it if ye'd take me into consideration."

"Consideration for what?" she asked as his hands slid down her arms to clasp her own.

"As a husband, ye daft lass. I wish to court ye."

Charlotte's head spun. She had gone from thinking Conner would never want to see her again to having him request if he could court her. It was all too surreal to be forgiven so swiftly and so completely. "Yes, Conner. I'd like that ever so much."

Grinning, he scooped her up in his arms, kissing her passionately. Charlotte melted against his lips while her breathing grew shallow and her knees buckled beneath her. When they finally broke their embrace, Charlotte could barely look at him. While she had welcomed his kiss wholeheartedly, she still wasn't used to such brazen presentations of affection.

"I suppose we should perhaps go down to dinner," Charlotte said in a breathless voice. "They might be wondering where we are."

"Ach, they'll wait. I want to show ye somethin' first." Conner went over to one of the units of shelves and tapped a rather old-looking novel.

Charlotte watched in awe as the bookcase swung open, revealing a dark corridor. "How amazing. It's another secret passageway."

"Aye, come have a look."

She took his hand and followed him into the darkness, jumping when the false door slammed shut behind her. The tiny hallway was pitch black now and Charlotte couldn't even see Conner before her. She clasped his hand tightly as they walked, touching the rough, stone, walls with the other. "Are there many passageways like this?"

"Aye." Conner's disembodied voice answered in the dark. "They were built with the castle so the family could hide if the keep was stormed."

"I thought you said the castle walls have never been breeched."

"They haven't." He brought her to a stop and a sliver of light brightened the hallway. "That's why they're secret once again. I found many of them as a child."

Charlotte blinked as her eyes adjusted to the light. When Conner brought her to their destination, she saw they were in a large, dimly lit bedchamber. It was similar to her own, with a four-poster bed covered in blood red bedding and a fireplace that crackled beneath the MacLeod crest. A display of swords hung upon the wall between two giant battle-axes. "Is this your bedchamber?"

"That it is." He left her by the secret door, which was little more than a false piece of paneling, and went to a large wardrobe in the corner. He opened it wide and slid aside the hung kilts and dinner jackets to bring out a large, flat box. "I have somethin' for ye."

"You don't need to give me anything."

"But I do." He placed the box on a trunk at the

foot of his bed. "If I am to court ye, I need to show everyone that you are attached to me."

"What do you mean?"

The box contained a large swatch of plaid, the very same tartan that Conner and all his men wore. Atop the fabric was a silver pin. Beautifully made, it boasted the fierce and angry bull of the MacLeod crest, encircled by a belt and buckle, the clan motto **'Hold Fast'** engraved upon it. It was slightly smaller than the palm of her hand. "This is the plaid of the MacLeod clan and this is the crest." Conner held the pin toward the firelight. "If ye really mean to enter into a courtship with me, then the pin is for ye to wear so all my men and everyone who sees ye knows that you belong with this clan as my equal. No matter where ye go in Scotland, or who ye meet, ye'll be under the shelter o' the MacLoeod name."

"Is this like an engagement ring in Scotland?" Charlotte asked warily. Although it exhilarated her to enter into a courtship with Conner, she wasn't all that sure if she was prepared for the finality of an engagement.

"Ach, no." He chuckled. "We Scots have engagement rings just like the rest o' the civilized world. This crest will just mark that ye belong to the Macleod's chief and merit respect. It's no' an obligation of marriage, but it is a promise o' my protection and fidelity until the day we do decide we are ready to wed. So, will ye wear it, Charlotte?"

She looked up into his eager face, his penetrating eyes uncommonly tender. "I would be honored."

Conner kissed the crested pin in his hand before fastening it to the silks just above her breast. He then brought her fingers to his lips. "You look beautiful, Charlotte. I'm proud to have you on my arm before all my men."

She smiled shyly in return, surprised at how the swiftness of their relationship didn't frighten her. "Then let us go down to dinner."

***

Gwen, Flora, and Ian were already seated in the feasting hall when Conner and Charlotte made their entrance. They walked arm in arm, following the piper. As before, the men cheered as they saw the MacLeod enter. It turned to a roar when the men saw Charlotte wearing the MacLeod pin. She couldn't help but smile at the men's enthusiasm. They looked more than pleased that their lord had chosen to court her and showed their excitement by rising from their seats and holding out their goblets of wine to them.

She felt strange with all of this attention directed at her, but tried to keep a warm smile on her face instead of an embarrassed one. They obviously accepted her as a potential member of their clan, but Charlotte still had a nagging feeling in the back of her mind. How she wished that her father, Penelope, and even Abigail, could be here to share in her joy.

No doubt her father was still fuming over her escape to Scotland. That is, if he even knew that she had gone to Scotland. Nonetheless, Charlotte decided to write to him that evening. Since she was in Scotland, and now courting Conner, there was no way he could still pressure her into marrying

Richard.

"You all right, love?" Conner asked as the servant began serving the feast. "Ye seem a million miles away."

She turned to him, her face brightening. "I was just thinking that it's time for me to write to my father. I want him to be glad for me and see how happy I am."

"I think that's a fine idea. Perhaps he could visit. I want his blessin' to court ye, although I'll do it with, or without, his permission." He speared a piece of meat with his fork. "The desk in your bedchamber is full o' ink and papers. Just give the letter to Maisie and she'll see that it gets sent out with the next rider."

The rest of the feast was even more jubilant and festive than the one before. The men were jollier, the goblets overflowing, and the pipers far more cheerful as they belted lively tunes. Charlotte saw the Scottish society as an enhanced, more vivacious version of the English one. The people seemed happy and at home in Conner's court and she shared their sentiments. She felt like a celebrated equal instead of a plain girl who was the property of men. Charlotte couldn't imagine ever going back to England.

Chapter Twenty-Three

The next morning, Conner was already seated in the library when she entered, a finished novel in her hand. "Oh, good morning. I just came to return this book." She slid the novel into an empty place on a shelf and came to his desk where he was poring over a map. "What's this?"

"Just getting ready for the spring survey. I go to each village and make sure they've come through the winter and see what their planting plans are. Every fall and spring I travel the same route."

"Do you own all this?" she asked, looking over his shoulder at a large portion of Scotland displayed before her.

"Aye, ye could say that." He put down the pen he held, giving her his attention. "Did ye sleep well? Ye look peaked."

"Oh, that's what every woman longs to hear," Charlotte stated dryly. "But, I did have a rather restless night."

"Aye? And why's that?"

Sighing, she dropped into the chair opposite

223

Conner's desk. "I don't know. I tried writing to my father but couldn't find the words. I wanted to tell him so many things—how angry I was, why I ran away, that I'm safe, that I'm here and being courted by you. I want to tell him about the beautiful horses and the hills that go on forever, but I can't bring myself to write a word. Then I tried drinking a cup of tea to calm me, but it didn't help."

"Do no' worry so. The words will come in time."

"I did write a note to Penelope telling her about my time here. I didn't tell her about the courtship, though. I trust her implicitly, but I can't take the chance my letter is intercepted and my father must hear about us from a third party."

"I understand. Would ye like me to write him for ye?"

"No, he must hear it from me. Richard must have him convinced you've kidnapped me so getting word from you wouldn't help a bit."

"Is that all on your mind keepin' ye up?"

"I just seemed to have strange dreams. As soon as I'd fall asleep, I'd have such queer visions that I'd wake from them immediately."

"Ye must just be terribly worried about your father."

"Perhaps that's it. But don't worry about me. I'm sure you're quite busy with your work."

"Ach, no." He waved a hand and straightened up his maps and ledgers. "It'll be some time before I go. I'd much rather test ye."

"Test me?"

"Aye. Remember the passageway I showed ye last night?"

"Yes, of course."

"Can ye find the book again?"

Charlotte bit her lip and stood, walking over to the shelf. "I believe it was over here somewhere."

"Are ye sure?" he asked, following her, bemused as she poked and prodded the worn spines.

"Fairly. I remember the book was quite old and red, maybe, or purple."

"Red."

She peered at each shelf beside the fireplace. "No, I don't think it's any of these."

"No, it's no' any of those. But you are close."

The next shelf held the same numbers of volumes and Charlotte looked at each one before settling on a particularly battered one. "Ha! This must be it!" She pulled the book from its seat, crestfallen when the shelves didn't move.

Conner chuckled. "Go on, lass, ye almost have it."

Charlotte shoved the book back into place and inspected the rest of the shelf, deciding to try another volume. Upon pulling it, the bookcase swung open, showing the familiar tiny hall. "I knew I could find it!"

"Well done." Conner stepped past her and beckoned her to follow. "Remember where it is. Now come with me."

They walked through the dark tunnel and exited in Conner's bedchamber. Charlotte looked around, confused as to why they came. "Why did we come here again? Are there any more secret passageways here or in the library?"

"Aye, there's one here." He crossed the room to

225

a tapestry, pulling it aside and tapping a piece of wood paneling, not unlike the exit of the library's tunnel. "Would ye like to see where this goes?"

"Yes, please," she said excitedly, scrambling to follow him into the darkness.

This hidden entryway led to a small flight of stairs that spiraled tightly down a mere twenty steps. She stumbled a bit, her hand firmly on Conner's shoulder for support. Conner had to exert a bit of force on the concealed exit, as it obviously hadn't been used in quite some time. When her eyes adjusted to the lights, she was stunned to find herself in her own bedroom. They had come through a large painting of a man atop a horse whose framework acted as a doorway.

"There's been a hidden tunnel to my chambers this entire time?" she asked as he helped her down the three-foot drop.

"Aye, but I have no' used it, I assure ye." He swung the painting closed. "My bedroom once belonged to my father and this one to my mother. It could be used to visit at night when he was alive."

"Is that why you put me in these chambers? So you could come to me in the night?" She wasn't sure if she was offended, flattered, or any mix of the two.

"I meant no impropriety. I only wished ye to have chambers that befitted ye as an honored guest and these were the second best," he guaranteed her, stepping closer. "I'd never come to you uninvited or improperly."

"You wouldn't?" She swallowed, breathing in his familiar scent. Charlotte tried to control her breathing but found that her heart and lungs had other plans.

"No." He brought his hands to her middle, his fingers tightening around her lightly corseted waist. "No matter how much I wanted ye, I couldn't abuse my knowledge o' the castle. It would no' be right."

"You…wanted me?" Charlotte's heart beat faster, pounding in her ears as she felt herself drawn closer until their torsos touched. With each breath, her breasts pushed against his brawny chest. She ached to be touched, though she didn't know where, but she did know that she shouldn't desire it as badly as she did.

"O' course I wanted you. I want ye still, every moment o' every day then again at night since the moment I met ye." His lips brushed her—a gentle caress that sent her spinning. "I want ye now, even more."

She grasped his broad shoulders, leaning her head back as his mouth found her cheek, her neck, her shoulder. "Oh, Conner!" She gasped, pulling him closer, relishing the feeling of his tongue on her skin.

They found themselves locked in a passionate embrace, moving together until they fell, as one, atop her bed. Charlotte lay on her back now, Conner above her, his body deliciously heavy upon her own. She cautiously touched the skin at his throat, following the edge of his shirt down the expanse of his chest, goose pimpled beneath her fingertips. She longed to touch more but her virgin hands knew not what to do.

"Oh, God, Charlotte," Conner groaned into her

mouth as his hand tentatively cupped her heavy breast. His grasp grew firmer as she arched her back to meet him. "You are so beautiful, so perfect." His thumb brushed a nipple beneath her blue silk gown.

Charlotte's mind muddled as she curved toward his touch, her body crushing against something hard, pressing into her inner thigh. She knew, at once, it was his manhood. She also knew that propriety stated that she should be scandalized at his hard member being so aroused against her. But she knew they were way past the lines of decency and found she hardly cared.

She opened her legs farther and pressed against him, making them both moan. Suddenly, she found her dress and corset too tight, too constricting and felt she needed to be released at once. Charlotte longed to feel his warm, calloused hands upon her bare skin. She yearned for strokes and caresses she hardly knew the meaning of, but craved all the same.

"Conner, my stays, please unlace me." She breathed throatily. "Please."

Without a word Conner reached a hand behind her, making fast work of the ribbons that held her silk dress closed. Then, he pulled away for just a moment, taking her gown with him, over her arms, and dropped it to the side, leaving her with just a corset and shift. Her breasts were concealed by nothing now but the thinnest of cotton, nearly transparent in its fineness.

"The corset," she pleaded, melting in his gaze. "Hurry and unthread it."

His usually steady fingers fumbled now as he

freed her from her bindings. She sighed, relishing the deep breaths she could savor without the restricting whalebone.

Conner peeled off his own shirt, exposing his bare chest to her. It was spectacularly chiseled, each muscle in proud display by long days of use. While she had seen him shirtless before, she had carefully trained her eyes away, not taking note of any part of his naked skin. Several scars flashed on his torso, white and faded with age, but they did nothing to mar his masculine beauty. In fact, the rugged lines highlighted his strength and made Charlotte gasp with unfamiliar feelings. She traced one with her finger, tenderly following it from below his collarbone down to his navel.

"Did it hurt?" she asked, as she reached the end of the long-healed gash.

"Aye." He brushed a loose curl away from her bare shoulder and gave her a small smile. "It hurt somethin' terrible. Does it repulse you?" He asked, his brows knit with sudden thought.

"Oh, no!" Charlotte flattened her palm upon the worst of the scar, looking up at him with faint surprise. The usually confident Scot had shown a kink in his armor. "Nothing about you repulses me."

"But your skin is so soft, so smooth and unmarred." He swiped a hand down her face and rested it on her bare arm. "Mine has seen battle and war. It's been hit by archers and cut with blades."

"And it's perfect," she said, savoring the steady beat of his heart under her hand. "It shows me you're a strong survivor and makes me feel safe. It shows me that you fight for your family and your people."

"And I'd fight for ye, Charlotte. I'd take any number o' men to keep ye safe."

"I know that, Conner."

He studied her, his eyes soft. "I love ye, Charlotte. I love ye somethin' fierce. I've loved ye since we met in London and I love ye all the more now."

Her heart was fit to burst as her lips found his. "Oh, Conner!" she whispered into his mouth. "I love you too."

Conner moaned and resumed the exploration of her body, newly awakened by their mutual confessions of love. Charlotte followed suit, leaving a light trail of kisses on his scarred chest while her hands grasped at his back and his lower body grinded gratifyingly against her own. Pausing slightly to look down, he slowly drew the shift downward, freeing her breasts.

"My God," he said as he stroked the newly shown skin. "Charlotte, ye are enough to kill a man."

"Is that a good thing?" she asked him breathlessly, her nipples peaking to his manipulations.

"I'd say that I'd die happy in this moment, bein' able to gaze upon a sight like you." He fell upon her then, his lips encasing a breast as he slipped a hand beneath her skirts to caress her leg above her silk stockings.

Charlotte panted as he moved his manhood against her sex, firm and stiff still between the layers of clothes. An unfamiliar wetness flooded her core and she openly moaned at each touch. Her fingers tangled in his blond locks, savoring his tongue on her breasts until he came up to her, kissing her roughly. Her beasts ached as they hit his solid chest, their skin both hot to the touch. Conner slid to the side, lying heavily beside her. His hand crept slowly toward her center, raising the flesh on her thighs in anticipation.

The tips of his fingers brushed the curls below her silks. Charlotte gasped as he gently swept against her slit, making her even more aware of how wet she was. These unfamiliar sensations were almost overpowering. With each stroke of his hand, a new stir built in her belly, growing with each movement. She pressed against his fingers, shouting out when she felt something enter her.

"Do no' worry," Conner said into her mouth, a grin on his full lips. "I will no' go further and take your maidenhead this day. I only wish to feel ye however I may."

"Please. Don't stop." Charlotte's voice was ragged as he continued his manipulations, her body heaving all the while. She felt vulnerable and exposed, but still found that she loved the feelings and raised her skirts higher to allow him more access.

"If I were a weaker man, I'd take ye right now."

"Do it, Conner." The forces within her began to heighten. The sensation was frightening and exhilarating, a confusing array that made her body weak. She closed her eyes in an attempt to ground her floating form. "Please, Conner."

"I can no'." He groaned, dragging his lips down

from her lips to her neck. "I can no' take ye until you are my bride. Be my wife and I promise to make ye mine entirely."

"Please," she whispered as she felt his teeth upon her nipple.

Her breath caught in her throat as the burning in her belly crashed down, giving her a feeling of delicious release. When the tender waves subsided, Charlotte opened her eyes. Conner slowly slid his hand from her sex and removed his face from her breasts. How easy it would be to move aside his kilt—to allow him to enter her, filling her to the brim with his body.

She tugged her shift, removing the fabric with her in a single brave moment. She was completely naked before him then, save for her stockings. She raked her nails down his chest as he hitched one of her legs over his hips, his eyes examining her form with a hunger she had never seen before. When she reached his kilt, she carefully touched his manhood through the fabric, surprised at its rigidity. Conner looked into her eyes as she caressed him, teeth gritted against a groan that threatened to escape his lips.

When Charlotte lifted his kilt and stroked the sensitive skin beneath, she could swear she heard the rumble of a growl deep within Conner's ribs. He pushed the newly bared member against her, this time rubbing against her wet slit, sending a whole new wave of pleasure through her form. The newly bared addition made Charlotte open her legs wider, inviting it in with her hips. But, still, he wouldn't enter her, instead teased her with his manhood, sliding it against her core, making both of them sigh in mutual pleasure.

"I want more, Conner." Charlotte gripped his torso, willing her lover to break through her maidenhead. She couldn't comprehend how something so foreign and new could provoke such beastly lust within her being. Her body understood just what it wanted and the pleasure clouded her judgment. She gripped him tightly, eagerly positioning him at her entrance, feeling the hard tip against her slit. "I need you. Take me now."

"Ach, Charlotte." He panted, breath hot on her cheek. "Lord knows I'd take ye this moment. But we can no' until we are wed." He took both her hands, pinning them above her head and pulled away slightly, careful to keep contact, but not endanger her maidenhead. Their grinding movements quickened and his free hand kneaded her breasts, teasing the point of one nipple with his thumb.

"Please." She gasped as a new wave of desire began building in her body.

He shook his head in the negative, his hips crushing against hers, his lips muttering Gaelic into her neck. While Charlotte had no idea what musings he breathed, his secret words melted her core fully and she had to sink her teeth into his shoulder to stifle a cry as she stood on the edge of pleasure.

They basked in mutual desire until, at last, they both collapsed, spent in their venture. Charlotte felt a peculiar tingling throughout her body and an odd stickiness on her stomach. She knew it to be the remnants of their gratification and reddened at the

233

thought.

They were so close to committing the ultimate act of defilement and yet, Charlotte hardly had it in her to care. Conner could have taken her there, in her borrowed chambers, and she would have been pleased. The wickedness thrilled her and the impure thoughts made her loins shiver with another soft wave of delight.

Conner kissed her softly. "I could stay here forever in this moment. I could look at ye like this and never regret a day in my life that brought me to ye."

Her color deepened further. "Did you mean what you said?"

"I said a great many things." He rested his body upon his elbows, grinning. "Do ye mean to ask if I truly love ye?"

She nodded, still too embarrassed to say the words.

"I do," he promised, kissing her again. "And I'd stay here forever if we could. But, we can no'." He pulled away and rose from the bed, dropping his kilt to the ground. He grabbed Charlotte's dressing gown from the nightstand and handed it to her, his eyes respectfully focused on her face. "I'll run a bath so we can get cleaned up before dinner."

Charlotte watched as Conner disappeared into the bathroom, his taut buttocks on full display as his kilt lay discarded on the floor beside her gown. When she attempted to rise from the bed, she found that her legs felt limp and she was suddenly so very, very, tired. She opted to pull the robe over her naked form and lay against the pillows. When

Conner returned, Charlotte could barely remove her gaze from the top of the bedspread.

"Are ye all right?" he asked, standing before her, midsection wrapped in a towel. "Did I hurt ye or scare ye in any way?"

"No," Charlotte assured him. "I'm not hurt, nor am I frightened."

"Then why do ye look so sad?"

"I don't know, exactly. I suppose I'm...disappointed."

"Disappointed? Did it no' please you?"

"Oh, no, it isn't that! I just wanted...more."

"Aye, me too." Conner bent to press his lips to her forehead. "If I had my way, we'd still be in bed together, but I can no' do that with a clear conscious without makin' an honest lass o' you."

"I know..." Charlotte drifted off, brushing disheveled curls from her cheek.

"Come now, Charlotte, we must bathe now or be greeted with a cold supper." He helped her from the bed and into the bathroom where the tub was already filled, steaming and fragrant with oils.

Charlotte pinned up her hair and turned her back to him before dropping her robe and sliding into the claw foot tub. While he had just explored her most intimate folds, the thought of him seeing her body now, once their fires had been quenched, seemed oddly indecent. Once she was submerged almost to her chin, she demurely turned her head, allowing for Conner to enter as well. She was rather glad the water was murky with oils and that the foam concealed their nakedness.

She had always thought the tub to be quite large,

but now, with two people soaking in its depths, the quarters were undoubtedly tight. They sat on either end, her arms crossed over brought up knees, loose tendrils clinging to her skin. Conner lounged back, his elbows resting on the tub's edges and his legs tucked on either side of her body. He studied her, his face calm and placid.

"Ye sure you're all right?" he asked, his voice echoing off the stones.

"Quite." Her lips twitched as she checked again that her body was concealed. "I'm just nude in a bath with an exposed Scot."

"Aye, I can see how that might be a wee bit strange for ye." He offered a lopsided grin and looked at the array of bottles and jars alongside the tub. He dumped the contents of a blue bottle into his hands. "What is this concoction?"

"It's shampoo. You could have just read the label."

He shrugged and began massaging the goop into his hair. "Need a hand, Charlotte? I'd be more than happy to scrub ye up!"

She shot out a hand, splashing him with the bubbly water. "Conner, do stop embarrassing me! I'm not entirely sure how to feel at this juncture and I'm a bit more than a little mortified."

"I'm sorry." He stopped washing his hair and took her hand in his soapy one, bubbles comically piled on his head. "This is all a bit new to me as well. I never meant to make ye feel badly. Ye have nothin' to be ashamed o'. You are a beautiful lass and I'm right pleased ye chose to share your body with me. If I—"

A sharp rap on the door startled them both, their eyes wide.

"Lady Charlotte!" Maisie called through the door. "Lady Charlotte, are ye all right?"

Charlotte bit her lip and leaned toward Conner. "What do I do? What do I say?" she hissed.

He shook his head, his face a mix of amusement and discomfiture. "Just talk to her as ye would normally. She'll go away."

"Yes, Maisie?" Charlotte answered, her face beet red.

"Are ye well?" The maid sounded worried and tried the locked door. "No one has seen ye for hours and your room is in a terrible state."

"I'm fine, just taking a bath!"

The maid gasped. "My lady! There's a kilt on the floor!"

"Shite," Conner swore under his breath.

"Lady Charlotte!" Maisie continued, banging on the door. "Who was in there? Shall I call the guards? I'll run to the MacLeod's chambers straight away for ye. He'll skewer the bastard!"

"No need, Maisie," Conner answered, making Charlotte blanch.

"MacLeod? Is it you?" Maisie's voice quieted.

"Aye, that it is." Conner shot a look of apology at Charlotte. "Do no' fret about Lady Charlotte. She's fine."

Maisie hesitated. "Do ye…is there anythin' ye need?"

"No, Maisie. We'll be down for dinner shortly. Ye can go downstairs," Conner ordered.

They waited with bated breath until they heard

the familiar click of the bedroom door's latch from afar. When it was certain that Maisie had gone, Charlotte let out a stifled moan. "Oh, Conner, now everyone will know what we did!"

"Do no' fret. Maisie is no' one for gossip. She'll keep her tongue in check," Conner promised, dunking his head in the water to rid it of shampoo.

"I'm so horrified!"

"Ye have naught to fear." He wiped the wetness from his eyes and pulled her through the bathwater to be nestled with her back to his chest. "Even if Maisie were to tell anyone, which she would no', it does no' matter."

"How? How doesn't it matter?"

"We're to be promised. The rules are different, more forgivin', in Scotland. Lads and lasses can live together as man and wife for a year before getting properly married. See if they are a good fit."

"But, Conner..." Charlotte was becoming exasperated. "We're not even properly engaged. We're merely *courting* and I doubt that is covered in your Scottish wedding handbook!"

Conner pursed his lips and folded his arms around her, his forearms pressing into her chest. "I see how that might be a problem, aye?"

She sighed, one hand idling fondling his fingers. "I'm sorry I'm so out of sorts. I'm just so very embarrassed that Maisie found us in such a state and I'm acting rather harshly."

"I understand." He kissed the top of her dry hair. "Should I leave ye to wash on your own?"

She shook her head. "No, I'd like to just stay here like this for a while."

"Aye, me as well."

Charlotte settled against his body, trying to relax in the warm water. She regarded his tanned forearms, noting another long-healed scar. She had known that Conner was deemed a formidable warrior among his people, and apparently the English as well, but seeing the conflict etched on his skin before her made it clear that he lived up to his reputation.

She tilted her head back to lean in the hollow of his shoulder and was rewarded with a small kiss to her temple. "Conner, may I ask you something?"

"Anythin'."

"Is it dangerous living in Scotland?"

"Dangerous?" He sounded surprised. "Why would ye think that?"

"It's only…you have an awful lot of scars."

"Oh, aye, I've been in a few battles. I've been wounded many times over, but I always survive."

"But you're the chief now. Surely you wouldn't be fighting anymore?"

"Just because I am the chief today does no' mean I'll be the chief tomorrow if someone with a stouter army comes and dethrones me. Scotland is different from England. Those of us in power have to protect their place."

"Is that why you showed me the passageway to the sea?"

"Aye, but I doubt we'll see much more fighting for a few years yet."

"Why?"

"Well, sooner or later I'll be expected to produce an heir for my seat. If I get old withou' a son to take

239

my place, others will try to take it."

"An heir," Charlotte repeated under her breath, suddenly aware of the unspoken thought between them. When Conner spoke of having an heir, the thought of Charlotte giving him that son must have crossed his mind.

"But do no' worry, that's many years away and I promised you ye'd always be safe in my lands."

"I know. I just hate the thought of anyone going to war."

"No one likes war. It's just the way o' the world. The best I can promise ye is that I'll love and protect ye as long as I have life in my body. And if I fall before my time, ye will be well taken care of."

Charlotte paled at the thought of Conner falling in war. If the gash upon his chest was any indication, the fighting in Scotland could get brutal. For a moment, she longed for the safety and tranquility of England where quarrels were settled with words and men argued over the expanse of tables in libraries. But, still, she knew that Conner would not be the same man if they had been in England. His calloused hands would be as soft as silk, his unruly hair would be slicked back, and his bronzed skin would be pale and covered with a gentleman's suit instead of swathed in rugged tartan.

Conner tightened his hold on her. "But I can try to see that I'll die old in my bed and not young on the field leaving ye a widow."

"In order for me to be a widow, I'd have to agree to marry you first," she teased.

"Oh, I'll have ye marry me," he growled in her

ear, his hands drifting toward her naked breasts.

She arched in response and sighed when his fingers encircled the full mounds.

He hardened behind her as his hands slid over her skin in the water, caressing her chest and stomach before one hand came to her neck, turning her head to display her pulse to him. He nipped at the skin, laying his mouth over her shoulder and neck. He stopped at her ear as a hand paused above her hip bone. "I'll have ye be my wife, share my bed, bear my bairns, and be the happiest woman in Scotland." His fingers found her opening and began a manipulation that made her moan.

Charlotte dug her nails into his arm. Her mind went blank and she struggled to regain her breath as she cried out in ecstasy, his lips upon her neck. She could feel him grin against her skin.

"I think I'd make a bonny husband."

Charlotte panted, pulling away from him slightly to avoid further temptation. "We really should get down to dinner," she said weakly, her body already missing his touch.

He laughed a bit. "Aye, whatever ye wish." Conner stepped out of the tub, taking his towel and wrapping it around himself before fetching a fresh towel for Charlotte. He held it up for her to take as she rose, hiding her.

"Thank you."

"You're verra welcome." He winked, making Charlotte blush.

Conner left the bathroom, leaving her alone with her thoughts. As Charlotte dried and perfumed her body and hair, she attempted to compose herself.

The feelings of passionate flight she shared with Conner were replaced with embarrassed nausea. She knew that her father was a world away, and would never hear about her actions, but she still imagined the look his face would have if he heard about her afternoon tryst with a Scottish king. Charlotte prayed that Conner knew, for a fact, that Maisie would never breathe a word to anyone.

When she exited the bathroom into her bedchamber, Conner was already redressed in his kilt, shirt, and boots. "I have to say, ye look lovely fresh from the bath with your hair a tangle and your flesh warm and fragrant."

"Oh, do stop." Charlotte blushed as Conner put his arms around her, drawing her close. He brought his head to the gap in her robe, kissing her shoulder.

"I can no' stop. I must tell you when ye look so radiant." His hands brushed her silk covered back. "Come, I'll help ye dress."

"You're just hoping for another peek, you cad." She slapped his stomach lightly, a smile on her lips.

"Guilty." He spun her toward her wardrobe. "Now, pick a frock so we might go down. I've worked up quite a hunger."

Chapter Twenty-Four

The next morning, Charlotte awoke with a splitting headache. As soon as Maisie opened her drapes, she begged them to be shut again so she could stay in bed.

"Are ye well?" the maid asked carefully, straightening the covers about Charlotte's shoulders.

"Yes, my head just pains me."

"Should I fetch the MacLeod?"

Charlotte sat up in bed, ignoring the sting in her skull. "Maisie, about yesterday—"

She held up her hands with a blank look. "I do no' know what ye are talkin' about. Nothin' happened yesterday. Ye stayed abed readin' all afternoon until I dressed ye for dinner."

She breathed a sigh of relief. "Thank you, Maisie. It's just that...well..." Charlotte longed to confide in the cheery maid.

"My lady, I'm here to dress ye, care for ye, and keep your confidences. If ye need a bit o' tonic for an unwanted bairn or an ear to listen, ye can come to me."

"Unwanted bairn?" Charlotte knit her brows. "Whatever do you mean?"

Maisie gasped. "Ach, ye poor lass! No one ever told ye what happens when a man and woman lie together. I'll tell ye now, as if ye are with child, it can no' be born a bastard."

"Oh! Oh, goodness no! There is no child, there can't be!"

"It only takes a time, or two," Maisie said knowingly.

"Maisie, I know how women get pregnant."

"So ye already have a tonic?"

"There won't be a child."

"Are ye barren?" Maisie covered her mouth with a hand. "Oh, my lady!"

"Maisie, stop!" Charlotte yelled out, thoroughly exasperated with the maid's musings. "Conner and I didn't…we didn't lie together in that way. I'm still a maid."

"But, your clothes, his kilt…"

"Maisie, I can trust you, yes?"

"Absolutely," she swore, perching upon the bed at Charlotte's feet. "I'll never betray ye, even to the MacLeod."

Charlotte lowered her voice even though she knew no one outside of the bedchamber could hear her. "You know that Conner and I are courting, yes?"

"Aye."

"Yesterday we began kissing and things got out of hand. It's true that we overstepped boundaries that are meant for the marriage bed, but he was a gentleman and wouldn't take my maidenhead. We are both still virgins and plan to be until marriage."

"You've agreed to wed him?" Maisie beamed.

"Well, no, not as of now," Charlotte admitted. "We just got carried away in the moment. Neither of us began the day planning on that."

"Wait…did ye say that the MacLeod is…that he never…" Maisie struggled with her words.

"He never what?"

"That he never laid with lass?" she blurted out.

Charlotte pinked. "He *says* he hasn't."

"I see." The maid raised her eyebrows, which threatened to disappear into her cap. "So he is a skilled man?"

"One might say that," she said delicately, turning away.

Maisie pursed her lips knowingly. "Ye know, I had me a lad once."

"You did?"

"Aye." She looked down at her hands, weathered with work. "It was a long time ago. I was still a young lass with big ideas about love and marriage. He fell in battle before we were wed."

"Oh, dear, I'm so sorry."

Maisie smiled softly. "Do no' worry for me. The time we had together is something I would no' trade, short as it was. He fought along with the MacLeod and when he did no' return, the MacLeod gave me a place in his house. I meant it when I said I would no' betray ye."

"I know, Maisie. Things are just so different here. In England you couldn't even be seen with a man to whom you were not related. And here, you can court openly without fear of judgment."

"No, there will still be some who look down on a lass for layin' with a lad before marriage. It makes the tongues wag a bit, but no one would dare gossip about ye and the MacLeod."

"Is anyone saying anything about us?"

Maisie glanced off to the side. "Nothin' too terrible. Some o' the lasses are a bit disappointed that the MacLeod has given ye his intentions, but it's naught to worry about."

Charlotte thought a moment. Conner hadn't said that anyone else was in the running for courtship, but she could assume that many other women, and presumably their fathers, were hoping that Conner wouldn't turn his affections toward a British lady on the run. Everyone must have assumed that he would eventually marry a fellow Scot.

Maisie lifted a hand to Charlotte's face, placing a palm on her cheek. "You are burnin' to the touch."

"Yes, I awoke not feeling very well."

"Then back to bed with ye!" She pushed Charlotte back against the pillows. "Should I call a doctor to tend ye?"

"No, I'm all right," she said, gratefully borrowing back into the blankets. "I just need a bit more sleep."

When had filled her teacup and made her promise to rest in bed, Charlotte tried to fall back into sleep but found it much harder than she would have liked. Her temples throbbed and she felt a light sweat dampening her nightdress. She was far too uncomfortable to fall back asleep. But, despite her discomfort, she felt a bit better having told Maisie about her improprieties with Conner.

As the clock crept slowly toward noon, Charlotte found that sleep was merely a notion and she was no closer to finding it than she had been when Maisie first woke her. Swinging her legs off the bed, she ignored her headache to splash her face with a shock of cold water. She then donned a pale green day gown and slid on her slippers. Feeling a shiver run up her spine, she pulled on a thick woolen shawl.

The castle was quiet and nothing echoed in the halls but the faint padding of her feet on the stones. Thankfully, it seemed she was just in time for lunch as the girls, and Ian, were seated at the table laughing over bowls of stew.

"Charlotte! You're awake!" Gwen dropped her spoon in surprise.

Flora smiled as Charlotte sat and summoned a footman to serve her a steaming bowl and slice of fresh bread. "Are you feeling any better?"

"Not particularly." Charlotte took a long gulp of watered down wine. "I've been feeling rather queer in the mornings lately."

"How odd. Is your room drafty? We could see that you're moved into a room farther in," Flora offered.

Charlotte thought back to the secret hall that connected her chambers with Conner's and shook her head. "No, thank you. The room is quite cozy. I'm just feeling a bit ill now and then."

"You're sick?" Ian squeaked, eyes wide with worry.

"No, dear, just not feeling well." Charlotte

touched the boy's hand, trying to look as cheerful as possible for the poor orphan. His parents had been taken by a sickness and Charlotte hadn't thought of how her words might worry him. "I'll be better soon with lots of rest and food."

"I eat lots of food!" Ian brandished his spoon and grinned. It was true that the boy had certainly filled out in his days at the keep. When he wasn't studying with his newly appointed tutor, he could be seen sneaking cakes and pies from the kitchen to share with the stable boys.

"Does Conner know you feel better?" Gwen asked.

"I haven't seen him, no," Charlotte said between bites. "I may go back to bed after this. If you see him, could you tell him that I'm all right?"

"I'm sure Maisie's keeping him well-informed," Flora promised. "Would you like some tea sent up to your room when you're settled?"

"That would be lovely." Charlotte tried finishing her bowl but found that after several bites, her appetite was almost fully gone. "I do think I'll retire now, though."

"Are you all right?" Flora leaned forward.

"Yes, I...I just need to lie down." Using the table as a crutch, Charlotte forced herself upward, her knees buckling beneath her.

Gwen stood up and hurried to her side. "Charlotte, you look as if you're about to faint!"

"Help!" Flora shouted as Charlotte fell back into her chair.

One of the men rushed into the room, scanning for intruders. "Lady Flora, what's amiss?"

"Johnny, Lady Charlotte is exceedingly unwell. Do help her back to her rooms and ride out for the village doctor immediately," Flora ordered.

Charlotte waved an unsteady hand. "Oh, don't worry about me so, I'm just a bit under the weather."

"Come, Charlotte." Ian rose from the table, his little face very grave indeed. "You must go to bed straight away with my wee pups and take a nap."

"Must I?" She managed a small smile. "Well, if you think I should, then go collect your dogs and I'll meet you in my bedroom." She allowed Johnny to help her from her seat and guide her back to her bed, his hands fully supporting her weight. "Thank you," she whispered to him as a frantic Maisie ran into the room, a shaky tea tray balanced in her hands.

"Oh! What have ye been doing out of bed! Ye poor dear!" Maisie shooed Johnny out of the room to go for the physician and deposited a steaming cup of tea on the nightstand.

Charlotte gratefully took the cup and sipped. "I'm fine. Everyone really must stop fussing."

The maid touched Charlotte's forehead. "You're hotter than before. Shall I help ye into a nightgown?"

"No, I'm fine for now. I'd rather not get up right now."

"Do ye think ye can stand a bite to eat?"

As hungry as she was, the thought of food made her stomach turn. "No, I don't think I could, just now."

"I'll wait downstairs for the doctor," Maisie said,

leaving the room.

Ian slipped in before the maid could shut the door, his dogs scrambling at his heals. "Bear and Pie are here to keep ye company," he announced.

"Bear and Pie?" Charlotte giggled. "Is that what their names are now? I thought it was Twig and Cow?"

"I like bears and pies better than twigs and cows," Ian explained in all seriousness as his dogs jumped on the bed.

"Oh, naturally."

"Are you going to die?"

Charlotte's eyes widened. "Oh, goodness no! I've just a bit of a cold. With a bit of rest, I'll be just fine."

"Good. I don't want you to leave."

"Oh, Ian, I'm not going anywhere."

"Do you promise?"

"Yes, I promise." She brushed his unruly hair from his eyes. "How about you go down to the kitchens and tell the cook I've said you're to have a treat for being such help."

His little face brightened considerably. "Hot chocolate?"

"Hot chocolate," she agreed, smiling after him as he clambered out of the room. His dogs bounded behind him, hoping for some kitchen scraps.

The door had barely closed behind him when it swung open again. Maisie entered with a man carrying a large leather bag.

"Charlotte, this is Doctor Carragh," Maisie said.

"How do ye feel?" the doctor asked, placing his bag on the bed and peering at her closely.

"Not well," she answered. "I have a splitting headache and my stomach churns terribly. The only thing I can keep down is tea."

Carragh pulled a listening scope from the bag and pressed the wide end against her chest, listening closely. "Strong heartbeat. They've told me ye fainted?"

"Nearly."

He pressed against her neck. "It feels a bit swollen. Havin' any trouble swallowin'?"

"Perhaps a bit."

"Just a wee bit o' weakness and a sore throat," he announced, turning to Maisie. "Do no' be alarmed, she's just in need o' rest and more tea. Give her a bit o' broth if she can handle it. She'll be right as rain in a few days' time."

"Thank ye, doctor," Maisie said, walking him to the door. "Charlotte, I'll go fetch ye a new pot o' tea. Stay in bed."

Once again, the door swung open as soon as it was closed. Conner rushed in, his wolf-skin cloak falling from his broad shoulders and face pink from the outside winds. "I came as soon as they found me. I was miles away seeing to a tenant."

"Everyone's making such a fuss. The doctor himself has told me that it's nothing more than a bit of a cold." Charlotte was secretly pleased at Conner's display of concern. "I'd heal a great deal faster if everyone would stop fretting so."

He sat on the edge of her bed and took one hand in his, pressing his lips to her knuckles. "Is there anythin' else that would help? Anythin' ye'd like to eat? Or I can get ye a book?"

251

"I'm fine, just tired."

Conner peered into her empty teapot. "No tea?"

"Maisie's fetching it now."

"Then I'll leave ye to rest." With a final kiss to her hot forehead, he left her alone to sleep.

***

The pillow was wet with sweat under her cheek when she finally opened her eyes. She felt groggy and thick as she tried raising her head and felt it better to stay lying down. But she did kick the heavy coverlet from her legs, rousing the figure that sat before the fire.

"Lady Charlotte!" Maisie rushed to the side of the bed, her cap askew. "Are ye well?"

"I feel ever so ill," she croaked.

Maisie was quick to bring a goblet of cool water to her lips. The liquid soothed her dry throat. "Are ye hot? Cold? Can I bring ye somethin' to eat?"

"No. I don't know what's wrong, though. Did I pass out?"

"Aye, ye have been abed almost three days. Ye've been in and out of it. I could barely keep ye sippin' tea and a bit o' broth. The doctors came to see you, but could no' find what ailed ye."

"Three days?" Charlotte was baffled. She had almost never been sick in her life and now she had been unconscious for half a week.

"Aye. If ye will be all right a moment, I'd like to tell the MacLeod that ye have awoken."

"Oh, he can't see me like this!" Charlotte brought a hand weakly to her tangled hair.

"Do no' fret. He's been here since ye fell into your first fit. He's only stepped out for a bite to eat."

"I feel disgusting," Charlotte groaned, pulling the damp shift away from her skin.

"He cares no'," Maisie assured her, pulled a sweaty tendril away from her fevered forehead. "He bade me to tell him when ye were awake."

"Then go, I suppose." Charlotte sighed, watching the maid hurry from the room. She debated crossing the room to the sink to wash her face, but found that she hardly had the strength to sit up. She didn't even turn toward the door when Conner came rushing in.

"Ach, lass, ye gave us all a fright. Are ye well?" he asked, kneeling by the edge of the bed to take her hand.

"I'm sorry." She smiled, touched by his eagerness. "I'm sorry I frightened you all and I'm sorry you have to see me in such a terrible state."

"Hush, lass, you are still beautiful and I'm just happy you're alive."

"I suppose it isn't just a cold, is it?"

"No one knows for sure. It was no' the bloody flux, the pox, or any other plague the doctors could find. No one knew what would become o' ye."

"Well, I doubt that I'll die."

"No, ye will no'," he said with some strength behind his words. "Do ye need anythin'? What would help ye feel a bit better?"

"Honestly? I would love to bathe. Could you perhaps ring Maisie to help me?"

"Ach, ye do no' need her." He straightened up.

"I'll help ye."

"Oh, no, you don't need to do that!" Charlotte made a grab for her discarded covers but was stopped when Conner grabbed her hand.

"I'll help ye," he repeated softly. Carefully, he slid one arm under her knees and the other beneath her arms. He lifted her as if she weighed nothing and carried her into the bathroom, seating her on the edge of the tub. He steadied her with one hand and filled the tub with the other, adding oils to the water at random until the room was fragrant with the smell of mint and flowers.

"I'll be all right. You can leave me here to bathe." She was already embarrassed enough that he had carried her limp, sweaty body that far.

"Ye know I can no' do that. Ye'd drown like a new ducklin' straight from the egg."

"I would not drown." Charlotte pouted. "And I'm not a duckling."

He tested the waters and turned off the faucet. "Now, let's get ye undressed and into the bath."

"I can undress myself!"

"Charlotte." Conner smiled patiently. "It's nothin' I have no' seen before."

She felt the heat creep up her neck and into her cheeks. "That...that was different!"

"I only wish to help ye. Trust me."

Charlotte nodded and allowed him to untie the front of her nightgown and lower her into the water. "Thank you," she whispered, still self-conscious but feeling more relaxed in the warm waters.

He sat on the floor beside the tub and brushed her cheek with his knuckle. "Charlotte, I do no' only love ye when you are healthy and decked in jewels. I was afraid when they came to me and told me that ye had fainted. I have no' slept in days for fear I'd lose ye. I do no' care how ye look as long as you are with me."

"I'm sorry. I'm just never so ill and I was embarrassed for you to see me in such a state," Charlotte said into the water. Speaking hurt her raw throat, but she knew he needed her reassurances now.

"Ye daft lass, I'm just happy ye are all right." Rising to his knees, he helped her wet her hair before washing it for her, his fingers massaging her scalp. "Do ye feel well enough to eat?" he asked as he rinsed the soap from her hair.

"I'm not sure." She felt a pang of hunger but could not be certain that she could keep any food down.

"Maybe a bit o' broth then," he said as he helped her from the cooling water and wrapped her in a towel. "I'll put ye in bed, aye?"

"I need a nightgown. They're in my wardrobe."

"We'll worry about that later." He lifted her again and settled her into the freshly changed bed, pulling away the damp towel once she was safely under the covers. He crossed the room to the tasseled pull to summon Maisie. When the maid entered, Conner ordered her to tend to Charlotte before leaving to fetch her some broth.

"I'll just brush out your hair," Maisie said, taking the ivory comb and brush set from the dresser and gently taking Charlotte's damp hair in her hand. "Are ye feelin' better after your bath?"

"Yes, thank you. I'm still tired but my headache has lessened a bit."

"Ye will be much better by the morrow. One more good night's sleep will fix ye up."

"It's so strange to have slept for three days and still crave more sleep."

Maisie took her newly combed hair and twisted it into a thick braid. "Do ye need anythin' else before I go down?"

Charlotte took in the maid's pale face, lined with sleeplessness. "No, I'm quite all right now. Conner will take care of me. Please go down and have supper and get some sleep."

"Aye, I'll see ye in the morn." Maisie dipped a small curtsey and slid past Conner who entered the room holding a covered tray. He lowered it onto the nightstand and lifted the lid that sheltered a bowl of steaming beef broth and a cup of tea.

"Do ye feel fit to eat?" he asked.

"Maybe later. I'd just like to rest a bit more first." She gripped the bedding over her naked breasts.

"Should I leave ye then? Or would ye like me to stay as ye sleep?"

"Could you stay?" she asked quietly.

"Aye, I'll pull up a chair."

"Don't," she said as he turned toward the seats before the fire. "Can you just...lay with me for a bit?"

"Aye, I can." He gently slid into the bed, barely moving the mattress as a testament to his skill as a hunter. He lay over the coverlet and held out his hand for her to take, which he brought to his lips.

"Ye gave me such a fright. I've ridden into battle and felled men in war, but when the doctors said ye might no' make it…I did no' know what I would do."

"I really am sorry. I don't know what came over me."

"Stop apologizin'," he said, reaching out and pulling her to his chest. He drew the blankets over her shoulders, offering his own body heat to warm her. "You are well now. Nothin' more needs to be said about it."

And Charlotte didn't say another word. She merely curled into him, savoring the feeling of his arms around her and listening to the beating of his heart as she drifted off to sleep.

***

Charlotte was suddenly jarred awake by several voices all shouting at once. There were maids and footmen in her bedchamber and Conner was gone from her bed, instead standing by the door, clutching something in his fist.

"Find out, now!" Conner growled, fire in his eyes. "I'll have the head of whoever did this, make no mistake!"

"Lady Charlotte!" Maisie broke free from the small party and hurried to her mistress's side. "I'm so sorry, I had no idea."

"Maisie, what's going on?" Charlotte asked with wide eyes. "Why are all these people in my room? I'm not even dressed."

"We can no' have that." The maid busied herself

257

with untying the drapes that were tied to all four bedposts. She pulled them shut, climbing atop the bed. She handed Charlotte a fresh dressing robe. "Conner thinks he's found what's made ye ill."

"Is that why he's yelling?" Charlotte tied the robe around her waist and peeked through the hangings. Conner was positively terrifying; his hand rested at his hip where a sword was sheathed and his face was red with anger.

"Last night, he awoke and drank from your cold teacup to quench his thirst. I did no' know I'd left one behind when ye fell ill. He tasted *witch's hand*. The village doctor confirmed it."

"What's that?"

"It's a poisonous plant that grows on the cliffs. When it's dried it looks like an old woman's withered hand. It's harmless enough to touch, but to ingest it is death."

Charlotte felt her blood run cold. "And there's no way they're mistaken?"

"No. To someone unfamiliar with the plant, ye would no' know the difference. But as someone who's grown with the flower and has ben warned o' it's sickly sweet taste for their whole lives, it's obvious." She grasped her hand. "Someone put it there on purpose to harm ye."

"To kill me," Charlotte corrected. "Someone in this castle wants me dead."

Chapter Twenty-Five

After the staff had been dismissed to find the attempted murderer, the warriors given posts upon the wall, and with Charlotte tucked back into bed, she was left alone with her thoughts. She had hoped that Conner would stay with her the rest of the night, but he had to rouse the men, promising he would return in the morning once he had settled things in the castle.

She had tried to find sleep again but was kept awake by fear and hunger. Not wishing to stew in bed with her own thoughts until Conner returned, she slid out of bed and slipped on her shoes to sneak into the kitchen for something to eat. Surely the kitchen would be empty and, if it weren't, the cook was always more than happy to feed anyone who came into her domain.

The halls were vacant but Charlotte could hear men in the distance and the tittering of maids behind various closed doors. No doubt everyone had heard about the witch's hand in her cup and it would be a topic of much conversation until the

259

offender was caught. She briefly wondered if she was safe, walking around with an attempted murderer, but assumed that with Conner and his men on high alert, the castle was safer than ever.

The kitchen was empty when she reached the landing. The smells of meat slow roasting for the next day made her mouth water. She began opening the cupboards and pulled out bread and a jar of honey. She had just taken the first sticky bite when she heard someone gasp behind her.

"This is no' possible!" a woman's voice cried.

Charlotte turned to see the kitchen maid, Nettie, standing in the doorway, her face contorted into a mask of disbelief.

"What's wrong?" Charlotte asked, placing her bread upon the wooden countertop.

"Ye should have *died*," Nettie muttered.

Charlotte's heart fell to her stomach. "What did you say?"

"You should be dead, but here ye are!"

"Nettie, was it *you*?"

The maid let out a short snort of anger. "O' course it was me, ye ugly English cow!"

"Why, Nettie?" Charlotte had never heard more than three words from the maid's lips and now she was admitting to trying to poison her.

"Because the MacLeod turned his favors on to ye! He picked you out o' all the lasses in Scotland. He picked an English whore when he could have had *me*!"

"I-I'm sorry it happened like that. I had no idea anyone felt that way about him. We never did anything to try to hurt you."

"But ye did. Ye lured him to your bed, made him love ye, and now he wants to marry ye!" Nettie pulled off her cap and tugged at her hair in frustration. "I wanted him. I *chose* him!"

"But, Nettie, you can't just go trying to *kill* me just because Conner wishes to court me."

"Do no' call him by his first name! Such disrespect."

Charlotte glanced around the kitchen, looking for an impromptu weapon. "I'm sorry, Nettie. But, you can't do things like that. Con—the MacLeod has everyone searching for the culprit. He's called for their head."

Nettie made a strangled noise deep in her throat. "The MacLeod knows?"

"Yes. Haven't you heard?" Charlotte began inching toward the block that held the butcher knives. "He's the one who found it and he plans on killing who did it. In this case, it'll be you."

"No," she whispered, her previous fury quite sated by the fear of death. "I thought that if I just got rid o' ye, he would be free from ye and come to me instead."

"This is it, then. He's going to have justice."

Nettie bit her lower lip hard enough to draw blood. "Do ye think he'd really kill me?"

"Yes," Charlotte answered evenly, her fingers brushing against the handle of a short knife. "If he finds that it was you, he will kill you."

"Ach! What am I to do?" Nettie buried her face in her apron.

Charlotte snatched the knife from the counter and slipped it into the pocket of her dressing gown

261

before Nettie uncovered her eyes. "Nettie, I'm sure if you go to the MacLeod and tell him how sorry you are, he'll take mercy on you."

"Ye do no' know him like we do," Nettie whispered. "I've seen him deliver his justice. He puts heads on the pikes before the keep!"

"Certainly not!" Charlotte could not imagine the man who tenderly washed her hair also decapitating someone and placing their head out for display.

"Aye, it's true. He'll kill me for sure and put up my head for my family to see."

"If you knew he would punish you like that, why did you try to kill me?"

Nettie shrugged, suddenly eerily placid. "I did no' think I'd be caught."

Charlotte frowned. As much as she hated Nettie for trying to kill her, she couldn't help but think that the poor maid was seriously unhinged. She had no idea if the woman would suddenly lunge at her to claw at her eyes or lie on the floor and go to sleep. She knew that Conner would rather her run for help, but she didn't feel as if she could have a part in the death of an obviously disturbed woman, even if she was guilty of a terrible crime.

Charlotte understood that in order to keep herself alive, and save her equally fragile conscious, she had to take a gamble. "Nettie, I'll help you leave the castle if you promise to leave and never come back."

The maid's eyes lowered suspiciously. "Aye? Ye'd help me escape?"

"Yes, but you need to leave now and you need to never enter MacLeod lands again." Charlotte's voice was steady and strong, but her fingers trembled against the knife in her pocket.

"Ye have a bargain." The maid untied her apron and laid it gently on a stool, patting it once and turning to Charlotte expectantly. "So, how do ye suppose ye get me out o' the keep, then?"

Charlotte hadn't thought her plan through. She knew the gates were well-guarded and none of the warriors were the kind to shirk their duties. But, she remembered, there was one more way. "Follow me."

Cautiously, the knife still tight in her hand, she led Nettie back up the stairs and down the halls to the door Conner had showed her during one of her first days in the castle. As she began the descent down the stairs, she wished she had the foresight to bring tinder to light the torch. The light would be invaluable in finding their way to the secret door, but she could not risk being caught helping Nettie escape.

"Nettie," she asked in the darkness, "do you know where we're going?"

"I know the jail cells are down here, and a cellar. Do ye plan on puttin' me in a cell? That's no' verra helpful."

"Heavens, no. Although what you did warrants a time in irons, we have a bargain." Charlotte gripped the wall to stabilize herself on the slick steps. "There's a door farther down that will take you to a cave at the cliffs. You will climb up the side of the cliff and run. It's still dark enough that no one will see you in the fields."

"Why *are* ye helpin' me?"

"Well, honestly, I don't want your death on my conscious. May I ask why you are so calm in all this? If I were in your shoes, certainly I would be a bit more emotional."

"What's there to fuss about? The deed is done and I've made my bed so there's nothin' more to do. My plan did no' fall into place."

She was still puzzled as to how the maid was so composed and didn't seem upset at all by these turns of events. She decided the situation warranted no more conversation and held up the hem of her robe as they reached the landing and she felt water seep into her slippers. Relying on a faint memory and the feeling of the stones beneath her fingers, she led Nettie through the pitch-black hallways until she felt the archway of stones that would take her to the cave.

"Here it is," Charlotte said, pushing the stone door aside. A faint shadow of light crept around a curve in the passageway. "Follow this to the cave and don't turn back."

"Ye will come no further?" Nettie's disembodied voice asked.

"And risk you pushing me into the sea?" Charlotte let out a rather unladylike snort. "I'm not a *total* fool."

"Aye, perhaps no'." Nettie brushed past her savior and began her walk toward the cliff. "Goodbye, Charlotte."

Charlotte shivered at the pleasant pitch of her voice. She was grateful when she pulled the fake door closed behind her, separating her from Nettie. Not wishing to stay in the darkness alone, she turned quickly on her heal and ran back down the halls, making her way back up to the light.

***

"Ye did *what*?" Conner's voice echoed in the library where he stood before the roaring fireplace.

"I did what I thought I had to do," Charlotte answered hotly, her hands on her hips. "She said you would have killed her and put her head out for the crows!"

"And what if I had? She tried to *murder* ye, Charlotte. Ye could have *died*!"

"But I didn't."

"Only because I drank the poisonous tea!"

"Stop yelling!" Charlotte stomped her foot. "What's done is done and I'd rather you dropped the subject. Nettie is gone for good."

"And how do ye know that?"

"I don't," she admitted.

Conner pushed a hand through his hair. "Charlotte, I have to send a scout after her. She tried killin' a member o' my family. It's no' just my law that says she needs to be punished. It's Scotland's law as well."

"I can't be responsible for someone's death. You didn't see her, Conner. She's not right in the head. She was so calm, it was unnerving."

"Mad, or no', I can no' have someone like that in my lands."

"Well, she promised she wouldn't come back," Charlotte offered weakly.

His jaw dropped slightly. "She promised—ach!

Charlotte, ye can no' make these decisions for me in my land."

"I'm sorry. I just couldn't have that kind of weight on my soul like that." She tried standing tall in her damp dressing gown and ruined slippers, but couldn't help the shivers that wracked her tired body.

Conner's face softened as he pulled her into an embrace. "Charlotte, love, I'm sorry. I just can no' watch ye shiver and shake like that no matter how angry I am with ye. Come, it's late. I'll take ye to bed." With an arm tucked supportively around her waist, he led her safely back into her bedchambers.

"Conner, will you stay with me tonight?" she asked, suddenly feeling the weight from the evening. "Please?"

"O' course." He smiled as she slipped off her shoes and turned around to allow her to put on a fresh nightgown. When she was clothed and tucked into bed, he went to move her soiled robe when he felt a curious weight. He reached into the pocket and pulled from it the short kitchen knife. He held it up with a raised eyebrow. "And what is this?"

Charlotte blushed at her pitiful blade. "It was the best I could do on such short notice. It's not as if I came upon Nettie in the armory."

He chuckled as he put it on her dresser alongside her toiletries and pulled his linen shirt over his head. "A wee little needle like that would do naught to stop someone. I'll get ye a nice blade for ladies. Both o' my sisters carry one."

"I don't think that's really necessary."

"Aye, I think it is." He unhooked the pin on his

kilt but paused, glancing at her. "Ye know, lass, Scottish men do no' wear nightgowns. I can go fetch a clean shirt if ye like."

She colored and busied herself with straightening the blankets over her legs. "I'm quite sure it'll be fine. I hate to have you make a special trip on my account."

Conner shrugged and grinned a bit as Charlotte turned her face away, feigning interest in the fire until he was safely tucked beneath the covers. "You're safe, lass. I'm fully shielded from view."

"Do stop teasing me."

"I can no' help it," he said, stretching under the silks. "Now stop bein' a stranger and come closer."

Charlotte glanced at him over the expanse of the bed. There was more than an arm's length between them. She debated keeping some space between them, but figured that since they had already disregarded most of the rules of propriety, actually sleeping together was the least of their transgressions.

She slid closer until their bodies curled into one another, her head on his chest and one of his arms draped around her back, his hand caressing her shoulder. They lay together in companionable quite with nothing but the sounds of the fire crackling and their own heartbeats in the early dawn.

"Charlotte, are ye too tired to talk?"

"No, I'm all right. Is something the matter?"

"The past few days have been hard."

"I'm sorry I gave you a fright."

He squeezed her arm and placed his cheek atop her head. "Stop apologizin' for somethin' done to ye. I just had quite a bit o' time to think and speculate what it is we're doin' and where it is we're headin'. I just got ye. I could no' stand to lose ye so fast."

"But I'm fine now. Nettie is gone and I'm right as rain." She traced the scar upon his chest, feeling a bit of the rough mark under her chin. "Things can carry on just as they were before."

"I do no' think I want them to carry on just as they were before."

Charlotte froze. "What do you mean by that?"

"Nothin' bad, I promise ye. I just mean to say that these days have shown me what ye add to my life. Ye've been here a month, but I already can no' picture what my home would be like if ye were to leave."

"Well, for the foreseeable future, I don't plan on leaving," she assured him. "I have so much here that I don't think I could ever turn away from it."

"I'm glad to hear it. Ye know I do love you, Charlotte."

"And I love you," she whispered in return.

"Charlotte, I know ye say ye can no' marry me yet. That you're no' ready."

"Well, I can't imagine marrying without my father, Penelope, and even Abigail in attendance."

"In Scotland there are many ways for a man and woman to be joined."

"You mean an engagement?"

"No' exactly." He shifted her off his body and slid down, turning to face her on the pillow. "Have ye ever heard o' a hand fastin'?"

"A hand fasting? What's that?"

"It's when a lad and lass decide they wish to be bound but can no' or will no' marry for some reason. They're joined together in a ceremony to live as man and wife for a year and a day."

"But what happens after that? They're just no longer married?"

"They can marry then, if they choose. Or, they can go their separate ways as if they'd never been joined." He took one of her hands in his, brushing the knuckles. "But I'd no go a separate way than you. I'd marry ye."

"I don't understand. Why not get engaged then, if you would wait a year to be properly wed in church by a priest?"

"If we were to be bound, ye would be treated no' as a guest o' the clan, or my companion, but as my wife. It would give ye the strength and protection o' my name in whole, and no' just by the pin on your chest or the orders to my men. Ye would no' quite be queen here, but—"

"Queen?"

"Well, there is no' exactly a name for the chief's wife but, in effect, that's what ye'd be if you decided to marry me at the end o' the year. Charlotte…" He dipped his head lower, bringing it closer so he could force her to look him in the eye. "I can only protect ye so much if we are no' wed. If we were to be bound, no one would dare touch ye, or even look at ye. Nettie would have never tried to harm ye if we had been hand fasted. Almost losin' ye has made me surer than ever that I can no' live without ye as my wife."

Charlotte bit her lip. Her head was still fuzzy

with fatigue and cold and the addition of being essentially married so quickly made her brain all the more muddled. "So you want to be, for the most part, married so that no other jealous maids try to poison me in my sleep? I assume that if someone wanted me gone, being married to you wouldn't stop them."

"It would. No one dares draw blade against the leaders o' the clan and, if they did, they'd face the most brutal o' punishments. If someone means to hurt us, they'd need to be prepared with an army, as well. Ye'd have the force o' my men to guard ye and me in your bed to keep ye safe at night."

"But you're in my bed right now."

He smiled wryly. "If ye no wish to be bound to me, just say it."

"It's not that." She sighed, turning on her back, looking up at the canopy above. "Things have just been so queer lately and I wouldn't want anyone to marry me, for a lifetime *or* a year, because otherwise I would be murdered. You must see how strange that sounds to me. I want someone to marry me for love, to build a home and family together out of nothing more than shared adoration and goals."

Conner sprung up on one arm, hovering over her. "And ye think I do no' love you? That I do no' desire a family with you? A life? I've told ye such many times over and I'll tell ye again if that's what ye need. I love you, Charlotte. I respect your mind and strength, the way ye care for wee orphaned Ian and ride the horses with abandon. I desire your body every wakin' moment and even more so in my dreams. I'll give ye my sword, my life, my body, my heart if ye say ye'll be bound to me. No' out o' duty or fear, but because I love you."

Charlotte stifled the small pinpricks of tears that threatened to burst from her eyes. "I just don't want you to feel pressured to marry me because of Nettie."

"I'd marry ye now, naked as a jay bird, in your bedchambers, if that's what ye wanted. Nettie or no Nettie." He pressed his lips to hers. "I'm no' askin' for forever right now. I'm askin' ye to be bound to me for a year and a day, at least. And *then* forever."

Charlotte smiled a sliver. "And if I say yes?"

"Then I'll be the happiest man and we'll be bound in the morrow."

"And if I say no?"

"Then I'll have to ask every day until ye can no' longer fend off my advances."

"How romantic."

"So, Charlotte, what say ye?"

She tapped her pointed chin with a fingertip, feigning deep thought. "Well, I don't know..."

"Ach, lass, ye tease me so. I'll give ye a taste of your own medicine." And with that he deftly untied the single ribbon that held closed the neck of her nightgown, allowing the fabric to drift to the sides, exposing her collarbones and the top swells of her breasts. "Say yes now or I'll have to make ye."

"And how do you suppose you could do that?" Her voice was but a breath, and he smirked in response.

"I have my ways." He flicked a tongue down her neck and bit the tender flesh at her throat. He ran his hand down her side and squeezed her thigh. He looked up at her, strands of blond hanging over his brow, but she could still see mirth in his eyes.

"Then I believe I'll still say no and see how effective your methods are."

Grinning, he swooped up and planted a peck on her cheek before falling to his back against the pillow next to her. "Goodnight then, Charlotte."

"Goodnight?" She blustered. Propping herself up on one elbow, she glared at him. "What do you mean 'goodnight'?"

"Testy now, are we?" He laughed, making her blush. "I told ye before, I will no' lie with a woman who is no' my wife. If you'll no be my wife, I'll no' share my body."

"You drive a hard bargain, MacLeod."

"But a fair one. Be my wife and I'll serve ye as a good husband should. But ye'll get no more than a kiss until then."

"Then I'll have to take you up on your offer."

"Aye?" He brushed the hair from his eyes. "Ye agree to the hand fastin' then?"

"Aye," she answered.

***

Charlotte awoke to the midday sun shining though the gap in her drapes and an empty, cold, spot that Conner had once occupied. She disliked that she awoke alone, but he was a busy man with land and people to care for. He couldn't laze the day away. And neither could Charlotte. After she had agreed to be bound to him, he told her that the hand fasting ceremony would be the next day at dusk.

She was to come, with his sisters, to the tallest mound.

She lay amongst the bedding for a time, unsure of how to feel about her upcoming nuptials. Conner had guaranteed her that the ceremony would be legal and sound in Scotland, giving her the rights as a full wife and without sin in the church. And, although it wasn't technically a *full* marriage, she felt rather odd at getting bound without her friends and family there to support her.

By the end of the year, she would plan on having a large wedding in her family's church in England. She would do it properly with her father to walk her down the aisle, Penelope as a bridesmaid, and an appropriate reception luncheon in her father's ballroom.

For the moment being, she had no idea what was to come that afternoon. Conner had given her no further instructions than to meet at sunset. She had no inkling of anything else about the actual ceremony, or what she would even wear. It was all rather befuddling.

She climbed out of bed and opened the shades. The waves below crashed against the cliffs but the sky was an icy blue, cloudless and clear. She splashed water on her face and brushed her chestnut hair before donning her shift and a yellow day dress. Taking one last look in her mirror, she attached the MacLeod pin to her breast and went down to see if anyone was about.

The rooms she passed were silent and the dining room was empty. It was past lunch, but her stomach still growled and she needed something to tide her over until supper. She could hardly remember the last meal she ate as Nettie had interrupted her last midnight snack.

The kitchen was bustling with movement. Maids stirred pots and chopped vegetables and the air was thick with the smells of roasting meat and burning wood. Cook was spicing skinned rabbits. The little bodies were lined up on a pan, surrounded by carrots and potatoes.

"Ach! Lady Charlotte! I'm so pleased to see ye are the picture o' health, once again and that ye'll be hand fasted to the MacLeod!" The cook crooned.

"Thank you, I'm feeling quite well. I see you're very busy.

"Aye, there's a feast to be had! Meat needs to be cooked, bannocks baked…aye, it's a busy day here. But all for a good reason!"

"Thank you for putting in so much effort. I'll admit that I'm not familiar with Scottish binding customs." The phrase felt odd on her tongue, but she was still unsure if she could call it a wedding. "Is there anything I could do to help?"

"No, no, the bride—" The cook paused and looked at her with wide eyes. "What is the bride doin' wanderin' the halls on the day of her weddin'?" Cook shouted over the din, slapping a raw rabbit to the countertop. "Ye should be upstairs lest the MacLeod sees ye!"

"Do no' worry so," a young scullery maid piped in. "I saw him ride off before luncheon. Her ladyship is fine for now."

"All the same, ye should be preparin' yourself! Where is Maisie?" The cook looked around at the busting gaggle of women. "Someone fetch Maisie!"

"I'm here!" Maisie shouted, a basket of vines and curious plants tucked under her arm. "I was just out fetchin' things for Lady Charlotte's hair."

Charlotte moved closer to the basket and poked about the stalks and tiny purple blooms. "What will I do with these?"

"Ye'll see." Maisie winked, patting her load.

"Maisie, daft lass, get Charlotte back to her chambers before The MacLeod returns," the cook ordered.

"Wait! I just came down here to fetch something to eat," Charlotte interjected. "I'm quite starved after my illness."

The cook glared at Maisie and wiped her hands on her apron before ordering a passing maid to make a plate. "Take the lady upstairs. I'll send up a lass with a bite and some tea."

"Come, we'll get ye bathed." Maisie took Charlotte by the arm and led her form the kitchen.

They passed the feasting hall where Big Angus was overseeing the movements of tabled and chairs, adding more seats to the already crowded space. The rest of the castle was still quiet but as they reached Charlotte's room, Flora poked her head from the door.

"Charlotte!" She squealed. "Are you gettin' ready now?"

"I'm not sure," Charlotte answered, glancing at Maisie.

Maisie pushed her into her bedchambers. "She's still in need o' a bath and a meal to tide her. I'll fetch ye when it's time for a penny and the hair."

275

"A penny?" Charlotte asked, slipping out of her shoes.

"Aye." Maisie shut the door behind her. "It's placed in your slipper for luck." She led the way through Charlotte's sitting room and into her bedroom, dropping the basket next to the small fireplace.

"Maisie, is it strange that I don't feel terribly nervous?" Charlotte asked as she unbuttoned her gown in the bathroom.

"No' a wee bit. The MacLeod is a good man and will make ye a fine husband."

"But if we aren't properly married, will we still be husband and wife?"

"Aye, it's just the Scottish way o' thin's." She filled the tub, sprinkling dried lavender into the water. "Ye'll be like a proper married couple until the year and a day has ended. If ye do no' get married by a priest by then, then you will no longer be wed. Until that time, ye are just as married as anyone."

Charlotte slid into the tub, dunking her head in the water to wet her hair. "I'm sorry if that sounds like a silly question. I'm just not all that familiar with Scottish customs."

"It's no' a silly question." Maisie told her as she massaged soap and oils into her hair.

"I have another silly question. What am I to wear? I haven't had time for a new dress."

"Do no' be angry with me, Lady Charlotte."

"Why would I be angry with you?"

"I took the lilac ball gown from your wardrobe. Some o' the lasses and I made a few alterations. It's like a new dress."

"You mean my coming out gown?" Charlotte perked up at the thought. "You know, that's the very dress I first met Conner in."

"Aye? Well, it's a totally different gown, in all respects, now. Are you quite cross with me?"

"Oh, no, not in the least bit! You're a wonderful friend, Maisie, to think so for me. But when did you find the time to alter the dress?"

"The MacLeod might have just asked ye to be bound to him, but I've known for some time. He's no' a man to give his affections lightly and I knew there would no' be any other balls for some time to warrant such a formal frock."

"Oh, Maisie, I can't wait to see it! I'm sure you've done a beautiful job."

The maid washed the fragrant lather from Charlotte's hair and placed a clean towel next to the tub. "I'll just go lay out your toilette. Ye come out when you're ready."

Charlotte piled her wet hair upon her head and continued to soak in the warm waters. As she washed her body, the reality of her upcoming began to build in her chest. She was going to be married in a few short hours to a Scottish chieftain in a strange land in an ancient ritual she had no real knowledge about.

She loved Conner, it was true, but she wondered if things were moving too quickly. A series of extraordinary events had led her to this moment. It was something out of a dime novel—English lady runs from an unfortunate marriage and into the arms of a dashing Scottish lord. Charlotte snorted at the thought and rose from the tub, wrapping herself in a towel.

No matter what circumstances led her to Conner, she was grateful. He was, in all accounts, the kind of man she had told her father she deserved. Conner was strong, kindhearted, a fair leader, and welcomed Charlotte's interests and dreams to a fault. He had given her a horse to ride freely, a library of books, and loved when she wore her hair down her back and debated politics and life. He gave her freedom and adoration, and feelings she had only imagined were possible.

"My lady, are ye all right?" Maisie asked through the door.

"I'm fine—coming out now." She pulled on her robe and exited the bathroom where Maisie was preparing piles of flowers on the dressing table.

She sat Charlotte down and began drying her hair with a new towel. When her hair was brushed, gleaming from many strokes, Maisie began intricately twisting the front of her tresses into small, twirling braids, pinning them to the back of her head with a handful of pins.

"Now for the heather." She picked up several delicate purple flowers and tucked them into the crown of braids, interlaced with a thin, green, leafy vine.

Charlotte touched the minute blossoms. "These are very pretty."

"Heather is abundant in the highlands. It's good luck for a bride to wear them in her hair and carry them, along with some thistle, on her weddin' day."

A maid slipped in with a covered tray. "Should I

put this on the dressing table, my lady?"

"Yes, thank you." Charlotte opened the lid and immediately began eating the cold chicken and warm loaf of bread. She took a sip out of the full teacup and sputtered. "Wh-what's in this?"

"Oh, a bit o' Scottish courage, I assume." Maisie laughed. "Whiskey will calm your nerves."

"I wasn't aware I was nervous." She muttered, taking a small sip of the vicious liquid.

"Not even a wee bit?"

"Well, perhaps a little."

"What's there to fret about?"

"Well, I've never been a bride, for starters," Charlotte pointed out.

"What's there to know?"

"How to be a good wife."

Maisie finished with her hair and began opening the tubs and jars on the tabletop. "He seems to like ye well enough now. I think ye'll be fine."

"Maisie..." Charlotte swallowed the bite she was chewing, trying to think of the words she meant to say. She had no mother to guide her and desperately felt she needed Maisie's advice. "There is something that I'm rather worried about."

"Aye, what's that?"

"The wedding night..."

"Ye said you knew well enough how bairns are made."

"I do, but how do I make it so he enjoys himself?"

She bit back a chuckle and stuck a finger in a jar of red cream. "Ye'll be fine. Do no' fret so."

The lip color was cold against her mouth but the

279

hue made her full lips glow healthily. If she weren't so nervous, she would think she looked more lively and lovely but, due to nerves, she thought she looked more like a vampire, fresh from the hunt. "But, I'm not experienced."

"All the better you're a maid on your weddin' night. Ye'll figure it out soon enough."

"I suppose so."

Maisie held up a container. "Ye do no' need anythin' on your lashes. Just a wee bit o' blush then."

The color added a healthy aura about her face, which was unusually pale that day. "Maisie, could you please get my emeralds?"

"Already done. I knew ye'd wish to wear them." She pulled the velvet box from a drawer in the table.

Charlotte fixed the heavy gems to her ears and draped the necklace around her. "Is it almost time?"

"Aye." Maisie glanced at the clock. "I'll fetch Gwen and Flora to finish ye. I've hung your gown back in the wardrobe."

When Charlotte was alone, she pulled on one of her finer shifts; it boasted a low neckline, edged in thin lace and had thin straps that could be hidden in the short sleeves of the gown. It might not be a new chemise for a bridal dowry, but it was clean and very well-made.

She opened the bureau to reveal the dress. It had been altered to look like a different gown. The lilac silk had pickups that showed off an underskirt of ivory. The swooping collar was trimmed with ivory as well and small capped sleeves hung to cup the shoulders in the same color.

"Oh, Charlotte!" Flora sang as she glided in, dressed in a gown of green. "Your hair is marvelous and that frock is to die for!"

"It was all Maisie's doing," Charlotte said.

"Can we help you dress?" Gwen entered, also in green, the same shade as her sister.

Charlotte held out the gown. "Of course. Let me just put on my corset."

As Flora and Gwen commended Maisie on her seamstress work, Charlotte began lacing herself into her corset. Her fingers shook with newfound nerves and she took a liberal drink of the spiked tea, now cold and bitterer than before. She unrolled her stockings, shivering a bit as the cold silk hit her legs. Another sip of the tea and it began to warm her stomach comfortably and ease her anxieties.

Gwen brought out a pair of ivory slippers and put a penny in the heel of one. Charlotte stepped into them, wriggling her toes against the odd feeling of the coin against her arch. The two sisters tittered to one another as they helped Charlotte button her dress, careful not to muss her hair. They adjusted the fabric and all giggled at the scandalous way her chest pushed against the neckline.

"You best be careful not to give everyone a show!" Flora jested, eyeing the exposed flesh. "If I ever wore a gown such as that, Conner would lock me in my chambers and I'd never see the light of day again!"

Charlotte looked at her reflection and frowned. She had thought it had been perfect in London— daring and alluring while still being at the height of fashion. Perhaps it was just too much in the Scottish highlands. "Do you think it's terrible? I wouldn't want to shame him before his people."

Maisie shook her head, folding a few more flowers into Charlotte's curls. "Do no' listen to her. While the MacLeod would no' want to see his wee sister dressed so, he'll be right pleased to see ye in it."

"If you're certain." Charlotte was still not convinced and tried pulling purple material upward, which snapped back into place, showing just as much skin as before.

"Stop fidgetin'." Maisie thrust the almost-empty cup under her nose. "Drink this and be done. It's just nerves makin' ye fuss this way."

She drained the last of the tonic. "You're right. I just need to put on my pin and I'll be ready." Charlotte scanned the tabletop, looking among the combs and cosmetic jars. "That's strange, I thought it was here."

"The MacLeod has it," Maisie said, straightening a few wayward waves.

Flora looked out the window at the dying daylight. "We should really get going or Charlotte will be late to her own wedding."

"Wait but a moment." Maisie grasped the remaining foliage and tied it deftly with a blue ribbon, handing it to Charlotte. "Are ye ready now?"

"Y-yes. I think." She cleared her throat and straightened her back, trying to look braver than she felt. "I'm ready."

"Ye'll do marvelously," Maisie assured her.

Charlotte froze. "Maisie," she hissed, "I have no idea what to do in a hand fasting. Are there vows? A special gift? A sacrificial offering?"

The maid chuckled. "Do no' worry so. All ye need to do is listen to the oaths and have your hands bound to the MacLeod."

"Literally bound?" Charlotte knit her brow. She had thought the binding was figurative, not factual.

"Aye, ye goose." Maisie laughed. "Now let's be off before it's too dark to see and we lose ourselves in the moors!"

***

Charlotte followed the three women through the halls, finding them empty and silent. "Where is everyone?"

"Already on the hill, I expect," Gwen said as they each pulled on a cloak.

When they opened the front door, three kilted men with bagpipes nodded to them, immediately starting a solemn tune. The music echoed in the courtyard and branched off once they had left the gates, spreading the song through the hills. The women walked in a straight line behind the pipers, towards the hill; Maisie, Flora, Gwen, and then Charlotte.

The beating of the war drums upon the hill reverberated in Charlotte's chest as they grew near. They resonated the feeling of her own heart's pulse giving an ancient feel to the ceremony at hand. The fading light illuminated a mass of people at the top of the knoll, all silent and watching, waiting for her to join them.

Charlotte saw Conner standing in the center of the group looking resplendent in traditional Scottish garb. His plaid looped about his shoulder and a jaunty hat boasted an eagle feather to highlight his standing in the clan. He grinned when his sisters left her alone in the circle—a smile that reached his sapphire eyes. The look alone comforted Charlotte who had, at that point, thought she might faint.

An old man stepped out from the crowd, lighting a small bonfire behind Conner, bathing him in a golden light. Conner beckoned for Charlotte to join him next to the blaze. The old man then came to them, holding out a thin length of the MacLeod yellow and black tartan. He nodded to both Charlotte and Conner before beginning his ceremony in heavily accented English.

"Before the four points o' the Earth. Before the sun, the wind, the air, the water, the ground. Before the people o' Scotland and the people o' the clan. Before the new God and the ones that came before. This man and this woman are enterin' into the ageless contract o' hand fastin' to become one mind, one soul, one body, one heart."

Flora slipped behind Charlotte and took her bouquet. "It's time to be bound," she whispered into her ear before she blended back into the circle.

Conner stepped forward and took her hands in his, his right with her right and his left with her left, their interlaced arms making a cross. He squeezed her hand in reassurance before tipping his head for the old man to continue.

"Conner Mackenzie MacLeod, do ye enter into

this hand fastin' o' your own free will, for the entirety o' a year and a day?" the old man asked.

"I do," Conner answered.

The old man turned to her. "Charlotte Lucille Holloway, do ye enter into this hand fastin' of your own free will, for the entirety o' a year and a day?"

"I do." Her voice sounded soft, but sure.

His eyes flashed back to Conner as he began winding the strip of tartan around their hands. "Do ye promise to live for this woman as your true wife, forsakin' all others?"

"I do."

The old man wound the cloth in another ring. "Do ye promise to live for this man as your true husband, forsakin' all others?"

"I do."

"Do ye promise on sword and life to protect and provide for this woman and all those who come from this union?" the old man asked Conner. "To fight, reap, and sow in her honor?"

"I do."

He held the final length of plaid and looked at Charlotte. "Do ye promise on home and hearth to care and provide for this man and all those who come from this union? To bear bairns, reap, and sow in his honor?"

"I do." Charlotte felt her mouth go dry as the fabric was knotted over their hands, signifying the finality of their union.

"Now you are as husband and wife for the time o' the hand fastin'. Ye must be married before the year and day end, or part forever once the period is gone." The old man addressed the crowd. "Let it be known, with ye as witnesses, this man and this women are bound in the right o' hand fastin'." He took their hands and gently pulled each from the tartan, amazingly keeping the knot fully intact. "Now the MacLeod will give her the protection o' the clan."

The man stepped back and a warrior took his place, holding a large piece of MacLeod plaid. Conner silently unhooked Charlotte's wolf skin cloak, passing it to someone in the throng. He took the tartan and wrapped it over Charlotte's shoulder.

"Charlotte, ye have entrusted me with your life for a year and a day in this hand fastin'. I promise that I will show you that I can be a good husband to ye and, God willin', ye will never wish to part from my side." He produced her silver crest pin from his sporran, attaching it to the ends of the plaid, creating a sash. He then took her hands in his, pulling her closer to speak quietly, but clearly. "I give ye the colors, the crest, the power and shield o' my name. As a MacLeod ye will never want, never crave, and never desire for anythin' as I will give ye all I have."

He bent down to kiss her then, his men and the other revelers cheering all around them. Charlotte felt the heat of the flames, but it was nothing compared to the intensity she felt within her. She was as good as a wife to Conner now—the spouse of the highland's leader and the best warrior in the land. It was almost too much and for a brief moment, she wished for Penelope to be there with her. The bagpipers then began playing, signaling an end to the ceremony and leading a sudden descent down the hill toward the castle. The guests had taken branches from the bonfire, giving them all a light to walk back to the castle in the darkness. They looked like dozens of little lightning bugs swaying to the beat of the drums.

As the crowd dispersed, she wondered if she was supposed to have given him a present in return—a token of sorts. "That's it, then?" Charlotte asked once Conner's lips left hers.

"Aye. That's it. Ye belong to me now."

She blushed at the implication behind his words. She *was* his, in a way. They would live together as husband and wife, sharing a home and a bed. Tonight she would share her body with him. Once they had lain together, she would no longer be a maid and while the thought frightened her, she was secretly brimming with excitement for the secret embraces that were to come.

"Come, we must go down now," Conner said, fingering the pin at her hip. "I've been too nervous to eat this day and now I've quite a hunger."

Charlotte looked out at the Scots. She could hear them laughing aloud at bawdy jokes and calling back to Conner in Gaelic.

"What are they saying?" she asked, taking Conner's arm. She was glad for the warmth emanating from his body. Without her cloak, the winter winds swept right through her silks and the plaid did little to conserve her heat.

"Ye do no' want to know," he said wryly. He helped her over the stones and held her close as they reached the doors where the pipers stood waiting to herald their arrival. "Are ye ready to enter…wife?"

Charlotte shivered at her new title, and nodded in the affirmative.

The feasting hall was bursting with guests. There were six long tables piled high with food and a band of musicians waiting for their turn to perform. Upon the small rise was a table set for two, encircled in branches, leaves, and heather, topped with a set of bells for luck.

The revelers lifted their cups and stomped their feet when Conner and Charlotte entered on the heels of the pipers. They shouted in Gaelic as the pair passed, some holding up their dirks in salute.

Flora, Gwen, and Ian were seated near the front of the hall. Ian waved at her and scampered from his seat, her bouquet in his hands. "Miss Charlotte! Ye forgot your flowers on the hill!" He held them up to her, grinning.

She knelt down a bit to reach him. "Thank you, Ian. I'm glad you've brought them to me." She plucked a burst of heather from the bunch and handed it to him. "Have a seat and be sure to eat well. I believe Cook's made many wonderful treats for dessert."

"Cake?" the boy whispered, his little face quite serious.

"Many different kinds!"

He beamed and tucked the heather into his miniature sporran and hurried back to his seat, delighted with the promise of sweets. Charlotte marveled at how he'd bloomed in his short time at the castle. She continued to the head table.

Once they were seated, she noticed that someone had placed the tartan hand fasting knot upon the table, a brightly lit candle tucked in its folds.

Conner noticed her interest. "We are to keep it with us for luck. We can place it on the mantelpiece in our chambers."

"*Our* chambers?"

"Well, aye. I just thought ye'd like to sleep in the same room now that we are wed." He studied her closely. "Unless you are more comfortable in your own chambers?"

"Oh, no." She waved a hand. "I would like very much to be in the same room. I just hadn't given any thought to it. It's a very new notion to be sharing chambers with anyone."

"I understand. Would ye like to say a few words before we begin the feast?"

"A few words? To everyone?"

"Aye. I'm sure they'd like to hear from ye."

Charlotte paled and bit her lip. "I…I suppose I should, shouldn't I?"

"Good lass." He winked and stood from his chair, drawing immediate silence. "My people," he began to the crowd, "I am honored you have come from your homes and farms to share in my hand fastin' to my new wife, Charlotte. I am blessed for your loyalty and fidelity to the clan, and to me. Now, my wife would like to say a few words."

Conner helped her stand and she uneasily looked out at the guests seated around the many tables, their eyes all fixed upon her. "Hello, everyone. Thank you all for coming to celebrate with us on this day. You have been nothing but kind and accepting to me and, for that, I could never repay you. Please eat, drink, and rejoice with us."

She sat down as the people erupted into applause and a great amount of stomping that shook the wooden tables. Conner had to bang the handle of his dirk upon the tabletop to call order to the evening. He then took the first sip of wine, signaling a start to the meal. The musicians began a lively tune and the scullery maids were quickly put to work keeping the goblets full.

"Ye did well," he said, kissing her knuckles as she took a shaky sip from her cup. "Ye'll make a find lady o' the clan."

"I suppose I am the lady of the clan now, aren't I?"

"Aye, but it's no' as scary as it sounds. Ye will just sit with me in the receivin' hall when guests come and be a good hostess. Ye do get a few perks with your new position." He placed choice cuts of meat and piles of vegetables on her plate.

"Oh? Whatever do you mean?"

"Now ye have the clan's colors as your own, so ye may wear them as ye like to show your status. This castle now partly belongs to ye, as well as the MacLeod jewels."

"I already have so many."

"Aye, but you're Lady MacLeod now, not just a titled maid," he said, biting into his food. "I'll have ye bedecked in finery befitting your stature."

"Lady MacLeod." She let the name wash over her as she spoke it aloud. It was a strange feeling, knowing that she was a new person now, in a way. No longer young Lady Holloway, an unmarried girl with no real prospects outside her father's graces, but a married woman akin to a queen in Scotland. It all seemed too extraordinary to be true, yet it was. There she sat in the plaid of a married woman, her husband by her side.

"Penny for your thoughts?" Conner whispered in her ear, jarring her from her contemplations.

"I don't need one, there's one in my slipper."

He knitted his brows. "Where've you got a penny?"

"In my slipper."

"Ye say that as if it's somethin' verra serious. Now, what's on your mind?"

"I was just thinking how…different it feels to be married. I'm still the same person yet, I'm not."

He nodded, topping off her cup with the pitcher left at his side. "Aye, it's strange to think o' me bein' a husband and you being my wife. Ye do no' regret it now?"

"Goodness, no." Charlotte took his hand. "I don't regret it a bit. It's just so new. I never thought that when I came here with you, I would end up being married, and so quickly!"

Conner smirked. "I knew ye'd marry me. I decided once I met ye at your comin' out ball that I'd make ye my wife."

"And how did you decide something like that? You hardly knew me."

"Aye, but I wanted to know ye more. You were like a rose, beautiful and pure, but if handled wrong, could sting most terribly. You have a fire in ye that I admire and I knew that if I showed ye all that I had to offer ye, ye'd give in to my askin' sooner or later."

"You are nothing but determined." Charlotte

291

laughed, sipping her wine. "But, I care for you more than what you have to give me."

"I know that, lass. But it does no' hurt to be able to give ye everythin' you deserve. I do have a weddin' gift for ye."

"Oh, you don't have to give me anything."

"But I do." He reached into his sporran and pulled out a ring. It was gold and delicate; twisting strands held a sizable emerald against the band amid a sea of tiny diamonds. "I know it's commonplace for the English to have an engagement ring, but since we never had a true engagement, I thought it would suit for a hand fastin'."

She held out her hand for Conner to slip it onto her ring finger. "Conner, it's beautiful. I don't even know what to say."

"Sayin' that ye like it is good enough for me." He placed his lips against the stone on her hand. "I told ye once, at New Year's, that you were my emerald queen and now I've made it so."

"Oh, Conner, I do love you so."

"Ach, I did no' tell ye how lovely ye look tonight. No' a verra good start."

"It's quite all right. You've seen me in this dress before anyway."

He frowned. "No, I do no' believe I have."

"Well, it looks different now. Maisie altered it to make it suitable."

"Ach, Maisie's a good lass."

"She is. I dare say she's become my truest confidant here."

He clutched his hand to his heart. "Charlotte, ye wound me!"

She giggled over the rim of her cup. "Oh, do stop. There are some things that need to be sorted out with a fellow woman! It's nothing against you."

"Aye, I suppose I have no fear o' Maisie takin' my place."

"And you shouldn't."

He glanced down at her plate, food still partially untouched. "Are ye no' hungry?"

Charlotte shrugged. "I suppose I don't have that much of an appetite."

"Is there somethin' else ye'd like? Quail? Stew? A beef pie? Cook has gone to great lengths to prepare everythin' in the highlands."

"No, I'm just a bit nervous, to tell you the truth."

"Nervous? Love, we're already wed, the time to be nervous is gone!" he said with a chuckle.

Charlotte blushed, her face slowly turning the shade of the ring upon her hand. "I was nervous for the wedding part and now I'm nervous for what comes next."

He paused, all mirth gone. "Charlotte, do no fret so. I'll no' force ye or frighten ye in anyway. Nothin' needs to be done this night."

"I know that, but it doesn't mean I can't be a bit nervous."

"We'll learn together, aye?" He brushed her flushed cheek with his hand. "For now, just enjoy your weddin'. The gifts will come soon and that's a rare sight."

"Gifts?"

"Aye, the chieftains o' the other lands, and some o' my more senior warriors, bring and send tokens to show their acceptance o' the match and their loyalty."

"How generous. It is such short notice, though."

"I sent messengers out as soon as I knew ye'd be bound to me." He glanced again at her plate. "Are ye sure you can no' eat somethin'?"

"I don't think I have the stomach for it," she said, playing with a small flower that fell from her hair.

"Perhaps ye have room for somethin' sweet?"

Her lips curled into a small smile. "That depends. What kind of sweets?"

He grabbed the arm of a passing kitchen boy, murmuring orders to him before releasing him. Conner turned back to Charlotte and, again, topped off her glass. "I can no' have ye faintin' from lack o' food at your own party. Besides, with naught in your belly, ye'd fall down drunk soon."

Maids began clearing away empty plates, cheerfully filling goblets and dodging the wayward hands that snatched at the pitchers of drink. The band still played with amazing joviality, playing up to the mood of the crowd and taking requests from drunken men who sang along with gusto, their voices uneven and pitchy.

Once the tables were reasonably cleared, they began bringing in desserts on silver platters. The array surprised Charlotte who made a mental note to give a gift of thanks to the cook when the wedding was through. Cups of fresh raspberry cranachan were placed before the guests, tart berries sweetened by heavy cream. Beside them came bread pudding, small carrot cakes drizzled with icing, apple scones, traditional bannocks, and shortbread cookies. Lastly cups of hot chocolate joined the dishes, which made the people gasp in delight.

"Quite the spread, aye?" Conner asked, heaping desserts upon a plate for her.

She took a sip of the hot chocolate. "Cook has outdone herself, really."

"Aye, that she has. I'm glad to see ye eat somethin', even if it is naught but sugary sweets."

"If I don't, I fear the wine will go straight to my head entirely."

"Do no' worry, you're quite charmin' when drunk." He grinned, popping a raspberry into his mouth.

"I'm not drunk," she said primly. Although, her head did feel a bit thick and her limbs slow and heavy. "I'm merely…tipsy."

He chuckled. "Tipsy? Is that what the proper ladies call it?"

"That's what *I* call it, and I have not been a proper lady as of late."

Shaking his head, Conner motioned forward one of his men, a skinny man called Tom, who held a fur-wrapped parcel. "Is that the first o' the offerings, then?"

"Aye." Tom bowed slightly and unwrapped his package to show a substantial broadsword. "The Macgregor sends his regards." The sword was then removed and a steady stream of gifts began.

"I think this one's for ye," Conner whispered to Charlotte as a small chest was opened to reveal a pile of freshwater pearls.

"From the lord o' the eastern ports," Tom

explained. "And this next one is from the Callaghans."

Dozens of packages were laid before them in turn, joining each other in a pile out of the way of the guests; jewels, a saddle, weapons, spices, and two new horses were added to the stable. Charlotte was overwhelmed by the ostentatious show of wealth and homage paid to Conner. In England, a newly married couple might receive a small monetary gift or one that was baby-themed in hopes of a child.

"Goodness, you must be rather well-liked," Charlotte whispered over the rim of her goblet.

"No' more than any other chieftain," he said, stretching in his seat. "I barely slept a wink last night for nerves."

Charlotte released a rather unladylike snort. "You, nervous? I don't believe it."

"Aye. It's no' every day a man marries. It can be quite the nerve-wracking experience."

Charlotte finished her fifth, or perhaps his sixth, glass of wine and found it nearly impossible to keep Conner's face in focus. To steady herself, and him, she pressed a hand to his face, frustrated when he still seemed to move about as if underwater. "Do stop moving. You look like you're about to melt into a puddle on the floor."

"Is that so?" he asked, brows raised in amusement.

"Aye," Charlotte replied in a serious, practiced brogue.

"We'll make a highlander out o' ye yet, lass."

Charlotte scanned the merry crowd. Ian sat on

the floor sharing cakes with his dog, Big Angus led a group in a jaunty jig, and Flora was tucked away in a corner, holding court with Jasper who looked at her quite tenderly. She briefly wondered if they could sneak away without anyone noticing. Surely they were all very preoccupied with drink and dace and wouldn't realize they were gone until they were quite hidden away in their rooms.

"Conner." Charlotte's voice was a loud whisper as she drunkenly attempted to be sly. "Let's go upstairs. We'll make a quick getaway while everyone is distracted."

"Ye do no' wish to stay at your own hand fastin' feast?"

"I just want to slip out before anyone sees us. I don't really want a whole parade up to the bedroom." Charlotte leaned in closer. "Also, I'm quite drunk."

"That ye are." He laughed. "We'll go down to the kitchens and take the servants' stairs up to our rooms."

"All right, just be very quiet. Like a mouse." Charlotte stood up faster than expected, promptly knocking over her small throne, creating a loud crash that echoed in the halls. She grimaced when she saw all eyes on her.

"Just like a wee mouse." Conner tipped his glass to her, an amused smirk on his lips.

"Time for the beddin'?" a boisterous voice called out.

"The beddin'!" roared the crowd in response.

"Oh, dash it all," Charlotte said, scowling at Conner.

He stood from his seat, much more gracefully than she. "Come, wife. Might as well get the dog and pony show over with, aye?"

"I suppose," Charlotte grumbled, taking his arm with one hand and the half-full pitcher of wine with the other.

The guests crowded around them, yelling in Gaelic and patting Conner on the shoulder. Charlotte squashed against Conner as the crowd propelled them up the stairs—a jolly, if not very drunk, group of Scots. Even timid Gwen participated in the revelry in her own way, holding on the small train of Charlotte's dress to stop people from trotting on the hem.

"I'll take it from here," Conner announced at his chamber's door. "Please, return downstairs. All that food is no' goin' to eat itself!" He pushed the door open and pulled Charlotte inside, barring the door behind them, firm to the jovial knocking of the guests.

"I spilled my wine." Charlotte frowned, sitting straight on the floor with a now empty decanter.

Conner laughed and pulled off his boots and stockings before heaving her up and helping her take a seat in a chair by the fire. "Do no' fear, wife, I've had some brought up for us, but I think ye might drink some water instead." He went to a small side table that was piled with cakes, cheeses, meat, and bread, and poured Charlotte a fresh glass of water. As soon as she had her lips upon the glass, Conner brought his hands to her hair, delicately removing each flower and vine from her tresses.

"Keep some for me, please? I'd like to press

some in a book."

"O' course." He put aside the least crumpled and moved to her bridal sash. "We'll keep this for ye in the wardrobe." That was removed and laid upon the free chair. "And now your slippers." The pair was placed carefully on the floor and he unrolled each silk stocking, placing a kiss on each calf as he bared it.

Charlotte, who was slowly sobering, began to realize where this slow undressing was leading them. "Are we going to go to bed now?"

"If ye wish," he replied quietly, still crouched on the floor before her.

"Will you help me undo my dress?" she asked in a voice much braver than she felt.

Conner stood and helped her up, turning her around to begin unbuttoning her dress. When the gown fell to the floor, his fingers began a careful ministration of her corset's ribbon. Her shift came last, thrown to the floor to join the rest of her discarded garments. She was left in naught but her emeralds.

"You are even more beautiful as my wife. I did no' know it was possible," Conner murmured into her hair.

Charlotte turned to face him. She trained her gaze at his striking face as her hands deftly unhooked his belt, allowing his broadsword to fall to the ground. Once his crest was unpinned, the kilt slipped from his shoulder, leaving his pressed linen shirt as the final barrier between them. He pulled it off himself, his lips finding hers the moment his head was freed.

Carefully, he gathered Charlotte up in his arms, laying her gently atop of his bed. The blue and gold silks were cold upon her back and she welcomed his heat beside her. He laid alongside her, running his hand from her neck to thigh, a satisfied smile on his lips. "I do no' think I could be happier. Ever since I saw ye, I dreamed of seein' ye in naught but jewels."

"Glad I could be of service," Charlotte said, fingering the emerald at her neck.

Conner's blue eyes raked her naked body and he made a small, choked sound in his throat before pulling her closer, his mouth finding hers in an instant. He tasted of wine and his hands caressed every curve of her figure. She felt herself grow wet and her already clouded mind seemed to detach from her body as she let herself be taken over by pleasure.

"We do no' have to do everythin' tonight."

Charlotte dragged her fingers through his hair. "I want to. I *need* to." It was true. While before he denied her out of his desire to only bed his wife, now there was nothing to stop them from consummating their passions.

His lips searched her body, making their way from the hollow of her neck to the swell of her breasts. Her breath nearly left her body as Conner cupped one heavy breast in his hand and began gently teasing her nipple with his thumb, making her moan in pleasure. He glanced up at her, shooting her a dimpled grin.

"Ye make the most bonny sound when you're pleased."

Her cheeks pinked. "Don't tease me just now, please."

"No teasin'. I like it." Conner leaned up into a crouch and pulled Charlotte by the hip, positioning himself between her creamy thighs.

Charlotte's heart thumped in her chest, waiting, wanting more. She swallowed, glancing down at the hard member pressed against her skin, wondering how something so large could fit inside her. Tentatively, she reached a hand down to stroke it. Much like before, the soft firmness surprised her and Conner groaned as her grip tightened.

"Charlotte, if ye go on as ye are, it'll be over before it's begun," he said, moving her hand away and kissing her palm. "We'll go slow, aye? Ye'll tell me if ye want me to stop."

She hushed him, squirming beneath his comforting weight. "Conner, I can't wait any longer."

"Ye'll wait just a moment more." His fingers found her warm core, slick with her arousal and tender to the touch. "You are so wet, Charlotte, so ready."

She gasped as he brushed against her most sensitive spot. Grinding against his hand, she felt the delicious sensation of release almost upon her. "Oh, God, Conner, I can't take it anymore. I need you now!"

She closed her eyes, moaning in frustration as his fingers stopped their manipulations. But soon the vacancy was filled in the form of his rigidity against her sex. The wait was torture. In desperation she pulled at his shoulders, wrapping her legs around his muscular hips, willing him to enter her. She was rewarded with the slow feeling of his hardness entering her. Each inch was a mixture of pain and delicious pleasure.

"Are ye all right?" Conner asked as he was firmly, and completely sheathed to the hilt.

She slowly opened her eyes, squirming a bit to the unaccustomed feeling of fullness. "Why did you stop?"

"I did no' wish to hurt ye."

"Please, keep going."

Conner pressed his lips tenderly to hers, beginning a steady rhythm that quickened with each thrust. Charlotte moved against him in time, her body taking on a primal beat that matched his. The concerto of desire hastened, as did her breath. When she felt herself at the edge of desire, she called out for him, her nails raking the tanned skin of his strong back, feeling each muscle as he moved within her. He released his seed inside her with one last powerful thrust. They collapsed into each other's arms, joined fully at last.

Conner lay beside Charlotte, pulling her onto his chest and stroking her auburn curls, breath still shallow with lust. "I did no' hurt ye?"

"Just a little," Charlotte admitted. She stretched a bit, moving her oddly sore muscles. "But I did rather enjoy myself."

"Is that so?"

"Just a little," she teased, nestling closer into the comfort of his shoulder.

"Well, if this is what it is to be a husband, I think I like it a great deal."

"I do hope you like being a husband much more than for just what happens in the bedroom."

"Aye, I'd like bein' a husband just as much in the library, at the loch, in the stables—"

Charlotte reached up a hand, silencing him with a laugh. "Goodness! Please stop."

"Fine, then," Conner said, nipping at her fingers. "Then I suppose I'll have to settle with bein' a husband again in the bedroom."

"You are an insatiable cad!" She laughed as she batted his roaming hand away.

"Aye, that's why ye married me."

"Aye," Charlotte replied playfully, hitching one leg over his torso, coming to a stop above him. "That's why I did."

Chapter Twenty-Six

Richard dumped the contents of his tin cup into the fire, disgusted at the hired soldier's poor attempts at tea. For the past week they had been wandering the damp countryside, waiting for word from the British authorities. Richard had come to Scotland expecting to leave with the Holloway girl, but the insolent boy who sat upon his chair playing 'king' rebuffed his legal rights to her.

Now he was trapped in the soaking countryside where even the moss grew moss and the cows were better educated than their masters. The whole situation would have been comical if it were not so insulting.

"Howard, we found someone." One of the men entered his private encampment, lit by the small fire. "A girl who says she wants to talk to you."

"What girl?" Richard asked. "It's not Charlotte Holloway?"

"No, sir. She says she worked for the Scot. She won't leave the camp without talking to you."

"Fine, fine." Richard heaved himself off the rock

he sat on and followed the man into the main camp where a girl sat alone by the fire, observing his approach with a blank look upon her face. The woman was young, pleasantly plump, and could pass for attractive if she had a good bath. She was positively covered in grime.

"Richard Howard?" She squinted up at him.

"The same. And you are?"

"Nettie. I worked in the MacLeod's castle."

"Oh? And why are you out here? And why search me out?"

"I did no' mean to search ye out. I just came upon the camp on accident. But, when I heard who the men worked for, I knew I needed to speak with ye."

"And why is that?"

"I know ye came for the English girl and I want her gone just as bad as ye want her to go."

He raised a pointed brow. "Any particular reason?"

"I want the MacLeod and that English whore stole him from me," she answered simply. "I tried killin' her, but the MacLeod found me out before the deed was done."

"You tried murdering her and he just let you go?" Richard wasn't fully aware of all the Scottish customs, but he was sure that MacLeod wouldn't just allow a murderer to roam free, even if she was obviously deranged.

"O' course no'. The MacLeod does no' look kindly at poisoners. Charlotte Holloway spirited me away and made me promise I'd leave the lands for good."

Richard let out an exasperated sigh. "So she helped you. What does this have to do with me and my efforts to reclaim my property?"

"Ye did no' ask how she got me past the guards." Nettie grinned, showing off a mouth of crooked teeth.

"I'm growing rather bored of your games. If you have something to offer me, speak now."

"I can get ye into the castle. I know a secret passageway that no one ever uses. Ye can slip in with no one bein' the wiser and steal back the English whore. Ye'd be long gone before anyone knew she was gone."

"And what would you want in return for your services?"

"No more than her gone so I might get back the MacLeod and make him love me again." Nettie's voice was calm and smooth, her face a mask of tranquil amusement.

Richard could assume she would never be allowed inside that castle again, but thought better against telling her the truth of her possibilities. As long as she was true to her word about the passageway, he couldn't give a damn what happened to her afterward. He held out a thin hand. "My dear Miss Nettie, I do believe this is the beginning of a beautiful relationship."

Chapter Twenty-Seven

Charlotte had no idea she could ever be this happy, especially not in marriage, if they truly *were* married. All right then, happy in hand fasting. She had left England in a hurry, with barely the clothes on her back, and now she was the wife of a Scottish king with all the power and notoriety that followed. It was all terribly exciting. And, even better, she was positively besotted with Conner in a way she never thought possible.

She smiled at his sleeping form, lit slightly by the early morning sunlight that seeped in around the window dressings. He looked so peaceful there; his golden hair lay strewn around his face, tanned and unlined with the health of youth. His lashes were dark, dark enough to make any lady jealous of his God-given charms. Conner slept soundly like a man fully trusting in the warriors who guarded his gates, confident in their loyalty and their love for him.

"Charlotte," Conner mumbled into his pillow, "are ye just goin' to ogle me all mornin' or is there a reason for your starin'?"

Charlotte pursed her lips, embarrassed at being caught. "I wasn't staring at you."

"You are no' a good liar, lass." He yawned, stretching like a cat.

"I'm not lying. I've just woken up, as well."

"Lies. Ye've been studyin' a good while now."

She pursed her lips and slipped from bed, taking one last look at her husband's shirtless torso, brawny limbs spread among the furs and blankets. Noticing the tenderness between her legs as she went into to the bathroom, she blushed, recalling the events of the previous night. They had been married a short five days, but as soon as the bedroom door was closed behind them each evening, they would immediately fall into each other's arms, stopping only for drink. Finally, when they were both exhausted, they would spend the rest of the night in a dreamless sleep.

Charlotte donned her silk dressing robe and sat at her small, mirrored table and began to sort out her tangled hair. The new clock on her dresser read almost nine in the morning and there was already too much to do. Today was the day the warriors and the other high-ranking men of the highlands came to reaffirm their allegiance to Conner. While everything was mostly taken care of by the team of maids, it was Charlotte's first official function as Lady MacLeod.

"Lady MacLeod." She shuddered at the sound of her new title.

"Gawkin' at me all night and now talkin' to yourself. Should I worry about ye?" Conner asked from the bed.

"Don't tease," she ordered, dragging a comb through her hair. "And do hurry and get dressed. You have to be presentable soon."

"I've naught to do but don a kilt and shamble down at some point."

"You must look respectable or I'll seem like a terrible wife who can't take care of her husband."

"Ye take care o' me right fine. Need I remind you o' last night?" Conner came up behind her, kissing the tip of her head and taking an ivory brush from the table, dragging it through his shoulder-length hair. "I'll dress now and go downstairs to see how thing are shapin' up for today. I'll meet ye in the throne room when ye're ready, aye?"

***

Charlotte entered the great hall in a pale gown of dove gray, the MacLeod tartan wrapped like a sash and her emerald earrings firmly on display. To top off the affair, Conner had sent Maisie up with a peculiar headdress to wear in order to show her station to the clan. It was rather plain, but beautifully made—a thin silver circlet of entwining cords of metal. They twisted about with small diamonds inserted intermittently and caught the light in a rather spectacular way.

As she glided toward the raised thrones, she felt much like she did on the day of her hand fasting. Conner stood upon her entrance in his usual plaid, smiling as she approached. On either side of her the men of the clan bowed to her as she passed, the women dropping into small curtsies. While

Conner's people had always been respectful toward her, the new reverence given to her as Lady McLeod was something almost unbelievable.

After Charlotte had been seated at the throne to Conner's right, the day proceeded largely in Gaelic, a language she only knew a few choice words in. Servants crept in and out, passing goblets of spiced wine, leaving Charlotte little to do but watch and drink. And as the day progressed, she felt stifled by her corsets and thick with alcohol.

"Conner." She leaned in toward him as the proceedings paused. "Could I leave a moment to get some air?"

"Are ye all right?"

"Yes, I just need to stretch my legs a bit."

He brought her knuckles to his lips. "Do no' worry about hurryin' back. Ye've made an appearance. But I'll see ye at supper, aye?"

"Of course," she answered with a small smile. When she stood to leave, all eyes focused on her and the curtsies and bowing followed her from the room.

As soon as she was back in the empty hallway, she decided to go back to her rooms and freshen up. Her slippers pinched her toes and she wished she had listened to Maisie and forwent the tight stays, but her old British habits remained. Her footsteps echoed through the deserted corridors and she rather liked having a moment to herself. Since the hand fasting, she had been given the task of caring for some of the larger decisions of the home—how many barrels of whiskey to set aside for trade, what to order from the larger ports that couldn't be made at the keep, and even some disputes between the servants.

She was looking forward to a short hour or two in silence with a book when an arm gripped her about the middle, violently pulling her into a doorway. She opened her mouth to scream but a hand slapped over her lips, forcing the sound back into her throat. She tried to kick her assailant, but another set of hands grabbed her feet.

The sound of a match made her pause. Her eyes adjusted to the new light in the darkness and she saw the tiny flame illuminate a familiar pointed face.

"Hello, Miss Holloway." Richard Howard sneered. "So nice of you to join us."

Chapter Twenty-Eight

Charlotte struggled against the two men who held her, trussed up like a freshly slaughtered boar. As they carried her down a narrow set of stairs, she realized they were going down into the dungeons. A ball of cloth had been shoved into her mouth, stifling another attempt at summoning help. Her hands and feet were bound, almost fully immobilizing her. Charlotte had wished, desperately, that she had taken Conner up on his offer of a sharp lady's knife and lessons on how to wield one.

Oh, Conner! She quietly grieved, wondering how long it would take for someone to notice her absence. He had told her not to hurry back and probably wouldn't even realize she was gone for many hours. Even more frightening was her unknown fate. Was Richard angry enough to toss her off the cliffs to be shattered on the rocks below? Would he spirit her back to England, dumping her in a vile sanitarium for wayward women? Would he ransom her back to Conner? That was certainly the most desirable option, but also the most unlikely.

While they continued their terrible journey in the dark, she questioned how Richard had found this passageway. While it wasn't necessarily a closely guarded secret, Conner made it seem that only a few knew of it—his family for the sake of safety in the event of a siege, her and…

Charlotte felt herself grow sick. She had shown the mad maid Nettie the way from the castle to save her life. While farfetched, the idea of Nettie and Richard making a shadowy alliance, plotting her ruin, seemed more and more likely. The maid had tried to poison her and failed. If someone else were on hand to take care of the matter, Charlotte was sure Nettie would take advantage of the fact.

As they came upon the mouth of the cave, Charlotte was unceremoniously dumped upon the damp floor, her headpiece falling from her loose hair. The men gathered around the mouth of the exit, pausing every so often to glance at her, as if to size her up. She reached up her tied hands and pulled the cloth from her mouth, letting loose a frantic scream that she hoped would echo through the caverns and corridors of the dungeons, somehow reaching some of the MacLeod warriors.

"Do something about her," Richard ordered, pushing one of his men toward her. "She's getting on my nerves."

Charlotte snapped at the hand as it neared her. "Don't touch me! Conner! Help!" She shrieked.

"Shut her up. But leave no marks. I cannot have my bride looking like a bruised peach on her wedding day," Richard said with a smirk.

Charlotte gasped, her blood running cold in her veins. She was just about to call out for help again when something hard came down upon her head, leaving her world black.

Chapter Twenty-Nine

Charlotte came to with a splitting headache. The world spun and she almost feared opening her eyes. When she did muster the strength, she opened them to darkness, making her panic for a moment before she realized she was in the midst of pitch-black night. Upon further investigation, as much as one might accomplish in such a state, she found herself draped over the back of a horse, her head thumping against the beast's side. The reality of her situation washed over her like a freezing bath, and although the gag had fallen from her mouth, she stifled a scream.

She knew that if she were to escape, it wouldn't be while traveling on the back of a horse, surrounded by armed guards. The flight would occur at night when the men rested or perhaps when she asked for a private moment to relieve herself among the sparse trees. But, then, she still wouldn't know where she was or how to get back to the castle.

She closed her eyes again, hoping none of them

noticed her quick assessment of her current location. What she once loved about the calming, steady landscape of Scotland, she now hated. All the hills, valleys, and homes looked exactly alike, especially in the almost full darkness, giving no sign as to her exact position.

Acting on a whim, Charlotte slowly moved her hands up to her ear, unhooking the heavy emerald and dropping it to the ground. She hoped, against all odds, that someone would soon notice her missing and scouts would be released onto the countryside to find her. As they changed direction again, she released another earing, lamenting her choice to not wear the necklace as well. She could have pulled each stone, if need be, but there was no point in mourning what could have been.

"Is that it, then?" a gruff voice near her legs asked.

"That's it." Richard's words seemed to have come from above her somewhere. She assumed he must have been upon his own horse. "We're expected and rooms in the old cloister have been made ready for us."

She opened her eyes a sliver to see lights in the distance. As they grew closer, she could make out a steeple and clusters of burial stones scattered about them. Her worst fears were confirmed: Richard was going to marry her with or without her permission. But certainly no priest worth his cloth would marry an *already* married woman to another man! Conner had assured her that being hand fasted was as good as being married in Scotland, especially to a man of his rank and standing.

When they reached the steps, the church doors opened, flooding the lawn with bright candlelight. A squat man came to the landing. "Are ye the man called Howard?"

"Richard Howard," he replied. "And I assume you're the one called Father Mack?"

"Aye, the same. Is that the lass, then? She looks dead."

Charlotte heard Richard dismount from his house and step toward her. He gripped the back of her hair firmly, making her wince as he lifted it to face him. He bent down to level with her. She gave in, opening her eyes, looking into his own wicked ones. "She's alive." Richard dropped her head, and walked over to the priest, giving him a roll of banknotes from inside his jacket. "A donation, of course."

"O' course," the priest agreed, pocketing his fee. "Ye can put the lass in one o' the containment rooms. The lad will show ye the way."

A small boy took his cue, silently motioning for the British guests to follow him. Charlotte was dragged from the horse, silently cursing the crooked priest for his weakness. The ties binding her feet were severed, leaving her to walk on her own, and she was shepherded inside the church by two burly Englishmen. She tried catching the eye of Father Mack in one last attempt at a wordless prayer for salvation, but the priest sat back in the pew, counting his payment.

The boy led them down the chapel, through several doors, and down a long hallway to a small room that held a single bed, a washbasin, and a large crucifix. Charlotte was shoved inside, scraping her knees through her gown as she hit the rough stone floor.

"Pity that dress shall be tarnished for tomorrow's festivities," Richard said from the open doorway, a look of bored displeasure on his face. "I'll see if I can find something more suitable, but I suppose that may have to do."

"Are you mad?" Charlotte asked, pulling herself to her feet. "What are you doing, kidnapping me and bringing me here for forced marriage? I've already been wed!"

He let out a laugh, a sound dusty from disuse. "Stupid girl, you've not been properly wed. Your nuptials weren't witnessed in a house of God, your names weren't announced in the London papers for prosperity, and you certainly didn't get your father's permission."

"My father wouldn't give his permission for you to treat me so monstrously. Just let me go free, Richard, and all will be well."

"Go free? Hardly an option. I told you some time ago that I intended to make you my wife and I'm a man of my word. I could have gone home after that Scot humiliated me, but his refusal of submission made it all the more personal. Getting you as my wife and making him wifeless is certainly a win-win for me."

"I've lain with him!" Charlotte announced in one last burst of bravery. If he refused to acknowledge her marriage to Conner, she hoped her admission of carnal knowledge would be enough to dissuade him. "I'm no longer a maid!"

Richard shrugged. "No matter. You've been selected for your capability to bear sons, not for your virginity. While I would have rather liked taking your maidenhead, I'll live without it. Perhaps I'll even still make you bleed."

She felt bile rise in her throat at the thought of Richard touching her. "I'd rather die than be your wife."

"Well, we can't have you go off and kill yourself now, can we?" He produced a worn iron key. "I'll just keep you nice and safe in here so no harm comes to you."

"Please." Charlotte turned her attention to one of Richard's hired men. "I'm Lady MacLeod now, and my husband has great wealth. Release me and I'll see to it that you're not prosecuted for your part in this and that you're handsomely rewarded."

The man scratched at his pockmarked chin. "Sorry, misses, but I've signed a contract. Wife or no wife, I work for Richard Howard."

Richard's look of victory was replaced with a dissatisfied frown. "You know, I've rather forgot something. If you've lain with the Scot, you might already be carrying his heathen bastard. We can't have that." He turned to the pockmarked man, motioning toward his lower navel. "Hit her in the stomach, hard, just here. That should shake any Scottish filth loose."

Charlotte paled, sitting back on the bed in disbelief, her hand on her stomach. She hadn't thought about the possibility of a baby until then. If she were carrying Conner's child, she could not let any harm come to it. "Please, I'm begging you."

Richard nodded. "I do regret things have come to this. Make sure you land a few good hits, just to be certain. I can't stand the sight of blood, so I'll retire to my chambers. Lock up behind you." He passed the key to the pockmarked man and turned on his heel, leaving without another word.

"You don't need to do this," Charlotte said hurriedly, drawing her knees to her chest. "You could let me go and I could leave without a word."

The man looked behind him, then back at her, leaning in closer. "I can't let you go, but I also can't hit a lady, especially not a pregnant one."

She let out a sigh of relief. "Thank you."

"If Howard asks, pretend. Say I hit you lots and you're in a bad state."

Charlotte spotted a bit of humanity. "Of course. I'll put on a good show and tell him that, Mister…"

"Chester," he offered.

"I'll tell him that you beat me fiercely. Although, I must ask, how did you come to be involved in such a severe crime? You must know how terrible this all is?"

Chester swallowed, suddenly looking rather weary. "Look, misses, I know what you're up to and I'm not a fool. You're lucky Howard asked me to beat you and not one of the others. I have to lock you up now."

"Chester, please. Don't."

"I'm sorry."

The door slammed shut with the sound of grating finality. Locked in the dark, in a cold, windowless room, Charlotte could not see any way out of her horrifying predicament. The door was solid, as was each brick that made up the wall. After several hours of crying, praying, and pleading, Charlotte fell into an exhausted sleep, wrapped tightly in her MacLeod plaid.

Chapter Thirty

Charlotte awoke to the scraping of her jail cell door opening, letting dim light into the room. Her head throbbed with each heartbeat and her stomach churned in dread. One of Richard's men silently slid a plate of bread and hard cheese into the room with a tin cup of water. She waited until the man had left again before consuming her meager meal.

She looked around the room with new eyes, hoping to see a secret escape hatch she hadn't noticed before. The walls were still just as solid, the door still just as locked, the small barred window still just as sturdy as it was the night before. She had just fastened both hands to the narrow bars, using her feet as leverage to get a good pull, when the door slammed open to reveal an uninterested looking Richard Howard.

"Interrupting, am I?" he asked, taking her in.

Charlotte glared at her keeper, dropping her hands. "What do you want?"

"Is that any way to speak to your husband on your wedding day? Charlotte, you wound me."

"If only," she mumbled.

"I do wish you didn't look like such a wild woman," he said, glancing at her tangled hair and dirty dress wrapped in plaid. Richard crossed the room and tore the tartan sash over her head, tossing it to one of the men behind him. "We won't be needing that ridiculous table cloth any longer."

Charlotte fought back new tears as she watched one of the men pocket her pin, obviously thinking of how much it might fetch him. "Richard, you needn't do this. You could go back to London and marry some other girl and leave me be."

"Aren't you bored of this conversation? Haven't you anything else to say?" He clucked in mock sympathy. "Why is every woman in my life so empty-headed? Would it kill you to have a decent conversation?"

"I shan't until I'm freed." She crossed her arms in a show of finality, slyly slipping her emerald ring from her finger and slipping it into her bodice. They had taken her pin and tartan. She would be damned if they got her ring as well.

He grimaced. "At least wipe that awful scowl off your face. I won't be having my guests see such a sour bride."

"Guests, what guests?"

Richard nonchalantly waved a hand. "Oh, just a few English friends, come in to see the happy occasion. Now, will you walk willingly to the chapel, or must I have someone carry you like an impudent child?"

Charlotte looked up at the dozen men behind Richard and caught Chester's eye. He looked away.

"I suppose I'll just walk," she answered, bringing herself up to full height. She hoped she looked more like the strong wife of a brave warrior king and less like a lamb on its way to the slaughterhouse.

She knew she needed to find a way to escape Richard, and the church, but time was running out. She assumed that the priest would marry them regardless of how resolutely she denied the marriage. Her only hope was to find a free moment when she wasn't being watched. Perhaps she would even have to marry Richard before her chance came. If she could make it back to Conner, he'd set things right. He, himself, said that the British laws meant nothing in his lands and, although she was in a Scottish church, there were dozens of highland witnesses to their hand fasting. Certainly he would have the power to void her forced nuptials. The weight on Charlotte's heart lifted. She could see a possible way out.

"Why are you smiling?" Richard asked suspiciously.

Charlotte brought a hand to her lips. "Am I? I hadn't noticed."

He grunted, grabbing an arm and pulling her along, down the hallways and toward the chapel they had walked through the previous evening.

The somber sound of a well-tuned organ wafted through the corridors making it feel less like a wedding and more like the funeral it was. When they entered the door next to the altar, the hired men all took seats in the pews, making up a rather gloomy guest list. Charlotte was dragged before the priest who looked at her intently over a pair of half spectacles.

"Do you know who I am?" Charlotte asked Father Mack.

"Oh, not this again," Richard grumbled, seeming fed up with her behavior.

"Aye, ye ran from your womanly duties and he's brought ye back to be wed," the priest answered.

"But I'm already married!" she cried. "I am wed to Conner MacLeod!"

The priest gasped, looking toward Richard. "Ye bring me a married woman who belongs to the *MacLeod*? Are ye mad?"

Richard picked a piece of lint off his jacket, rather unaffected by the Father's obvious concern. "Not married, merely sealed, or whatever it is those heathens do. She was never wed in a proper church."

"We were hand fasted," Charlotte explained, seeing a glimmer of hope in the shape of Father Mack's frightened face. "I was hand fasted to Conner Macleod several days past. He'll know I'm missing by now, and come for me."

The priest looked as if he had swallowed something foul. "I can no' do this. The MacLeod will have my hide."

Richard reddened. "Now, see here! I've paid you good money to marry us, and marry us you will! I have the proper paperwork from the high court of London and her father's permission. We *will* be wed!"

Father Mack bit a lip, obviously recalling the rather generous donation Richard had given him upon arrival. "Ye'll leave as soon as I marry ye?

Leave Scotland and never say a word that I was the one who wed ye?"

"Of course. I wouldn't stay in this soggy hellhole another night if you paid me a king's ransom." Richard reached into his pocket and shoved a crumpled pile of papers into the priest's hands. "Here are the legal documents proving my claim."

"But the courts of England have no standing in Scotland!" Charlotte cried, hoping against all odds the priest would refuse Richard's orders out of respect, or fear, for Conner.

Father Mack flipped through the papers and handed them off to an altar boy. "I did no' see anythin' from the lass's father."

Richard smiled. "Don't fear, I have her father here and he'll certainly support my claims."

Charlotte gasped, feeling her knees weaken. "My father? He's here? Does he have any idea what you've done?"

"What I've done is save you from ruin and your family from public embarrassment," Richard said before motioning toward the church's front doors. "Bring them in."

A man opened the front doors letting a pleased-looking George Holloway, Duke of Glenwood, enter followed by a thin Abigail who certainly looked as if she would rather be anywhere else. Her eyes widened as she saw Charlotte's bruised and dirtied state.

"Charlotte, my dear!" George hurried up the aisle, arms outstretched. "Thank the Lord that Richard found you!"

"Father, you don't understand, I—" Her father

threw both arms around her, silencing her with a rib-crushing embrace.

"Oh, Charlotte, we thought we lost you to the wilderness for good. When Richard wrote to say he had a plan to rescue you, I could scarcely believe it." George held back a few unmanly croaks of emotion.

Charlotte untangled herself from her father's arms. "He didn't rescue me, he kidnapped me!"

"See, George?" Richard's voice was smooth, even, and tinged with pity. "She was with the Scots for far too long. They've managed to convince her that *we* are the enemy. Poor girl."

"Charlotte, are you all right?" Abigail stepped forward. "You're not hurt?"

"Not badly. Richard had me knocked over the head into unconsciousness when he abducted me." She grasped her stepmother's hands, lowering her voice. "Abigail, please, I must escape. I can't marry him."

"Let's get on with it," Richard said, checking his timepiece. "We have a train to catch shortly."

"George, you really must talk to Charlotte," Abigail told her husband.

"There's nothing to talk about. When we get back to civilization she'll see a fine physician to undo all the Scottish brainwashing." George patted Richard on the back. "If it weren't for good old Richard, we might have lost our girl for good."

"Father, please, I can't marry Richard," Charlotte begged. "He's an evil brute. I want to stay here with Conner and his clan."

"Disgusting." The duke sneered. "You have a

perfectly good man willing to marry you, ruined or not, and you still are so delusional that you think staying in Scotland is the best choice."

"Father, I've married Conner. We've been hand fasted, which is as good as married. I'm Lady MacLeod now in a proper way with lands, a title, and someone who loves me. Isn't that enough?" Charlotte felt the tears roll down her cheeks, staining her torn silk gown.

George shook his head, looking at Richard with a great deal of sadness in his eyes. "You said that she would be unwell, but I had no idea how badly her time in Scotland would have affected her. She's almost beyond help."

Richard squeezed his friend's shoulder compassionately. "Don't worry, my dear man, once she's out of Scotland, properly wedded, she'll be back to her old self."

"I do hope you're right." George blew his nose into an embroidered handkerchief.

"Can we get on with it now?" Father Mack cut in. He tapped his foot below the hem of his robe, obviously anxious to get the entire ordeal over with.

"Of course, of course." George nodded, taking Abigail's arm. "Come, let's sit down."

"No, George." Abigail pulled her arm from his grasp, going to stand beside Charlotte. "I can't agree to this match. You've been blinded by Richard and his lies, but I know better."

The Duke of Glenwood blustered. "What, what, what! Abigail, sit down immediately."

Abigail's lips pursed. "You brought me here under the pretense of visiting Charlotte and now I find you're going to forcefully marry her off to Richard who is nothing but a false brute."

"George!" Richard clutched his chest. "Your wife's words wound me."

The duke looked between Abigail and Charlotte, unsure of what to do or who to correct first. "Abigail, I've been a good husband to you, and you a dutiful wife. Charlotte is ill and needs to be taken back to England for treatment. She was seduced by a trickster and—"

"No!" Charlotte stomped her foot. "Stop talking about me like I'm not here! I'm *not* ill, I *wasn't* seduced, and I *won't* marry Richard! He's hit me before on the night or our so-called engagement when he tried to take physical liberties with me and I refused his advances. If you force this marriage, you'll be signing me away for a lifetime of pain and humiliation."

"You want to talk about humiliation?" George's sadness was quickly turning to fury. "You ran off in the middle of the night with a Scot without a word, leaving us to wonder if you were dead or alive!"

"That's not true," Abigail interjected. "I knew she was leaving and she did so with my blessing. I saw Richard for what he really is—a monster. I needed to save Charlotte from the life I was obligated to live for far too long. If you force this marriage, I'll divorce you."

George's mouth gaped open, flapping about like a fish out of water. "You'll *divorce* me?"

Abigail nodded. "I will. I can't stand by and watch you lead a lamb to slaughter."

Richard threw his hands up in the air. "Enough!

All I'm trying to do it make an honest woman out of your stupid whore of a daughter and you're debating it as if she has other options!"

"Stupid whore of a daughter?" George bristled. "Now, see here—"

"No." Richard pushed George back with one hand, grabbing Charlotte roughly with the other. "Father Mack, marry us at once!"

George and Abigail stared, seeming stunned by Richard's sudden outburst. Charlotte saw this as her moment; Abigail was on her side and her father was finally starting to see what a beast Richard Howard truly was.

"No! I refuse this marriage!" she called out, pulling her arm from Richard's grasp.

"Silence!" Quick as a whip, Richard reached out a hand, striking Charlotte with such force that she slammed against the altar, scraping the skin of her back raw as she fell to the floor.

"Richard, how dare you strike my daughter!" George stomped toward them, but two of Richard's men grabbed him on either side, dragging him backward. "Richard, what are you doing? You've struck Charlotte!"

"See, Father?" Charlotte was sobbing now as Richard pulled her up, his hands like vices on her arms. "This is why I ran away!"

"Oh, God, I've been such a fool." George fought against the two men, but they were far stronger than the portly duke.

"Now, get on with it," Richard ordered Father Mack gruffly, struggling to hold Charlotte still. When the priest hesitated, he raised his voice. "I've paid you for your services, so you best well bloody serve your purpose!"

Father Mack cleared his throat, perturbed by the dramatics, but more interested in the money currently hidden in his robes. He opened his worn bible, his voice raised to be heard over Charlotte's heaving sobs and George's frantic pleading. "Dearly beloved, we are gathered here today to join this man and this woman in holy matrimony."

"Stop!" a voice called out, echoing around the vaulted ceiling of the cathedral.

"Jesus, will everyone just shut up?" Richard yelled.

The priest held up a hand. "Do not take the Lord's name in vain in the house of God."

"Really?" the bodiless voice interrupted. "That's the moral hill ye choose to die on while ye marry an already married woman to a monster?"

"Conner?" Charlotte looked around frantically. "Conner, where are you?"

"Here." Conner leaned over the balcony overlooking the altar where, normally, a choir would sing at Sunday service.

"What the bloody hell?" Richard blanched, his hold on Charlotte loosening.

Conner MacLeod deftly leapt from the balcony, landing on his feet next to Charlotte like a cat. As soon as his toes hit the floor, his broadsword was out, primed for use. "How dare ye come into my home and steal my wife?"

"You stole her first!" Richard shot back lamely, motioning for his hired men to help him.

Conner pulled Charlotte behind him. "Are ye all

right, Charlotte? You're bleeding."

She wiped away a smear of blood from her lips, unable to find the words to express how desperately relieved she was to see him. "Oh, Conner, I—"

"Charlotte, love, as much as I'd like to hear it, ye can go on about undyin' passion, and how ye can no' live without me, when we're safe at home," he said, his eyes trained on his prey.

Richard pulled a thin sword out of the scabbard of one of his hired men. He held it before him, faking confidence. "I'll have you know I'm a champion fencer in London!"

"And I'll have ye know my best hunting dog caught three hares this mornin'," Conner replied.

Richard paused and knitted his brow. "What do your hunting dogs have to do with this?"

"I suppose the same as your fencin' trophies. Nothing." He grinned, primed for a fight.

"Ridiculous," Richard growled. "I'll kill you, you dirty heathen."

"I'd like to see ye try." Conner chuckled, making Richard all the angrier.

Richard made the first move, lunging forward, missing his mark as Conner skillfully stepped aside.

"Is that it, then?" Conner asked, obviously in his element. "My wee sisters can wield a sword with more talent."

When Richard raised his weapon again, their swords clashed together, making their rapt audience cry out. Father Mack ducked out through the back door toward the cloister, his altar boy at his heels. Conner drew back his blade, swinging it from the left, cutting Richard's arm as he tried to dodge his blow. Richard retaliated, calling forth his hired men to aid him. Aid him they did; four drew their swords and fell upon Conner who managed to keep each at bay. Conner reached toward the altar, snatching a silver offering dish with his left hand and using it as an impromptu shield against his attackers.

"Richard Howard, you are a coward!" Charlotte cried. "You can't even fight your own battles!"

Conner glanced over at Richard who was watching the conflict from a safe distance. "Ha! Howard the Coward! What a lark!" He laughed, ducking to avoid a wayward punch.

Richard pinked. "You bloody Scot," he spat, throwing up his weapon and stabbing it blindly into the skirmish.

Charlotte gasped as she saw Richard's sword leave its target tinged with blood. A red splotch spread on Conner's shirt, staining the snow-white linen. "Conner, no!"

"Charlotte, no' now," Conner answered, not even pausing to check his wounds.

"But you're hurt!" she shouted, growing pale with worry.

"Is naught but a scratch from Howard the Coward's wee needle." Conner felled two of his foes in a series of moves so swift that Charlotte could barely see his efforts. He turned to his two remaining opponents, egged on by the spilling of blood. "Come, now, lads! Better earn your supper fightin' Howard the Coward's battles for him!"

The two living hired men lowered their swords, looked at each other, and then fled the church. Charlotte was oddly pleased to see that Chester was one of the escaping men. The only two of Howard's crew who remained were the men holding tightly to her father. Neither one looked too keen on attempting to defeat Conner for Richard Howard and kept glancing at the door, obviously eager to leave.

Conner sheathed his sword and pulled his bloodied shirt over his head, dropping it to the floor. "So, Howard the Coward, now that your men have abandoned you, are ye ready to face me like a man?"

"Stop. Calling. Me. That," Richard snarled through gritted teeth.

"Then prove to me ye are no' a coward, then." Conner held his arms wide. "Come, now, let's see what years o' fencin' have taught ye."

Richard jabbed his borrowed sword again, unused to the heavy weight in his hand. When Conner dodged his blade, Richard struck again, missing greatly and striking his sword against the stone altar, shaking with reverberations. Conner drew his weapon, slicing Richard's arm with one quick motion.

The Englishman yelped in surprise. "You've struck me!"

"Blood for blood," Conner replied. "Ye trespassed into my lands, spirited into my home, kidnapped my wife, and treated her most unkind."

"And what do you think you're going to do about it?" Richard spat. "I'll never be defeated by a dammed Scottish scoundrel."

"There's only one kind o' justice in my lands when a man goes against a king," Conner stated calmly.

Richard scoffed. "I see no king here."

"The penalty for those grave injustices is death." Conner looked at Richard intently. "Do ye understand?"

"Oh, come off it." Richard rolled his eyes, taking his practiced fighter's stance. "You bloody barbarians and your justice."

"Charlotte," Conner called, "I know ye do no' do well with killin', but ye must understand that he can no' live. I have to do my duty toward you, and my people."

Charlotte bit her lip. While she wished for nothing more than for Richard to just disappear without more casualties, she understood that death was his punishment. "Do what needs to be done," she answered like the highland queen she was primed to be.

Conner nodded in readiness, gripping the hilt of his sword. Charlotte glanced toward her father and stepmother; their captors had fled at some point, leaving them frozen in their pew, jaws open wide in shock. She briefly debated going to them, but still found her father was firmly out of her good graces. Instead, she lowered herself to her own bench, gaze focused on Conner, a prayer in her heart.

MacLeod made the first move, swinging his blade in the air in a powerful arc, knocking Richard off balance and onto the floor. Richard stabbed his sword upward, narrowly missing Conner's thigh before scurrying backward to avoid another assault. He leapt upward, cursing Conner and thrashing wildly with his weapon, always missing his mark.

Conner sidestepped each swing with graceful ease, although Charlotte could see the beads of sweat forming on his brow.

Richard's normally tidy hair was mussed and the arm of one jacket was torn, hanging down his elbow. Still, he continued his wild flaying, a primal glint in his beady eyes. He came close to striking Conner once or twice, but hardly took a moment to aim before swinging his sword again, swearing all the while. Charlotte clenched the silks of her skirts, cringing each time the blade passed by Conner without shedding blood.

Again, Conner deflected a blow, kicking Richard in the stomach, sending him sliding against the floor. Richard waved his weapon in the air, stabbing madly in toward the Scotsman. In return Conner brought up his broadsword, whispering something in swift Gaelic before bringing the razor sharp point down on Richard's skull with a sickening smash.

Abigail shrieked in horror and George cried out in dismay at having seen Richard Howard's life ended so suddenly before them. Charlotte released a breath she didn't know she was holding and ran to Conner, skirts flying behind her. He caught her in his arms, stroking her hair as she cried into his bare shoulder, blubbering about his cut skin and near death experiences.

"Dinna fash so, Charlotte," he crooned as he slid his sword back into his belt after a hasty wipe against the fabric of his plaid. "It's all over now and ye have naught to fear. We'll get ye home and into bed soon."

"Conner, I'm so sorry! I should have been more

careful. I should have fought back harder to return to you and now you're hurt."

"Ach, I've had worse."

"But this one is *my* fault."

He lifted her chin gently, kissing her softly on the lips. "I'd fight a thousand men to see ye safe but now it will no' ever come to it."

"How did you find me?"

"Ye left a mighty fine trail, lass. We saw ye were gone before supper and I sent the men out to search while I investigated the dungeons. I found the crown there and knew at once what must have happened. I had a horse saddled and tracked ye all night. Ye know, it's verra hard to find those emerald earrin's at dark." He reached into his sporran, giving her back her gifted jewels. "I might get ye new, bigger ones that'll be easier to find. If ye can no' see them in the dark, they're no' fit to be on my wife."

Charlotte laughed through her tears. "Oh, stop. I don't care about jewels at all. I'm just so grateful you found me!"

"I did no' find your ring though, and now I see I should have been lookin' for it," Conner said, looking at her bare left hand.

"I didn't drop it, I have it here." She reached into her corset, pulling the emerald ring from between her breasts and slipping it back on. "I didn't want it to be taken from me, no matter what happened. They had taken my pin and tartan. I didn't want them to take every last part of you."

"Charlotte, they could never do that. I'll always be with ye no matter what happens or how large the

337

distance between us." His voice was gruff with stifled emotion and he pulled Charlotte close, their lips crashing together, happy to have been reunited.

George Holloway cleared his throat behind them. "Charlotte, I—"

"No." Charlotte turned on her heel, glaring at her father. "You almost led me to as early grave by marrying me against my will. I want nothing more to do with you."

"Charlotte," George begged, "please, I had no idea what Richard was truly like."

She scoffed. "Really? You never noticed how terribly he spoke of his wife? His daughters? Did you not listen to my pleas as I begged you not to tie me to that beast?"

He clasped his hands together. "Believe me, I had no idea he was such a brute. I'm sorry I didn't trust you to make your own choices. I was such a fool, such a terrible father. I understand if you stay firm with exiling me from your life."

Abigail stepped forward between the two. "Charlotte, you know that I have always been on your side. But I'm asking you now to trust that your father truly didn't recognize what he had done. He was blind to Richard's evils and giddy with the idea of joining the two families. He loves you dearly."

Charlotte wiped away fresh tears. "Father, are you going to try to force me to go back to England with you, take me to see doctors and be hospitalized?"

"Lord, no." George cried openly now. "I give you my permission, and my blessing, to stay here and be Conner MacLeod's wife. I will contact my bank in the morning and have them send your dowry so you can set up house properly."

"That will no' be necessary to give a dowry to me when it could be put to better use in Charlotte's name." Conner spoke softly, his arm around Charlotte's frail shoulders. "I know ye do no' know me, but I love your daughter with all my being and would lay down my life for her, as ye have seen this day. As my wife, she'll be well taken care of and want for nothin'. My army, my lands, my castles, all of the highlands will be at her disposal as its queen. Instead, I'd ask ye to put the dowry in a trust to be used for openin' a home for orphaned youth."

Fresh tears brimmed in Charlotte's eyes. "Oh, Conner, that's so brilliant of you!"

"If that is what you both desire, then consider it done. Charlotte's dowry also includes two country houses for her use. If she decides to stay here with you, those are at her full disposal. But..." George swallowed. "She will always have a place at home in England with us."

"This is my home," Charlotte said, gripping tightly to Conner's arm. "I'm happy here and it's where I choose to stay."

"And I truly couldn't ask for anything more." George stepped before the couple, lowering himself to his knees, arms outstretched in atonement. "Conner MacLeod, you are truly worthy of my daughter and I am full of sorrow that I didn't see it in time. Although I don't deserve it, I ask for forgiveness...from both of you."

Charlotte bit her lip, placing a hand on the top of her father's head. "I forgive you."

Epilogue

"Charlotte, you look so lovely." Penelope sighed, shaking out her friend's bridal veil and taking a step back to admire her.

Charlotte studied herself in the mirror, ready for her walk down the aisle. She wore a snowy silk gown, edged in gold lace. It had a sweetheart neckline, a gently nipped-in waist, and a billowed skirt, wide with carefully placed hoops. Over her powdered shoulders sat delicate gold puffed sleeves and her arms were bare. She wore a small gold ribbon woven through her curls, interspersed with traditional orange blossoms. Her slight lace veil was held in place with an emerald clasp. Lastly, she wore a pair of new emerald earrings, gifted to her upon their return to the MacLeod castle. Conner had promised her bigger jewels and he certainly did deliver.

"I can scarcely believe it." Penelope giggled. "You were once so opposed to marriage and now you're possibly ready to run down the aisle!"

"It feels rather different when you're marrying

for love. Conner's everything I could have hoped for in a husband."

"I do hope I can find a great love like that."

"Perhaps next season. You've already denied so many men."

"Well, since Conner doesn't have a brother, I suppose I'll have to keep looking in London for someone who worships me like he does you."

Charlotte laughed, squeezing Penelope's hand. "You will visit me, yes?"

"As often as I can," she promised. "Although, I do suppose you'll come back quite frequently to oversee the running of your children's home."

"Of course." And Charlotte meant it. George Holloway was good to his word; as soon as he came back to London, he immediately signed over the rights to two county estates, and the dowry funds, to Charlotte, allowing her to hire nursemaids, a physician, and buy all the necessities the dozens of children would need. "I'll be visiting after my honeymoon to christen the opening of my orphanage."

"And then you can tell me all about your wedding night and your wonderful time in Paris!" Penelope said with a grin.

"My *second* wedding night." Charlotte looked back on the first fondly, remembering the tentative caresses and the slow build to a beautiful, mutual, release.

"You're blushing!"

"Well, I should be blushing. I'm a bride."

"We really must go. Your father's waiting to walk you down the aisle and we're almost late."

"Do I look all right?" she asked, starting toward the door.

"Like a positively delicious confection!"

Charlotte felt her heart beat faster with every step toward the Holloway family's church. When she was a young girl she had never dreamed of being a trussed up bride, waltzing down the aisle to a wedding march. But, here she was, living her new dream. When she arrived in the small foyer of the chapel, she could hear the tittering of the wedding guests—proper King's English mixed with thick Scottish brogue, two worlds colliding.

"I'll go in now," Penelope whispered, passing Charlotte a large bouquet of orange blossoms.

"Charlotte, you look like an absolute vision." Her father stepped forward, taking her free hand. "I'm giving you to MacLeod with a full heart, my only regret being that I didn't get to see you wed the first time."

"You're here now and that's all that matters to me." The organ struck up Felix Mendelsohn's wedding march, signaling their time to enter. "I suppose that's our cue."

Two attendants opened the cathedral's doors, allowing George and Charlotte a grand entrance. She smiled as she took in her family's church, dressed in leafy vines and fragrant blossoms, the colorful guests all rising as she passed them. Little Ian sat with Flora and Gwen, upon the lap of Conner's mother, the Dowager Lady MacLeod. Abigail cried openly with happiness, gripping Penelope's hand as she stood. Conner stood by the altar in full chieftain garb, a wide smile on his handsome face. He was bathed in a colorful array of light from the ancient glass windows that allowed for a generous influx of early morning light.

Conner mouthed, "I love you," when she took her place beside him, the priest obviously pleased at seeing a happy couple marry for love instead of the usual contractual obligations.

The priest cleared his throat, beginning the ceremony. "Dearly beloved, we are gathered together here in the sight of God, and in the face of this congregation, to join together this man and this woman in holy matrimony…which is an honorable estate, instituted of God in the time of man's innocence, signifying unto us the mystical union that is betwixt Christ and his Church, which holy estate Christ adorned and beautified with his presence, and first miracle that he wrought." He looked at Charlotte and Conner.

"Conner MacLeod, will you have this woman to be your wedded wife, to live together after God's ordinance in the holy estate of matrimony? Will you love her, comfort her, honor, and keep her in sickness and in health, and forsaking all others, keep yourself only unto her, so long as you both shall live?"

"And far into the afterlife," Conner replied, gazing down at Charlotte.

"Charlotte Holloway," the priest addressed her, "will you have this man to be your wedded husband, to live together after God's ordinance in the holy estate of matrimony? Will you obey him and serve him, love, honor, and keep him in sickness and in health, and forsaking all others, keep yourself only unto him, so long as you both shall live?"

Conner snorted, making the priest cast him an offended glare. "Sorry, Father." Conner struggled to keep his face straight, his striking features twitching comically as his body shook with mirth. "It's only that I've never know any woman who'd be less likely to obey her husband, nor any man for that matter. Give her the man's vows. She'll keep to those."

The priest, looking rather confused, again cleared his throat, beginning again with a careful voice. "Charlotte Holloway, will you have this man to be your wedded husband, to live together after God's ordinance in the holy estate of matrimony? Will you love him, comfort him, honor, and keep him in sickness and in health, and forsaking all others, keep yourself only unto him, so long as you both shall live?"

"I will," Charlotte replied, struggling to keep her own giggles at bay.

"You may present the ring," the priest ordered, watching as Conner slipped a gold band from his sporran.

Conner, suddenly much more serious and earnest with his words, said, "With this ring I thee wed, with my body I thee worship, and with all my worldly goods I thee endow: In the name of the Father, and of the Son, and of the Holy Ghost. Amen."

The priest closed his bible as Conner slipped the wedding band onto Charlotte shaking finger. "By the power invested in me by the Lord almighty, I now pronounce thee husband and wife."

Charlotte and Conner smiled, kissing to the roar of the Scots and the polite applause of the English—two worlds, two people, two lovers, joined at last.

Acknowledgements

A special shout out to my fellow Limitless author Sarah Fischer for pushing me to actually finish something, for once, and helping me bring my #HotScot to life.

And thank you to my lovely editor Rosa Sophia and the rest of the Limitless team who made this book possible.

About the Author

Kelsey McKnight is a university-educated historian from southern New Jersey. She has married her great loves of romance, history, and literature to create her newly finished works. Her first books, *The Scottish Stone Series*, take readers on a journey through the bustling streets of Victorian London and into the lush hills of the Scottish Highlands. Her second work, a contemporary romance titled *The Non-Disclosure Agreement,* will also be available in May of 2017, and feature a bad boy politician and the small town girl that could change his ways. When she's not working, Kelsey can be found reading, drinking too much coffee, spending time with her family, and working with two different non-profits, *Hole High* and the *No You Cant'cer Foundation.*

Twitter:
http://twitter.com/KelseyMMcK

Goodreads:
https://www.goodreads.com/Kelsey_McKnight